FOR WHOM THE SHOFAR BLOWS

A Rabbi Ben Mystery

Marvin J. Wolf

For Whom The Shofar Blows

Publishing History:

Antenna Books eBook edition © 2013 by Marvin J. Wolf;
Antenna Books eBook edition © 2011 titled *The Tattooed Rabbi*
by Marvin J. Wolf

Rambam Press Paperback Edition Copyright © September 2013

Also By Marvin J. Wolf

Family Blood

Fallen Angels

Perfect Crimes

Rotten Apples

Cons By Pros

Where White Men Fear To Tread

Buddha's Child

Beating The Odds

The Japanese Conspiracy

"When the ram's horn soundeth long, they shall come up the mount."

—Exodus 19:13

What was that noise? Ben wondered. It was faint—barely louder than the roaring in his ears. But it sounded almost like people screaming—how could that be? And why did his hands feel sticky?

The scream-like noise was louder now, and there was something else, a strange rising and falling tone, like from one of those old European movies his *zaideh,* his grandfather, used to watch. But why were his hands so sticky?

The screaming—it was clearly screaming—got louder. The odd tones, Ben realized, came from an ambulance siren.

But why was he covered with gore?

He raised his head, looked around. Dozens of people, dead and dying, lay in the ruins of a café. A few staggered outside into the street. He must help them, he realized, and turned to kneel beside a pale young man. Choking sounds came from his ruined face.

Ben saw that the man had swallowed his tongue. Reaching into the man's mouth, he realized that he, too, was bleeding—that his hands and arms bore numerous cuts. Blood dripped into his eyes. It was hard to see, but he must get his tongue out. Somehow. The screaming was overwhelming, crowding out even the sirens.

It must have been a bomb, he realized. That was it. A suicide bomber! Rachel was visiting and they had just ordered dinner. Where was Rachel? Where?

Oh God! Please! Please! No! No!

Ben sat up in bed, dripping with sweat.

Again.

Kicking off the sopping sheet, Ben turned to look for the alarm clock. The glowing red digits should have been to his left on the nightstand next to the bed.

Nothing there but his glasses. He put them on, then swiveled his head until he saw blue digits glowing in the darkness off the foot of the bed.

Of course. He was in a hotel room. In California.

It was a little after five. He'd slept almost six hours. His meeting was at nine, and they'd probably be a little early. Might as well get up, he told himself. Find the gym, get his heart pounding, a nice sweat going, a long hot shower, some coffee.

***

It was ten to nine and Ben was on his third cup when the Beit Joseph people entered the hotel coffee shop. He was expecting only three, but there were five people. They hesitated at the door, looking around, unsure of themselves. The tables were filled with noisy families with young children; the lone solo diner was a robust, red-headed, fair-skinned, smooth-shaven man an inch or two under average height and dressed like a tourist in an open-necked sport shirt, faded jeans and well-worn Nike running shoes.

The newcomers looked at each other—had they gotten the wrong hotel? Was it the Red Lion Hotel Anaheim or the Anaheim Plaza Hotel Suites? Or were they simply too early?

Ben stood up and waved.

They trooped over, four men and a woman, all over forty and under sixty, neat and tidy in business attire. Ben decided that the bearded man about fifty had to be Rabbi Hank Kimmelman. The tall, graying, blue-eyed, good-looking fellow? A lawyer—probably the congregation's president, he concluded. The short, very pretty, dark-haired, slightly *zaftig* woman—an educator. Perhaps a college professor. Maybe the synagogue treasurer. The other two were older. More reserved, harder to read. Probably the money guys, he thought. Businessmen.

"Rabbi Ben Maimon?" ventured the bearded man, extending his right hand. "I'm Hank Kimmelman. We exchanged emails—"

"Call me Ben." They shook hands.

"This is Dr. Tova Levine, our immediate past president," Kimmelman continued. "Gary Burkin, our president," he said, indicating the tall, handsome man. "And board members Aaron Ferguson and Manny Seddaca."

Ben shook each hand in turn, and then looked around the room. "We'll need a larger table."

"I'll handle it," Ferguson said. He headed for the cashier's desk, all but breaking into a trot.

"I apologize for meeting in such a *goyishe* place," Rabbi Kimmelman said.

"I understand. We're fifty miles from your shul in a place no Jew would come to eat. I'm getting that whether you hire me or not, discretion is vital."

Kimmelman and the others exchanged guarded glances.

"You come very highly recommended."

"Thank you. Your email said that you knew my grandfather, of blessed memory?"

"*Olav hashalom*—may he rest in peace. He taught Talmud my first year at J.T.S. Just before he retired."

"So he would have been in his eighties. By then he was bald and his beard was white. Otherwise, I look just like him."

Everyone smiled.

"So, Dr. Levine—"

"Tova."

"—you're still at UCLA in...the Political Science Department?"

Tova's mouth dropped open. "How did you know that?"

"When I got Rabbi Kimmelman's email, I visited Beit Joseph's Website. It hadn't been updated in a while, but you were listed as a board member."

Tova smiled. "But—"

"I Googled Tova Levine and discovered five in Southern California. Two were very young, judging by their Facebook pages. One was awaiting sentencing on drug charges, one a pediatrician and one teaches at UCLA."

Kimmelman said, "But I introduced her as 'Dr. Levine.' How did you know she wasn't the pediatrician?"

"Because she's put on a few pounds lately—forgive me, Dr. Levine—Tova—but your jacket is a little tight—and the sleeve has a faint odor of old tobacco smoke. So I guessed that you might be trying to quit smoking—"

"—and no *pediatrician* would smoke," Kimmelman finished. "I told you he was good."

"Okay, what do you make of me?" Burkin asked, as Ferguson returned with a waitress.

"I can seat you now," she said, and the group followed her to a booth across the room.

After everyone had ordered, Burkin looked at Ben.

"Rabbi Maimon—" Burkin began.

Ben said, "You're an attorney. Managing partner in Burkin, Turner and Overstreet. You've made a reputation handling criminal cases, and you seldom go to trial."

"You've done your due diligence."

Ben shrugged. "Now please, before we go any further, can you tell me why I'm here? What is this all about?"

Burkin and Kimmelman exchanged glances.

"Someone got into our bank account," Kimmelman said.

"How much did you lose?"

"That's the crazy thing. He didn't take anything."

"Then how do you know that—"

Burkin said, "Someone deposited over two million in one of our accounts. We'd like you find out who."

"And why," Tova said.

"And if we can keep the money," Ferguson added.

CHAPTER 2

Ben glanced around the table, feeling the eyes on him.

"Why not call the police?"

"No police," Burkin said. "It might create a false impression—our community will misunderstand."

"We prefer to handle this quietly," Kimmelman said. "I was given to understand that you have, uh, special expertise. And that you were very, very discrete."

Ben said, "Before I agree to anything, and before we discuss my fee, I'd like to know exactly why you don't want law enforcement involved."

Again the five people exchanged glances. Burkin gave an almost imperceptible nod. Kimmelman cleared his throat.

"Ben. We're a small congregation in an old, poorly maintained building that's falling down around us. Half our families are older people who've been members for years. Not enough young people. We polled the congregation—"

Tova said, "Twice!"

"—and we're virtually unanimous that we don't want to leave Burbank or merge with another shul. We like the way we do things. We have, we think, a very special culture. Nobody wants that to change. But if Beit Joseph is to survive as a congregation, it needs to attract more young families with children. And that means redeveloping our campus. Making it more attractive, more family friendly. We've got enough space, but it no longer fills our needs. Most of our campus is either underutilized or over-crowded.

"So we're talking to architects and fundraisers, and it's going to take three million dollars for a minimum—"

Burkin interrupted. "We really need more like five."

Ferguson said, "I'm chairing the capital committee."

"And I'm co-chair," said the heretofore silent Seddaca. "We think we could raise, at most, two, two-and-a-half mil over the next five years."

"Not enough, not nearly enough," Kimmelman sighed.

"You're telling me that you'd like to find a way to keep the money that turned up in your bank account?"

Ferguson said, "Rabbi Kimmelman convinced us that if we set our hearts and minds on this, if we do all that is humanly possible—and really put our faith in God—*HaShem*— will show us a way to keep our congregation together. Now suddenly here's this money. It's a miracle, is what it is."

"Then why do you need me?" Ben asked. "Move the money to a new bank, a new account, and get on with it."

Burkin shook his head. "We can't take that chance," he said. "What if some criminal is hiding money there? What if it's part of a drug deal? What if its stolen money?"

Tova said, "What if it's part of some anti-Semitic scheme? There are plenty of people in this country who would do anything to discredit the Jews."

"You want me to determine who put the money there—and then what?"

"We're hoping it was deposited by a philanthropist," Kimmelman said. "Someone with a good heart, acting out of good motivations. The Rambam says an anonymous contribution to a good cause is a higher, elevated form of *tzedakah*, charity or justice to the poor."

"Higher still, says the Rambam, is *matan b'seter*, giving in secret, where the unknown giver doesn't know who receives his gift," Ben said. "But do any of you really think an anonymous donor deposited that money?"

Kimmelman said, "It's possible." The others nodded agreement. Looking from face to face, Ben saw only people desperate to believe in a miracle.

Ben knew he must move them off that kind of thinking.

"In your experience, Mr. Burkin, do people make contributions of this magnitude without also taking a tax write-off? And doesn't that require acknowledgement of the gift and its purpose by the recipient?"

"There are ways to claim a deduction—" Seddaca began.

"Things look one way if you think only with your mind," Kimmelman said. "But if you think with your heart..."

Ben looked around the table again, meeting the eyes of each individual in turn until they looked away. There's something else, he thought. Something they don't want to tell me. Not yet, anyway.

"And if I discover who the money belongs to?"

Burkin said, "Then we offer to return it, of course."

Kimmelman spoke up. "Unless it's stolen money. Then we must call the police."

"I would need access to all synagogue records. And I would have to be able to enter every room in the synagogue, every cabinet, every desk, and every closet. Any time."

Burkin nodded. "Certainly. But there has to be some way to explain your ongoing presence in the building. You can't just show up, and start poking around."

"On previous occasions, I've been a cheder teacher, a scholar-in-residence, a researcher, a cantor, or—"

"Previous occasions?" Tova asked. "You've done this sort of thing before?"

Burkin said, "I told you, Tova. He's a detective who happens to be a rabbi as well."

***

Ben's investigative career had begun by chance, six years earlier, when a friend of his grandfather, a former student, had learned of his long, frustrating search for a congregational pulpit, and asked him to teach a semester of Talmud at a high school yeshiva.

After a time, Ben was asked to keep an eye on a teacher accused of molesting students. Ben determined that the teacher was innocent. His accuser, however, the school's IT manager, was using its powerful computer system to run Web-based scams, and reaping huge sums. Suspecting that the teacher knew this, the scammer tried to discredit the teacher by inventing the lie and spreading it as a rumor.

With careful planning, a little kosher skullduggery and a bit of luck, Ben helped the yeshiva ease the scammer out of his job and exonerate the accused teacher. Then Ben anonymously identified the man to each of his victims and to authorities.

The following year, one of the two elderly rabbis aware of Ben's covert activities passed on a request for similar services, a task that consumed almost a year and afforded him multiple satisfactions. Ben still dreamed of having a pulpit, but he accepted that it was unlikely. He settled into his new profession and stayed surprisingly busy for a man who never advertised his services.

Ben said, "Actually, I consider myself a rabbi who has some additional skills. Sometimes Jewish institutions encounter problems that call for finesse and discretion in solving them. And, sometimes, I'm able to help them."

No point in over-selling, in building up false hope, Ben thought.

"Excuse me, Rabbi, but exactly what are those skills?" Ferguson asked. "*How* will you do what you do?"

"A fair question. A lot of what I do is the application of Talmudic logic to complex issues. I also use people skills to get cooperation, computer skills, my skills as an administrator and educator and my knowledge of secular and non-secular subjects. I have studied aberrant psychology extensively; I have some mechanical talent and artistic accomplishments. And I can draw upon a nationwide pool of scientific experts."

Seddaca said, "How old are you?"

"Older than you were when you made your first million."

Seddaca laughed. "Good guess."

Burkin said, "But what—*how* will you—"

"I don't know yet. And it may be better if you don't know details. I may deceive people, borrow things and return them. I don't carry a gun or any weapon. I seek the truth and harm no one unless it's necessary to stop them from harming me or others," Ben said.

Ferguson said, "We can figure out what to call you later. First we have to decide if we can afford to hire you. How do you bill your time?"

Ben leaned over to Rabbi Kimmelman and passed him a napkin and a pen. "Please write your annual base salary," he said.

Kimmelman hesitated.

"This is how I operate. If it doesn't suit you, I'll go to Chicago as quickly as I can change my flight."

Burkin said, "I thought you lived near Boston?"

"I do. What's it going to be, Rabbi?"

15

Kimmelman sighed, then wrote a number on the napkin and passed it to Ben, who glanced at it.

"I would have thought much more," said Ben.

Burkin said, "We have only 280 families. We're very fortunate to have a rabbi of Rabbi Kimmelman's stature."

"Indeed." Ben passed the napkin to Ferguson, who showed it to Seddaca.

"Okay," Seddaca said. "How much do you want?"

"That's my fee," Ben said. "Payable in advance."

Burkin jumped up. "Hold on a minute! You could figure this whole thing out in a couple of days—a week."

"Or it could take me a year. Which would be preferable, Mr. Burkin? A day, a week, or a year?"

Rabbi Kimmelman said, "Don't be silly. The sooner the better," and everyone nodded agreement.

Tova said, "What if you don't find anything?"

Ben hated this part of the job, but he had no choice. He lived modestly but his medical expenses were high and he had to put money away for retirement. He wished he didn't have to ask for a fee—but he did. Bitter experience had taught that those unwilling to pay either didn't actually want the problem fixed or would be impossible to work with. He researched each potential client before setting a fee and he knew that Beit Joseph could afford what he asked.

Ben said, "Isn't that what you want? Isn't the best possible outcome for the synagogue that I try everything I know, pursue every possible avenue but can't determine whose money that is? And do all that quickly?"

Burkin said, "But why must we pay in advance?"

"Mr. Burkin, do you represent accused murderers?"

"From time to time."

"And what's your usual fee for defending someone charged with murder?"

"Whatever the market will bear, but never less than a hundred thousand dollars."

"Cash?"

"Sometimes I'll accept a deed of trust."

"In advance, right?"

"I see where you're going with this, Rabbi. But it's not the same thing."

"It's precisely the same. When you accept an accused murderer as a client, what's his best possible outcome? Would he prefer to spend months or years in jail awaiting trial before being convicted, or that prosecutors drop all charges and release him immediately? For that matter, what would be the best possible outcome for you, personally?"

"The faster I can make it all go away, the better it is for everyone involved."

"And does it ever happen that you get a charge dismissed before trial or even before entering a plea?"

"Sometimes."

"I get it, I get it," Ferguson said. "If his client gets out of jail without even a trial, then the guy wants to know why he should pay all that money for Burkin making a couple of phone calls. If he doesn't front the money, Gary, you're gonna have to chase him for it."

Seddaca nodded. "So he gets his fee up front. Smart."

Ben said, "Any other questions?"

Ferguson said, "What about expenses?"

"Roundtrip coach from Boston, a week in a motel until I find a place to live, and a rental car until I can buy or lease one. The rest is included in my fee."

Burkin said, "Rabbi, can you give us a few minutes to discuss this?"

"I'll be up in my room," he said.

***

Ben was zipping up his carry-on when the phone rang.

"Rabbi Maimon, this is Gary Burkin."

"Did you come to a decision?"

"You're asking for an awful lot of money."

"Less than five percent of what fell into your account."

"Actually, we checked a few minutes ago, and there's almost $3 million in there now. But that's irrelevant."

"Mr. Burkin, there are any number of fine detective agencies in Southern California. Any one would do an outstanding job for you. They charge by the day."

"But what do we tell members about a detective poking around, asking questions? How do we keep this secret?"

"Compartmentalize and control that information. I'm sorry to be short with you, but my plane leaves in about an hour and there's airport security and so forth."

"Would you be open to a counterproposal?"

"I have no shortage of clients, Mr. Burkin."

"We'll give you the whole sum up front, but if you wrap this up to our satisfaction in under a month, you donate 10 percent of your fee to our capital campaign," he said.

"What if you have to return that $3 million?"

"Either way. If you finish in less than a month, you make a tax-deductible donation to Beit Joseph."

"I can do that. I'll need a few days to go home, pack some clothes and personal things, and arrange for someone to look after my apartment," Ben said. "I look forward to meeting the rest of your congregation."

"Of course," Burkin replied. "The clock starts when you return. *Nesia Tovah*—a safe journey."

CHAPTER 3

Tova gripped the wheel of her three-year-old Prius with both hands, doggedly keeping to the second lane from the curb, dodging mammoth 18-wheelers with the aplomb of a Drivers Ed student in a Formula One race. Rabbi Kimmelman sat beside her while Seddaca, Ferguson and Burkin were crammed into the back, a trio of olives in a claustrophobic jar.

Tova said, "I liked him," intending her remark for Kimmelman's ears.

Ferguson leaned forward until his head was between the front seats.

"Like, shmike—we're paying him a fortune."

Burkin said, "What's done is done. We'll call him a visiting scholar. People know that I have connections with the Federation. Let them think we got a grant. Of course, if anyone really wants to know where the money came from—"

Ferguson said "—they can talk to me."

"Excellent," rumbled Kimmelman in his throaty bass. "We'll move the interns into the cheder office and Rabbi Ben can use their room. He can give a couple of Shabbat sermons, teach an adult seminar—maybe take over my Talmud class once in awhile."

Burkin frowned. "Will he be here that long?"

"Even if he isn't, we have to make it *look* like he's engaged with our community."

Seddaca said, "We should get *something* for our money."

"When are we going to tell him about—" Tova began.

Burkin cut her off. "What was all that about his grandfather, Rabbi?"

Kimmelman swiveled to look into the backseat. "Rabbi Salomen Maimon. A great scholar. For many years he taught Talmud at J.T.S., the Jewish Theological Seminary, in New York. A close friend of Abraham Joshua Heschel—truly, an elevated soul. The Chelmnicker Hassids considered Maimon almost a saint."

Seddaca and Ferguson exchanged looks. Out of Kimmelman's view, Seddaca rolled his eyes.

Tova said, "What about his parents? Was his father a rabbi, too?"

"I don't think his father was Jewish."

"So Rabbi Salomen was his mother's father?"

"Ben was lost his father when he was a little boy."

Tova sighed. "His father died young—cancer?"

Kimmelman frowned. "I seem to recall something about a plane crash. Overseas somewhere. Something like that. Rabbi Salomen never spoke about his son-in-law. I saw Ben's mother once, in his office. At least I think it was her."

Tova said, "So he was raised by his mother?"

"Mostly by his maternal grandparents."

Ferguson said, "His father was a *shaygetz*? That's not easy for a kid."

Tova said, "Then Ben Maimon is his Hebrew name?"

Burkin said, "Wait a minute! Ben Maimon means 'son of Maimon.' That's not his *whole* Hebrew name?"

Kimmelman shook his head. "I think his legal name is Mark. His *Hebrew* name is Moshe Benyamin. He goes by Ben."

Burkin laughed. "Are you kidding? We just hired Rabbi Moshe Ben Maimon—a second Rambam?"

Tova said, "I didn't want to appear stupid—in the coffee shop—but tell me, what's a Rambam?"

Kimmelman said, "An acronym for Rabbi Moshe ben Maimon. The Hebrew letters Resh, Mem, Beit, Mem—Rambam."

Seddaca said, "The Greeks called him Maimonides. He wrote the Mishnah Torah—our greatest scholar and theologian since Moshe led us out of Egypt."

Ferguson leaned forward "How much longer with this freeway?"

"There's so much traffic!"

Seddaca said, "Maybe if you moved out of this lane."

"If you wanted to drive we could have taken *your* car."

Ferguson said, "I didn't get breakfast. What do you say we get off downtown and grab lunch at Langer's?"

***

Ben, too, was hungry. He'd barely made American's 11:30 flight to O'Hare; by then the hotel's third-rate bagel was ancient history. The airline offered no meal on his flight, much less a kosher meal. There was nothing to eat except peanuts, coffee and juice; as the Boeing dropped into the Chicago pattern, Ben's stomach was rumbling and he was annoyed with himself for not packing granola bars.

Descending over rush-hour-packed expressways, Ben pulled out his iPhone and as a loudspeaker message instructed passengers to turn off their phones, composed two text messages.

Later, as the plane taxied toward the terminal, he sent both.

CHAPTER 4

Ben sat down at a table in a noisy Skokie restaurant.

Mitch looked up and said, "If I'd known you were coming to Chicago, I'd have picked you up at the airport."

Tall, pale, balding and building a paunch, Mitch Katz was Ben's closest friend, his roommate for two years at M.I.T. Ben majored in computer science while Mitch took a double major in biology and Semitic Literature. Two years after graduation they had met again at New York's J.T.S. Upon ordination, Mitch became assistant rabbi in a Long Island synagogue. Less than a year later he left his job, enrolled in medical school and now practiced psychiatry as part of a suburban Chicago medical group.

Ben said, "I'll remember next time."

Mitch grinned. "Your visit is personal or professional?"

"Both. I'm hungry. Let's order—then we'll talk."

Mitch looked up and caught a passing waiter's eye.

The waiter mumbled that it wasn't his station. Mitch indicated Ben.

"The rabbi is starving."

"I'll send your waiter over."

"These waiters get worse every year," Ben sighed.

"Yeah, but where in this town can you get food like this— steaks, lamb chops, ribs, fresh fish, spaghetti, duck—anything you can imagine, and all glatt kosher."

"They give you a discount for promoting the place?"

"They should!"

A slender young man in crisp whites arrived to take their order.

Ben said, "An order of pot stickers right away, and then I'll have the citrus duck with a salad."

"Vitelli di Marsala," Mitch said. "And French onion soup. With real soy 'cheese,' of course."

"An excellent choice, Doctor."

"And a plate of Angel Hair Siciliano," added Ben.

The waiter's plucked eyebrows arched upward. "That's a lot of food, sir."

"I hope so. And I also want a chicken schnitzel sandwich to go. Wrap it twice, please."

As the waiter disappeared Mitch took a sip of water then peered at Ben intently.

"You look a little thinner. Ben, are you—"

"I'm fine. Been on the move the last few weeks. Missed a few meals. But I always get in my workout. Maybe I'll enter the L.A. Marathon next year. If I'm still there."

"So you'll be on the Coast for awhile?"

"Could be. I just accepted a job; I have the feeling that it's either going to take a few weeks or many months."

"So that's the personal part?"

"Yeah. You know I can't talk about my clients. I'll just say that it's another dysfunctional shul with two problems, one they've told me about and another they'll get around to as soon as I cash their check. But they seem like nice people."

Mitch brightened as the waiter set a plate of steaming, meat-stuffed Chinese-style dumplings before them. For several minutes only chewing and swallowing sounds were heard at the table.

The pot stickers vanished.

"So you could be in Los Angeles for quite a while?"

Ben nodded. "Could be. By the way, I'm buying dinner. And I'll expect a bill from your practice."

"We'll see about a bill. I bring a lot of business in to those boys."

"I insist. Any job I take means walking a legal tightrope. There's always the possibility of a lawsuit, or—you gotta be able to assert doctor-patient privilege. Billing for a session proves that our relationship and conversations are privileged—the billing is your insurance policy."

"But you never tell me about your cases."

"And I'm not going to. But, trust me, if someone comes after me, some lawyer somewhere will dig up the fact that we're friends and that we see each other from time to time. He'll try to put you on the stand, and that's lose-lose."

"I guess you're right. By the way, you didn't come here to see me, so what brings you this time?"

"David. I hope to visit him tomorrow."

"David...Siegel? That schmuck?"

"He's a crook, but he's still my friend. *Our* friend. I don't know if I would have made it through *Mishnah Nezikin* without his help."

"That's his Orthodox upbringing. His grandfather was one of those Hassid miracle-workers, wasn't he?"

"I thought it was his *great*-grandfather. And I thought he was actually a bigger flimflam artist than David—I just realized something: *Mishnah Nezikin* was his strong suit—"

"And he turned out to be a thief."

Mitch laughed. "So he studied first-century Jewish criminal law to learn how to scam Jews?"

Staring at each other, both men burst into laughter.

Bearing an enormous serving tray and assisted by a second waiter, the slender young man set a feast before them. Salad, soup and the duck vanished, as did the veal. Over Mitch's half-hearted protest, Ben shoveled half the spaghetti onto his friend's plate.

Ben laughed at himself. "Big eyes, small stomach."

"Wish I could say that." After a pause he dug into the plate with gusto.

When the coffee was poured, Ben sat back.

"Mitch, I had the dream again. The last two nights."

"Israel?"

Ben nodded yes.

"And Rachel, is she—?"

"Both times I woke up before that. Knowing what was coming, not being able to handle it."

"We've been through this. You suffered a triple trauma—the bomb, the loss of your wife and child, and..."

"Yeah. I know."

"Talking about it helps. I'm glad you came."

"Mitch, if only I hadn't had a second beer that night."

"Then you wouldn't have had to go pee, and you wouldn't have been in the restroom hallway when the bomb—"

"I'd have been with Rachel."

"You'd have been killed."

"Maybe. If God willed it. But I just—"

"Do you believe God has a plan for each of us?"

"Sometimes. Sometimes not. But I can't believe in a God that kills innocent babies. Or young brides."

"That makes you a Jew, instead of a Christian. You have work to do. We've talked about it. It starts with finding a woman."

"I can't, Mitch. I just can't."

"It's been eight years, Ben. Are you prepared to spend the rest of your life alone?"

"I may have to."

"Just *date* a girl. Go out and have a few laughs, take her to dinner. Go to a club. A concert, a play. Whatever Jewish girls and Jewish boys do on dates now. Let it happen if it's going to. If not, then just enjoy her company."

"And what do I tell her when we're naked?"

"Every responsible man uses a condom these days. And there are many ways to reach orgasm."

"So, mutual masturbation?"

"And cunnilingus."

"And if I meet someone that I really like? How do I tell them what I do for a living? That I'm a roaming rabbi, gone six months at a time, two weeks at a time? What smart woman is going to sign on for that? Especially after they see my medicine cabinet."

"Ben. You'll never find someone if you don't even look. Get out there. Get your heart broken a few times."

"And then I'll just forget Rachel?"

"Not at all. But when you put new relationships between Rachel and the present, you'll gain a different perspective. Rachel's gone. If you believe in a heaven, that's where she went. If you stick to Jewish tradition, she lives on in your memory. You can't change that. But you can stop behaving like you're still together. Start treating her as the memory she has become."

"I know. You're right. I know."

"Listen, I know a woman you might like."

"I'm only here for tonight," Ben said.

"It's my mother's cousin's daughter. A young widow. Very cute. See, you've got something in common already."

"I'm going downstate tomorrow, then back home to pack a couple of suitcases."

"You'll be back. A month, six weeks, whenever. I know you."

"I don't know, Mitch. Long-distance relationships—"

"If something jells, if you feel a spark, you take it to the next level. One day at a time."

"I'll give you a call before I come back."

"Come home with me tonight. We've got plenty of room."

"I checked into the Airport Hilton. Left my bag."

"Next time, then."

"Next time."

They rose from the table and Ben grabbed the check.

Mitch said, "I'll send you that bill. But promise me you'll go on a date. Just one. Any kind of a date."

"Maybe. I don't know..."

"Say the words!"

"Send the bill first. It might be awhile before I even meet a suitable woman."

"Drive safely! *Nesia Tovah.*"

CHAPTER 5

WEDNESDAY: MAY 5

Ben rose at six; by eight he had put in five, eight-minute miles on the gym oval, showered, downed two cups of black coffee and was headed south in his Avis Chevy Malibu hybrid while munching on cold chicken schnitzel.

Most of the traffic was headed north, toward Chicago; in less than an hour he turned off onto I-55. Soon he saw the first signs for Stateville, a maximum security prison north of Joliet.

He was headed not for the Big House but for The Farm, the minimum security lockup south of the main prison. At ten minutes to nine, just as his off-ramp came into sight, the iPhone rang. He let the call go to voicemail, took the off-ramp and pulled into a strip mall to play back the message. As he'd hoped, it was from Marcus Lowenthal, the Chicago lawyer he'd text-messaged upon landing. The message was brief: Ben was cleared to see Lowenthal's client David Siegel, an inmate at The Farm.

Siegel had used his status as a rabbi as cover for an impressive string of confidence swindles. They ended with a single conviction; he was serving eight years for an elaborate charade involving a mythical condominium complex in Eilat, Israel's Red Sea resort.

By ten Ben had been cleared through prison security and escorted to the visitor center, where he sat at a narrow table with a center barrier to prevent visitors from passing things to inmates without a guard's approval.

Siegel appeared in a violently orange jumpsuit, a large, ornate yarmulke covering his head. His full beard was starting to go gray and he sported long side curls. He smiled when he saw Ben, then took the seat opposite.

"So, now the Hassidic look?"

"What do you think? Can I get over in Williamsburg?"

"If only you could find a black jumpsuit."

"Three years, eight months, 27 days."

"How have you been, David?"

"I survive. And thanks for the food."

"It comes every month?"

"I don't know when it comes, but they give it to me twice a month. Tenth and twenty-fifth. I may be a criminal, but I am a strictly kosher inmate."

"You are a criminal. The food doesn't change that. Only you can change."

Siegel held up a hand. "I don't need to be reminded. I've had a long time to think, to begin teshuva. And I know HaShem can only forgive me for sins against God. When I get out I intend to spend the rest of my life making amends to all the people that I hurt."

"That's great, David. I hope you mean it. For your sake, if not for society's."

"I do. I also want you to know that I don't eat all that kosher meat. I give about half to our Muslim brothers."

Ben responded with a searching look.

"It's not exactly halal, but they say it's close enough. And it's a lot better than what they feed us."

"*Give* it to our Muslim brothers?"

"Trade it."

"For...?"

"Cigarettes. Favors. Whatever."

"So I break my balls to get you kosher meat in prison and that makes you a player."

"It does. And I love to hear you say things like 'break my balls.'"

"You haven't changed, David. You're still looking out for David. And only David."

"Ben. This is a prison. Most of the Muslims here are converts, black guys doing long stretches for murder, rape, arson. How long do think a Jew—a rabbi—survives in this place unless they have a good reason to leave me alone?"

"And the cigarettes? Since when do you smoke?"

"They're currency. I buy personal protection from the Aryan Nation, the Mexican Mafia and all the other anti-Semite tribes in here. So thank you for that, too."

"You're welcome."

"I can't believe this is strictly a social call," Siegel said, looking deep into Ben's eyes, as if searching for information.

"It isn't. You're the only con *artiste* I know who is also intimate with the workings of synagogue politics."

"*Former* con artiste."

"We'll see. Anyway, I need to pick your brain."

"So now I'm a consultant. Shall we discus my fee?"

"A two-pound Hebrew National salami. Like the ones I send every month."

"Point taken. What can I help you with?"

"Can you think of a scam that begins with depositing money in someone else's bank account?"

"Maybe a twist on the old 'pigeon drop.'"

"Explain."

"You let the mark—the pigeon—find something valuable, usually money, at the same time that you appear to find it. So you assert a joint claim, then suggest that you help him find the rightful owner and jointly claim the reward. To keep everybody honest, you say, you both need to put up some of your own money. A show of good faith. Kind of like putting it into escrow. The scammer stops a passing stranger and asks him to hold both your money and the mark's. Then something exciting happens. Maybe the cops show up, a man waving a gun comes around the corner—street theater, in other words. The stranger throws the envelope at the mark and everybody scatters. The stranger, of course, works with the scammer. When the mark opens the envelope, it's old newspapers. His earnest money is gone."

"How would that work with a bank account?"

Siegel thought for a long moment.

"I've never done this, but here's how it *could* work. Intercept the mark's mail and switch his bank statements to show a mysterious deposit. If he's computerized, hack into the guy's computer and install a virus that redirects every attempt to log into his bank to a fake site that mimics the real one. When he checks his balance, it looks like someone made extra deposits.

"He calls the bank and they say he's mistaken, that there's no extra funds in his account," Ben said.

"So the mark goes to the bank to try to straighten things out," David continued. "Pretending to be a bank officer, I intercept him in the lobby. I convince him that there really is windfall money in his account but the evil manager is trying to steal it. I tell the pigeon that I can get into the bank's computer and transfer the money to another bank, but I'll need his password."

"Ah. Then you loot the account."

"Exactly."

"But why doesn't the mark go to the police?"

"Greed. He thinks he's getting something for nothing. If he calls the police, he loses it."

"That makes sense," Ben said. "But it requires inside information about the mark."

"You get a pal to apply for a job—anything, a secretary, a janitor—that puts him inside. He goes through wastebaskets and assembles a dossier. Or you hire someone for a black bag job and plant the virus on their internal network. I've spent as long as two years setting up a big con. Patience is the name of the game."

"Okay," Ben said, thinking. "What if it isn't the pigeon drop. What if it's something else?"

"This is an actual case?"

"In Atlanta. A friend of mine called. He says there's almost $15,000 in three mysterious deposits in his bank."

"And he doesn't want to call the cops."

"He wants to keep the money."

"What's stopping him?"

"He's not sure if it's a scam, or something darker. So what else could it be?"

"Oh, all sorts of things. Depends on what kind of account we're talking about. A checking account with a lot of cash flow, maybe you don't notice it for a few weeks, and then it's gone. That's somebody at the bank looting a dormant account. Move it to one account, move it to another, wait for somebody to complain. If they do, move it back. If they don't, move it out of the bank."

"That would work with an account that doesn't have much activity?"

"Maybe. Some guys stash ten or fifteen thou in a savings account and pretty much forget about it. Get-out-of-town money—catastrophe insurance. Or long-term savings and they make one or two deposits a year. Then you rarely check your balance."

"Can you think of anything else? Like somebody trying to discredit a business, get them in trouble, by making it look like they swindled somebody?"

"It might be worth fifteen large to get a competitor busted on fraud charges, or for bribery. Even if there's no arrest, once the word is out, you're in deep shit. What kind of business did you say your Miami friend was in?"

"Atlanta. A general insurance agency," Ben said, as casually as he could. He began to regret his visit. Who knew what kind of strings Siegel could pull from prison?

"That might work. Anything where there's a fiduciary relationship. A stock broker, an escrow outfit."

Ben got to his feet. "Thanks, David."

"Appreciate you coming down. I don't get many visitors. Come back soon, as they say in Atlanta."

"Keep working on teshuva."

"Where you headed now?"

"Miami—I mean, Atlanta."

David signaled to the guard. "*Nesia tova,*" he said.

CHAPTER 6

Ben headed north, back the way he'd come, but instead of taking the O'Hare turnoff he continued for several miles along the expressway. Two hours after leaving the prison he stood before the grave of Mark Moses Glass, who had died the day after he was born, two months prematurely, in an ambulance outside a Jerusalem restaurant. Mark for the infant's paternal grandfather, Moses for Ben's maternal grandfather.

His son. Rachel's son.

Ben first saw Rachel as she kibitzed with other freshman girls at an M.I.T. Hillel event. It was far from love at first sight. Ben was sensitive about his height and Rachel was an inch taller; that first night, in heels, she towered over him. But there were things about her that he couldn't quite forget—not her long, dark tresses with their hints of auburn, nor her slender, athletic figure or even her laughing brown eyes. And her nose, Ben had decided, was especially interesting.

Later he would be intrigued to learn that Rachel had rejected her mother's bat-mitzvah-gift offer of rhinoplasty. With a little nip and tuck, Rachel's nose might have perfectly complemented her otherwise perfect face. But she had rejected the offer and insisted on keeping her old nose. As Ben looked at Rachel he saw a nose that was a little too long, a little too wide—too big for her other features—but it lent character to her face and to her whole personality.

Rachel's nose said, "This is who I am. I'm not perfect. Take me as I am or get lost."

And so, the next time they met at Hillel, Ben made a point of introducing himself. He asked her out; she made an excuse. He asked again the following week, and the week after that, until Rachel ran out of excuses.

For months they enjoyed a casual, comfortable if chaste relationship. And as their courtship progressed to intimacy, Ben saw that he was right about her nose, that it was a metaphor for her approach to life.

They married two years later, just after his first year at J.T.S. She remained in Boston to finish an engineering degree, arranging classes to leave Fridays open so she could arrive at Manhattan's Penn Station before noon and they could spend Shabbat and most of Sunday together.

At J.T.S., third-year rabbinical curriculum was conducted in Jerusalem; in her seventh month of pregnancy, Rachel flew over for the Pesach break. The day after she arrived, they went to dinner.

Their son survived the blast, survived Rachel's death, survived Caesarian delivery—and succumbed the next day.

Ben thought about this, and about Rachel, as he stood before the grave. Rachel's parents, Esther and Murray, who lived in the Chicago suburb of Evanston, had begged Ben to let them bury mother and child where they could easily visit her grave. Ben knew that a young rabbi seeking a pulpit must be willing to relocate anywhere in the country. He let Rachel and Mark go.

After ordination he looked in vain for a pulpit in the Chicago area. Over the next seventeen months he had eight job interviews around the country but no offers.

Ben knelt to place a pebble on the tombstone, recalling as he did that this Jewish custom traced its origin to the Biblical account of another Rachel's death, when each of Jacob's sons left a stone on her grave.

His own Rachel lay next to Mark. Ben gently laid a bouquet of yellow tulips, her favorite, on the grave and said Mourner's Kaddish for both.

***

By early evening Ben was in his own apartment wolfing down faux *treif* carryout from Qing Dao Garden, a Cambridge vegetarian restaurant that did a credible job of making soy paste taste like food no observant Jew would eat—*treif.*

As he ate, Ben played back his voice mail but heard nothing that couldn't wait.

He'd read a little, he decided. Go to bed early, and work out in the morning before heading back to Los Angeles.

He kept a bag of clothes packed, along with a special carry-on for his prescriptions, which were expensive and not easily replaced if an airline should lose his luggage.

When Ben traveled with prescriptions, he did so under his legal name, the one on his diplomas and other documents, Mark Thompson Glass. He'd been named by a father that he didn't remember, a father whose mysterious death had haunted his mother until she could no longer endure this world and hastened her own transit to the next. The year before Ben's Bar Mitzvah he'd gone to live with her parents, with Bubbe and Zaide, grandma and grandpa.

Ben was drifting off to sleep when his iPhone rang. An unfamiliar voice rasped in his ear.

"Ben—it's Hank. Rabbi Kimmelman, from Beit Joseph."

Ben came fully awake.

"How are you, Hank?"

"Fine. We're all fine. Ben—the money, the $3 million that shouldn't have been in our account—it's gone now."

"Gone?"

"As if it was never there in the first place."

"So you no longer require my services?"

"On the contrary. There's another matter, completely separate and unrelated, that we'd like you to deal with."

"What is that, Hank? What other matter?"

"Not on the phone. Especially not on a cell. Come out as soon as you can. We'll have two checks waiting for you, one for your travel expenses and other for your fee."

After hanging up, Ben wondered if there had ever really been mystery money in Beit Joseph's account.

CHAPTER 7

SUNDAY: MAY 9

"On my solemn oath! There was nearly three million dollars in that account," Rabbi Kimmelman said.

Ben looked around the shabby conference room, at each of the faces staring at him—Tova Levine, Gary Burkin, Manny Seddaca, Aaron Ferguson and Kimmelman. Tova wore tight slacks and a silk blouse that displayed her impressive cleavage but otherwise the group was much as he remembered them from the Anaheim hotel.

Ben saw two envelopes on the table. Both had his name; one said "Travel Expenses," the other "Fee."

Ben watched their faces. "And now that money is gone?"

Seddaca said, "I'll explain it. We have seven accounts, all told, at three different banks. Our operating account is at WestBank, where it's been for thirty years—"

Ferguson said, "Fifty years. The bank used to be called First National of the Valley, and then they merged with Southern California Bank of Commerce, and then, five, six years ago, they became WestBank. We've got records going back to the sixties. Same bank, same account."

Ben said, "And that's where the mystery money turned up before it disappeared?"

Ferguson and Seddaca shook their heads. "That's the operating account. We have an emergency reserve at Bank of America. They also have our building maintenance fund, which is an automatically renewed certificate of deposit—"

Ben interrupted. "Which one got the mystery deposits?"

Burkin said, "Sorry, Rabbi. For years, since our member, Mr. Rosenfeld, *olav hashalom,* he should rest in peace, remembered us in his will, we've maintained an interest-bearing account at The Bank of B. Cohen that includes the principal and interest from that bequest."

"What's the name on it?"

Kimmelman said, "Cheder Halakha. Our Hebrew school, where kids ten through twelve study for their bar or bat mitzvah. Most of those students don't belong to a shul."

Ben said, "So the cheder is a source of income for the congregation?"

Seddaca said: "An important source of income. It allows us to keep dues low."

Burkin said, "We can take ninety percent of the interest on the Rosenfeld bequest; the rest adds to the principal to allow for inflation. Every year the interest brings ten to fifteen thousand dollars. We use that to award two or three cheder scholarships to deserving students. Those were the terms of Rosenfeld's gift."

"The Bank of B. Cohen?" Ben said. "Really?"

Kimmelman said, "It's a community bank with only two branches. A few of our older members keep personal accounts there. They feel like they'd rather do business with a member of the tribe, so to speak."

Seddaca said, "Actually, Mr. Cohen's been dead for years, and his family sold the bank quite a while back. I'm not sure who owns it, or even if they're Jewish."

Tova said, "Anyway, the balance doesn't change much from month to month. Just at the end of each quarter, when the bank pays interest into the account. When we give the scholarships, there's a withdrawal. Nobody pays attention to monthly statements—we just file them away."

Ben thought about how David Siegel had described bank accounts with infrequent activity. And, he reasoned, there was a greater chance of pulling off a scam in a small local bank than in a big corporate operation. It all fit.

"How was the mystery deposit discovered?"

Ferguson said, "We were looking at maybe moving that account to another bank that would give us a better return. I asked the office gal—"

Tova hissed, "She's the Synagogue director! We pay her over sixty thousand a year, plus benefits. And you call her 'the office gal.' No wonder she gives you a hard time."

Burkin said, "Not now, Tova, please."

"I asked her—LaShonda—for the last statement, to check the interest rate. She couldn't find it, so we asked the bank for a duplicate and that's when I saw it."

Burkin passed a statement to Ben.

"Can I see a statement from last year?"

When it was located, Ben placed the two side-by-side and compared them. If the newer statement was a forgery, he decided, it was first rate. Everything seemed identical—paper, type, ink, color, layout, even the corporate watermark. The newest statement, dated three weeks earlier, showed a seven-figure balance.

"Okay, I believe you. Now, why am I here?"

Burkin said. "We'd still like to know who got into our account and how they did it."

Tova said, "And why."

Ben glanced at the statement. "There's almost a quarter million in there now?"

Ferguson said, "The original bequest, plus accumulated interest. The bank verified the balance—all kosher now."

"So leave a few bucks in the account and transfer the rest. Your downside is minimal, and the upside is it's easier to get information on an active account."

Burkin said, "I'd rather just move the money to a different bank and close the account. We've got too many accounts at too many different banks as it is."

"That's your choice. But it makes it harder to backtrack deposits because once an account is closed the bank has no incentive to keep records."

Ferguson said, "That makes sense."

Burkin shook his head. "I still don't like it."

Tova said, "We'll discuss it later."

Ben said, "Now, why am I *really* here?"

Everybody looked at everybody else.

Burkin said, "Rabbi Kimmelman?"

"Here it is, plain and simple. The shul owns some burial plots in Shabbat Tamid. A Jewish cemetery."

Burkin said, "Members buy them when the need arises."

This was like pulling teeth, Ben thought.

"And?"

"And we think there might be bodies buried in some of our unsold plots."

CHAPTER 8

Ben looked around the table again and saw five people staring at him as though he was a pastrami sandwich at sundown on Yom Kippur.

"That's it? You have unsold cemetery plots and you think there may be bodies in them, but you're not sure?"

Burkin said, "Correct."

"What does Shabbat Tamid's management say about it?"

"They say that the gravesites are empty and that they have no record of any unsold plot being opened."

That's what they'd say if they'd illegally sold the plots, Ben thought. Then they'd quietly remove the buried caskets and hide them elsewhere. Of course they'd have to phony up records, but that wasn't so difficult in an age of computers and word processors.

Ben looked directly at Rabbi Kimmelman. "What makes you think that there's bodies in these plots?"

Kimmelman said, "There was a death—not someone from here, but many of our members knew her. She was a sort of *melamed*, a freelance Hebrew teacher—she tutored b'nai mitzvah students from all over the Valley for many years. Out of respect, we went to her funeral,"

"Go on."

Seddaca said, "My father is buried there. And as long as we were at the cemetery, I thought I should go visit his grave and say Kaddish."

Everyone, including Ben, nodded to themselves. It was the right thing to do.

"Well, I bought his plot from the shul maybe eighteen, twenty years ago. Dad is there near some of our other members, in a row with six or seven unoccupied graves."

Ben kept silent, allowing Seddaca to tell his story in his meandering way.

"And...?"

"And three graves looked like they'd been opened and then closed."

Tova said, "There was no grass growing over them. The soil had been turned recently. And there's no good reason to do that, unless you're burying someone."

"Or doing maintenance on the sprinkler system."

He said it a little too sharply and Kimmelman flinched. Burkin's face became a paper mask.

Seddaca said, "Tell the truth, we never thought of that. But it doesn't matter. I'll tell you why. See, they're expanding their mortuary. Construction's my business; I have eight crews rehabbing apartment buildings. So when I see how the empty graves look strange, I walk over to the construction site and look around and sure enough I find a long piece of rebar."

Ben began to understand. "You poked the rebar down into the grave," he said, and again everybody nodded.

"There was nobody around. I'm sure. Anyway, the rebar was four or five feet long. I stick it in the ground, and it goes in pretty easy—the dirt was loose, not compacted. At maybe three feet down I hit something solid. Sounds like wood. I pull the rebar out and stick it in again maybe a foot away. Same thing."

"And the other suspicious graves?" Ben asked.

"I want to check them, but then one of the funeral directors came walking by and I threw the rebar away."

Ben shook his head. "Cemeteries have to bury caskets much deeper than three feet."

Then he had a sudden thought. "Unless there's more than one casket in the grave."

Kimmelman frowned. "I checked with the California Funeral and Cemetery Bureau. Caskets must be buried at least five feet below grade. You put a second casket in, they're required to dig a deeper hole."

Ferguson said, "It doesn't matter. There ain't supposed to be anything in those plots."

Ben said, "I don't see why you don't call the police. They'll get a court order to open the graves. Then you'll know."

Burkin shook his head emphatically. "No police."

Ben suspected that the five people across the table shared some dark secret. It was time for some theatrics. He rose and put the "travel expenses" envelope in a pocket.

"Tell me why you won't call the police."

They all looked at Kimmelman, fidgeting in his seat.

"Please, Ben, it's not what you think. Hear us out."

Slowly, Ben sat down again.

Kimmelman said, "Actually, this all started back in the Fifties when this was a much bigger congregation. The board decided to buy a bunch of plots at Shabbat Tamid, which had just opened. First Jewish cemetery in the East Valley. They negotiated a price—five hundred each—that included opening and closing the grave when the time came."

"How many?"

"Triple *chai*—fifty-four plots."

"That's too many for a shul this size."

"It *was* too many. Even for a congregation of, then, almost a thousand families. Now, Shabbat Tamid is almost full and everybody uses Mt. Sinai or Eden—and we've got nine plots left. But back then, Beit Joseph had plenty of money and nobody seemed to care if we bought too many. That's the sense of what I get from the minutes."

"You have board minutes from sixty years ago?"

Tova said, "They were in storage. Four years, when I was treasurer, money was tight. I went through the monthly bills looking for anything we didn't need. I found phone lines that were no longer even connected to phones, an annual retainer to a law firm nobody knew—and a monthly deduction for a storage locker. Nobody knew where it was or what was in it! When I stopped the payments we heard from the storage company. That's when we found the minutes, along with old photos, furniture, a sefer torah that needed repair—and lots of other stuff."

Seddaca said, "But when we started reading those old minutes we discovered that the cemetery deal wasn't quite kosher. When somebody was buried, the cemetery charged them extra for opening and closing the grave, even though that was supposedly included in the original price.

"The guy who negotiated the purchase was chair of our *Chevra Kadisha*, the burial society, and he was taking a kickback on every funeral. He also took a cut every time he sold a plot. After six or seven years, he got caught."

Kimmelman sighed. "It was a *shanda*, a big scandal."

Ferguson said, "Because by then this guy was our president. "So of course they called in an auditor. Sure enough, he was cooking the books, skimming off donations. Thousands and thousands of dollars he took."

Ben said, "But that was almost fifty years ago."

Burkin said, "It all but ruined Beit Joseph. Hundreds of families left. We really never recovered from that."

"Are there any members who remember that far back?"

Kimmelman said, "Maybe four or five. But last year was our diamond jubilee—seventy-five years in Burbank. When Tova found those boxes full of old board minutes... "

Tova said, "The Jubilee Committee put together a memory book as a fund raiser. Actually, it sold out and we did quite well. But Leticia Silverman—"

Seddaca said, "She chaired the Jubilee committee—"

"—Leticia couldn't resist a juicy story about a crooked president and the burial plots," Tova continued. "She wrote a long article, with photos, about the scandal."

"So everyone knows. It's part of our history."

Ferguson said, "I was just a kid when all that happened. The scandal—it was terrible for our family."

Unexpectedly, he began to sob. "He was my mother's brother. My Uncle Jake. When the news got out, he killed himself."

Kimmelman said, "Now there's trouble with the same cemetery plots. And the treasurer is in charge of selling them."

Ferguson burst into tears. "That's me—I'm the treasurer. Will you please help us, Rabbi?"

CHAPTER 9

Ben said, "So because it's burial plots and because the first time around it was his uncle, if anything gets out about this, you're worried that so many families will leave that it's could be the end of Beit Joseph?"

Kimmelman nodded, grim. Ferguson continued to weep quietly until Tova handed him a tissue.

"You may be right about that. I hate to ask this, Mr. Ferguson—"

"It's Aaron. Please call me Aaron."

"I have to ask: If you're in charge of the burial plots and there's a possibility that someone sold them and pocketed the money—why should I think it *wasn't* you?"

Ferguson nodded. "That's fair. And the reason is that today a burial plot at Shabbat Tamid goes for around eight grand. I've sold two in the last six years and we're supposed to have nine left.

"But even after what that gonif Madoff took from me, and after the beating I took in the market the last few years, and even after real estate fell through the floor—I'm still worth about eight million, net. Give or take."

Burkin said, "Seventy thousand dollars isn't much to Aaron. He's given us way more than that, over the years."

Ben turned to Ferguson. "You put up the money to hire me?"

Seddaca said, "Half. He put up half. We raised the rest among ourselves."

Ben frowned. "It looks bad when the prime suspect pays the investigator. Even half, it doesn't look good."

Burkin said. "Then we hope you can straighten this out without involving police. With no publicity. The quieter and faster the better."

It was a strange situation, Ben realized. But at that moment, and not for the first time, he was immensely proud to be a Jew. Jews like to think that they are more honest than gentiles, but human nature isn't changed by circumcision. Exhibit A: David Siegel.

Ben knew there were many Jewish crooks, not to mention those whose business practices bordered on the criminal. There were Jewish prostitutes and Jewish pimps, Jewish burglars, Jewish wife beaters—every kind of schemer and low life. He had met more than his share of them. But these five people were what he hoped all Jews would be, less concerned for themselves than worried over their congregation's fate.

Then came the annoying thought that it was possible that one or more of the five was not quite what he seemed. Or maybe even all five.

Ben turned to Burkin. "I must be free to work on this without any oversight."

"No micromanaging. Agreed."

"No managing, period. When I need help, I'll ask you. If you think of any relevant information, no matter how inconsequential it may seem, tell me privately. Agreed?"

Everyone nodded in agreement.

Ferguson said, "You run the show. No interference."

"One more thing. From time to time I might ask one of you what seems like a strange question. Maybe even a crazy question. But I will need your best answer in any case."

The room was perfectly silent for a long moment.

Ben stood up and took the second envelope.

"I'll need a notarized letter authorizing me to view all your financial records, including bank accounts. I need to look at every scrap of paper in your office and in your cheder, and I'll need all your computer passwords."

Tova said, "I wonder if he's gay." Her head swiveled around the Starbucks, where people of all ages and every identifiable sexual permutation drank coffee, sipped tea, surfed the Web, wrote screenplays, read or chatted.

Across the table Burkin and Kimmelman shook their heads. Burkin said, "No way. And my gaydar's pretty good."

Kimmelman frowned. "*Loshon hara* doesn't help anyone," he said, referring to a Leviticus prohibition against gossip, literally "going up and down as a talebearer among thy people," sometimes called "the evil tongue."

Tova looked peeved. "I'm just saying... it makes me wonder. He dresses well. He's good looking, single, no kids, never had his own pulpit. I just wonder about him, that's all."

A wicked grin twisted Burkin's mouth. "Also, he never once stared at your breasts last night."

Tova blushed. "There is that. But he's four years younger than me."

"Seven. Or more."

Tova was annoyed with Burkin. "I never understood all that. Boys with Oedipal fixations grow into men obsessed with younger and younger women. What does a young girl know about pleasing a man?"

Burkin said, "Why don't you ask your former spouses? Didn't they—"

"What chutzpah!" Tova hissed. "From a man who left his wife to *shtup* a gold-digger half your age? Younger than your own son?"

Kimmelman tried to suppress a smile. "Calm down. Both of you. And if I may interject, there's much more to relationships than sex."

Tova said, "I wasn't talking about sex!"

She was so loudly passionate that heads turned and the café's noisy hubbub paused.

She lowered her voice. "I meant exactly what the rabbi meant. What does a young girl know about making a man feel wanted but not needed, and both secure and important? All they know is the bedroom. And maybe not even that so much."

Burkin let his exasperation show. "Why don't we talk about something relevant, such as creating some sort of contingency plan if Ben fails. Or if the story gets out."

Tova said, "What do you think about hiring one of those PR firms that specialize in crisis management?"

Burkin snorted. "They charge more than he does. And we'd have to tell them everything."

Kimmelman said, "More to the point, our target audience is 280 families—our own community. If we hire a PR firm, our members would wonder how we're spending their money and they'd be sure that we're trying to cover something up."

Tova threw up her hands. "You're right. But seriously, what do you think he'll find? What are the possibilities? If we can anticipate them, we could plan for each."

Burkin said, "I've been thinking about that. The first thing that comes to mind is that the cemetery is in cahoots with someone and they sold our plots again."

Kimmelman said, "My first thought also. But there could be a much more innocent explanation. In the Fifties, when we bought those plots, all records were paper. I understand that the cemetery's management changed hands last year. I'm sure they must have computerized all the paper. Maybe someone made a mistake in the process."

Tova said, "Sure. Garbage in, garbage out. Or they could have lost or misplaced paper records. Shouldn't we have checked that before we spent all that money?"

Burkin shook his head. "Give me credit for a little common sense!. "Ferguson and I discussed all this with Seddaca before we told anyone else. And Seddaca checked with the cemetery," he said. "Their records show exactly what ours show. Seven plots in one row, and two more in two other rows."

"So if the plots are supposed to be empty, and they're not, isn't the onus on the cemetery? Isn't it their responsibility?"

Burkin said, "Legally, it is. But if one of their employees is involved, he'd certainly alter the records. And someone from our community might be in on it."

Kimmelman said, "Maybe we're not the only victims. Maybe this has happened to other shuls."

"So we need to know more facts before we accuse anyone, before we get the congregation all riled up."

Kimmelman put on his sport jacket and stood up. "And that's why he hired Rabbi Ben."

Tova and Burkin also rose. "Are you both coming tomorrow night" she asked.

"Of course," Burkin replied.

Kimmelman said, "I invited Ben. We'll introduce him to the board."

Burkin hoisted a bulging briefcase from the floor. "I'd like to talk to him before the meeting. Do you know what he's doing today?"

***

Ben was driving around Burbank looking for an apartment, a furnished place that he could rent for a short period.

He also needed to return the rental and buy a car.

That turned out to be easy: He found a private seller with a ten-year-old Honda. It was dented but mechanically sound and the air conditioner worked, and Ben was sure that when the time came, he could sell it quickly for almost as much as he'd paid—far cheaper than any rental.

Later that afternoon he found a furnished studio and sublet it from a junior studio executive about to leave for filming in Thailand for at least two months. It was in a huge, security-gated complex that offered a degree of anonymity. Ben would need to kasher the kitchen, but it was near Beit Joseph, had a microwave oven and a broadband connection. He could move in at once.

CHAPTER 11

TUESDAY: MAY 11

Burkin tapped a ceremonial gavel on a felt-lined anvil. "The meeting will come to order."

As the room quieted the officers and directors of Temple Beit Joseph noticed Ben, sitting next to Burkin at the head of the long conference table.

Burkin said, "Please welcome our visiting scholar, Rabbi Ben Maimon, who through the generosity of an anonymous donor, will be with us for the next few months.

"Rabbi Ben Maimon, would you care to say a few words?"

Ben rose, taking in the scene with a glance, not much surprised at the unexpected invitation: Burkin seemed like the sort of man who enjoyed testing others with unexpected requests.

"The honor is mine, Mr. Burkin.

"Master of the Universe, we thank you for this opportunity to serve our community and our people by conducting the business of this congregation," he began, unfeigned emotion infusing each word.

"As we perform this mitzvah, help us to remember that we are here not for any selfish purpose but to do our part, however small, in *Tikkun Olam*, to heal the world, and work toward the completion of your purpose of Creation.

"Help us to listen as well as speak, to consider our words and ideas carefully, to treat each other with the respect due each member of a holy assembly.

"Master of the Universe, help us to recall that we are but the latest small link in a chain stretching back through the ages, through our people's times of travail and our days of triumph, an unbroken connection to *Har Sinai,* Mt. Sinai, and *Moshe Rebbeinu,* Moses our teacher, and to our fathers Abraham, Isaac and Jacob, and our mothers Sara, Rebecca, Rachel and Leah.

"And let us say, Amen."

"Amen!" came the response. "*Yasher Koach*! *Koach*! May you have strength."

Around the long, scarred, walnut table, tears glittered in more than a few eyes.

Ben acknowledged their applause with a nod. "I look forward to getting to know each of you in the days ahead."

Burkin got to his feet.

"Thank you, Rabbi Ben."

"Now, if you've all read the minutes of our last meeting, I'll entertain a motion to accept them."

"So moved," Tova said.

"Seconded," Seddaca called from across the table.

"Additions, corrections, any other discussion?" Burkin asked, and the meeting was underway.

***

Two hours later the meeting ended and Ben was surrounded by people anxious to exchange a few words. A tall, thin man with a goatee pumped his hand.

"I'm Gene Englander. I'm so pleased that you're here." But tell me, what does a visiting scholar actually do?"

"I'm doing research for what might turn into a book, Beit Joseph is a base, a place to work from. While I'm here I'll be pleased to participate in the community in whatever ways are open to me."

A dark, burly, handsome man of perhaps forty, whose eyes seemed vaguely Asian and whose hands were adorned with the calluses and scars of an artisan or skilled laborer, spoke up. "What's the subject of your research, Rabbi?"

"*Chevra kadisha*," Ben replied. "Burial societies in Twentieth Century Southern California."

"I'm Chang Rosenfeld—call me Chang."

Ben tried not to look surprised.

Chang laughed. "My grandfather Chang, of blessed memory, was born in Korea. His parents died in the war and when he was about ten he was adopted by a Jewish family. He had his bar mitzvah right here, at Beit Joseph. Zaideh Chang served on this board for years. He wanted our family to remember its Asian roots, so when he died I changed my name—Chad—to his, Chang."

"All that explanation wasn't necessary, but thanks."

"People get confused by the name. I'm used to it."

They shook hands.

Ben said, "You seem young to be on a synagogue board."

Chang laughed. "This is my tenth year. Carrying on the family tradition. I chair the *tefila*—ritual—committee. And I just started teaching a weekly shofar-blowing class."

"I might come by and watch that."

"Please do. Excuse me, but burial societies sounds like an odd subject for a rabbi."

"Many societies evolved into community prayer groups and in time acquired their own building, hired a rabbi—"

"—and became synagogues," Chang finished. "Now it makes sense. But how do you research a subject like that?"

"Public libraries, community records, period newspaper articles, death notices. Things like that. I'll be trying to locate archives or old documents that might be stored in synagogues and temples."

"No poking around in cemeteries?"

"Maybe. Depends on what my research turns up."

Chang dug out a card. "If I can help, call me."

Ben glanced at the card. "You're a cabinet maker?"

"Custom interiors. Paneling, built-ins, cabinets. Anything that requires good craftsmanship. In my spare time I've started building a new ark and a Torah table for the chapel. A gift to the synagogue in my zaideh's memory."

"Excuse me, Rabbi," interrupted an older woman, her wrinkled face hinting at faded beauty. "I'm Dvora Klein and I was so moved by your prayer. Where did you find it?"

"It was my grandfather's."

"Well it was just wonderful, and I thank you for it," Dvora said. "Thanks again."

By the time he broke free, Ben had chatted with the entire group and was impressed with their sincerity.

Ben felt that this was an unusually close, warm and open congregation. Few synagogue boards had been quite so effusive in their welcome.

Yet he was troubled by Burkin's insistence on avoiding police and wondered what that was really about. Was he still hiding something?

CHAPTER 12

WEDNESDAY: MAY 12

Something was buried in a cemetery plot. Someone was moving money through a little-used bank account. Both the plot and the account belonged to the same institution and both came to official notice about the same time. Ben wondered if could be mere coincidence. Or was there some connection between them?

At Beit Joseph, Ben asked Rabbi Kimmelman to find the Cheder Halakha account records. He brought him an accordion folder with checks and statements going back to the establishment of the fund fifteen years earlier.

At the desk of the cramped cubicle that had been the rabbinical interns' office, he went through the canceled checks, noting that each bore two signatures—synagogue policy for amounts over five hundred dollars. Checking signatures against board rosters, he saw that with two exceptions, each check was signed by those then serving as president and treasurer.

The exceptions were nine and seven years earlier, when one Sanford Feingelt co-signed in place of the treasurer. Feingelt's name didn't appear on the board roster either year but he was listed as a director the year between the two checks he signed and five years before the first check.

Ben decided to go to the bank and look at the old signature cards, if they were still on file. But that could wait, he thought. The cemetery was a more pressing issue, and he would first need to learn more about cemetery management in general. Before leaving, he put the accordion file on Kimmelman's desk, with a note that he'd looked through the canceled checks but might want to go through the statements again.

Stepping into the corridor Ben was startled by the sound of a shofar. He stopped to listen to a virtuoso performance; never had he heard a ram's horn blown through three octaves, and never with such a sweet, pure, distinctive tone.

He found Chang Rosenfeld in the chapel with an enormous shofar made from a curving, knobbed horn nearly four feet long, the biggest shofar Ben had ever seen.

"*Yasher koach*! May you have strength to repeat your mitzvah! I've never heard a sweeter sound from a shofar."

"Thanks, Rabbi Ben. A good horn helps."

"You know the *Akeidah*? The Binding of Isaac?"

"Of course."

"When *HaShem* stopped Abraham from sacrificing his son, Abraham saw a ram whose horns were caught in a thicket."

"Sure. And he sacrificed the ram instead of Isaac."

"There's a Midrash, a teaching, that this ram was an ibex, because if his horns were smooth and straight, like most ram's horns, they wouldn't have gotten caught."

Chang smiled. "I like that."

"We also know that the shofar that was blown in Solomon's Temple, and later in the Sanhedrin, the Supreme Court of ancient Israel, was the same—from the *yael*, or Nubian ibex. So that's not *just* a shofar. It's a wonderful piece of Jewish history. *Koach*."

"Would you like to try it, Rabbi?"

"I'm not much of a musician, but yes. I'm honored."

Ben put the horn to his lips and after an abortive trial blew "*Tekiah*," a short blast of three seconds. Then he blew *Shevarim*—three quick blasts. Finally he blew nine quick, staccato blasts—"*Teruah*," before admiring the instrument and handing it back to Chang.

"You have potential, Rabbi. Come to my class and we'll turn you into another Joshua—walls will tremble and fall for your shofar."

Ben laughed. "Amen. You're teaching today?"

"A little later. Please join us."

"Maybe next time."

En route to the Bank of B. Cohen, Ben marveled at the variety of skills and education he saw at Beit Joseph.

The bank, a sturdy brick corner building in downtown Burbank, was closed. A discreet sign announced public banking hours of nine to noon Monday through Thursday. Ben was disappointed but intrigued.

***

Dealing with synagogue officers, Ben had learned, it was usually easier to speak with them individually and privately. He decided to start with Tova.

Tova was surprised and pleased when Ben invited her to dinner. And a little off-balance—was this personal or professional? Was he interested in her? She liked the idea.

They met at the Contented Cow, a Studio City eatery offering innovative vegan fare and a selection of faux meat dishes made, skillfully, from textured soy protein.

Tova handed Ben a menu. "It's vegetarian, so I hope you're not disappointed, Rabbi."

"Ben."

"Ben."

"Not at all. Good kosher restaurants are hard to find. At home I often eat fake *treif* Chinese carryout."

"It's just that I had classes at UCLA this morning and I wanted to avoid shlepping back to Kosher Canyon."

Ben smiled. "Kosher Canyon?"

"Fairfax Avenue, near Hollywood. Where most of the kosher restaurants are—there, and on Pico, in West L.A."

"This is fine. What do you recommend?"

"The Salisbury steak is excellent."

A beautiful young waitress in a low-cut blouse came to take their order. Tova saw that Ben seemed to pay little attention to her and wondered again if he was gay.

Tova ordered a big salad with a side of cheese bread, and Ben the Salisbury steak in mushroom sauce.

Tova said, "Was there something you wanted to talk about, or is this just to get acquainted?"

"Both. And I'd appreciate it if you keep not only what we discuss to yourself, but also the fact that we met."

Tova felt crushed. She had hoped – but no, she told herself, that was silly. He was only here for a short time. Why would he want to get involved when he'd soon be gone?

Still, she'd hoped there might be more to it. Hoped, after far too long, to enjoy the warmth of a good man's arms around her. To feel desired and desirable.

"My lips are sealed."

Ben smiled. "You can unseal them to eat, I hope."

When the food came Ben wolfed it down appreciatively. Tova picked at her salad wondering how Ben stayed so trim.

Ben said, "I run five miles every morning."

"My God—you read minds?"

"I'm fairly intuitive. For example, I get the feeling that you'd hoped that this was more personal than business. And that we might become, well, close."

Tova blushed down to the scoop neck of her dress.

"Why on earth would you imagine that?"

"Just a vibe. Maybe I was wrong. In any case, I do notice that you're an exceptionally pretty woman, and very intelligent. But I can't get involved under these circumstances, much less with someone I'm working for."

"And you have a girlfriend back in Boston."

"No. I travel constantly. That just wouldn't work."

"You've never been married?"

A cloud drifted over Ben's face. "Very briefly. Less than a year."

"I'm sorry it didn't work out."

"Me, too."

"I tried twice. I was too young the first time and too needy the last."

"So we move on."

"We move on, yes."

"I'd like to talk about Beit Joseph."

"What about it?"

"Can you give me some idea of who the machers are? Aside from Burkin, Seddaca, Ferguson and yourself?"

"I'm hardly a macher!"

"You're a mover and shaker. You served two terms as president. Close enough."

"The real machers never show their faces at a board meeting. Except for Aaron Ferguson."

"So they're machers because..."

"Because they're deep pockets, and they like the idea of being asked to open their wallets for us."

"So they're more into the *idea* of a synagogue than into actually participating in one?"

"You could say that. If the sanctuary needs a new roof, or when we wanted to start a day school, or buy new computers—we call one of them. And if they need a *sefer Torah* for a private bat mitzvah, or a rabbi to *kasher* their kitchen, they call us.

"And if they don't like the way the board runs things, we hear about it."

"Who are they?"

"There's Marcus—Marcus Pinsky. And Efraim Jacobs, Richard Martel, Miriam Levine, and Sandy."

"Tell me about them. Are they all older?"

"Richard and Sandy are in their early sixties. Miriam is close to eighty. Marcus and Efraim are in their seventies."

"All married?"

"Richard is gay. He made a fortune in software and retired. He travels a lot. Miriam is a widow. She paints and gives a lot of money to art museums. The others are married. But why do you have to know all this?"

"I told you that sometimes I'll ask what seem to be strange questions. This is one of those times, Tova. I have my reasons."

Tova looked torn. "I don't want to be a gossip."

"Nor do I. I just need to know who I'm dealing with."

"I suppose."

"By the way, do any of these people, these machers, know about me and why I'm here?"

"Not unless Aaron said something—but I'm sure he didn't. After all, he's got the most to lose if people find out about the cemetery. Or the money, for that matter."

"Okay. Let's start with Sandy. Tell me about him."

"Sanford Feingelt. Probably the richest Jew in the Valley, not counting a few of the movie folks. He's old money, dabbles in law—estates and trusts, and owns all sorts of businesses. I even heard he owned a bank, or he used to own one, or was a partner in one—something. But I don't know which one."

"Married?"

"His first wife divorced him about five years ago. Right after that, he married someone quite a bit younger. He has grown children from the first marriage."

"What about Marcus?"

"Retired. A land developer—he owns apartments, mini-malls, shopping centers. His sons run all that now. He plays golf, goes to Las Vegas, travels. Comes once a year."

"A Yom Kippur Jew."

"Bless them. He makes a nice donation every year."

"That leaves Efraim."

"Efraim Melendez. He's got clothing stores. Or did. I think he may have sold them a few years ago."

"Melendez?"

"He's from Ecuador. I'm guessing his mother was Jewish. Or maybe he's from a *converso* family—they all took Spanish surnames."

The *conversos*, as Ben knew, were Spanish Jews of the Fourteenth and Fifteenth Centuries who converted to Christianity to escape persecution. Many continued Jewish practices in secret; in recent decades some had openly returned to Judaism.

"Thanks Tova, this has been very useful."

"I can't think how. But if it helps..."

"It does. By the way, have any of those people, the machers, have they ever served on the board?"

"I don't know. I've only been a member eight years, and a board member for five. I became treasurer, because nobody else would do it, and then became president for the same reason. Until my second year as treasurer there wasn't much interest in serving on the board."

"Bickering, infighting..."

"You don't know the half of it! They argued over everything, even things that didn't matter. Nobody wanted to go to a board meeting and stay past midnight deciding where to hold the Purim party. And they micromanaged every committee chair until they quit."

Ben smiled. "I've seen that in other synagogues. How did you deal with it?"

"I wouldn't serve a second term as treasurer if certain people remained on the board."

"That must have gone over like a lead balloon."

"Not really. Manny, Aaron and Gary got together and it was like a coup d'etat! Six board members left the shul and joined Chodosh Agudath in Van Nuys."

"How did the rest of the congregation react?"

"A few families left with them, but for the most part it was 'good riddance.' Now we have a harmonious, very cohesive board. We don't agree on everything, but we work things out. There's no bullying, no shouting. More like needling or teasing. That's why your prayer resonated so well last week."

"I'm pleased that it did. Can you get me a list of the board members that left Beit Joseph?"

"You don't think that they—"

"I need to look into every possibility."

The waitress brought the check and Ben grabbed it.

Ben said, "I've really enjoyed this, Tova."

"Thank you, Ben."

"Tova, if things were different..."

"I'm not looking for commitment. Just somebody—"

"You're beautiful and talented—I'm sure someone—"

"Please."

Ben took her hand for a moment.

"Really, I wish that our circumstances..."

Tova pulled away and half-ran for the door.

A few minutes later, behind the wheel of her Prius, she watched Ben drive away. She wasn't sure why, but she wanted to cry.

CHAPTER 13

THURSDAY: MAY 13

Still damp from the shower after a morning run, Ben opened his Mac Book Pro and logged on to Google, where he checked email and replied to two friends. The third message was from Bert Epstein, another M.I.T. classmate and now a Harvard virologist.

News to share. Important, not urgent. Call me!

Bert

It was mid-morning in Burbank, noon in Cambridge. Maybe he's at lunch, Ben thought, and called Bert's cell. The call went straight to voicemail, and Ben hung up without leaving a message. Important but not urgent.

Back on the Mac, Ben Googled Shabbat Tamid cemetery and found a single-page website with an address and phone number and an announcement that the mortuary was closed for modernization.

Not much help, Ben thought.

He Googled **Jewish cemeteries + Los Angeles** and got several hits. The oldest was Home of Peace, he read, a successor to the first Jewish burial ground in Los Angeles, whose remains and headstones were in 1910 moved from Chavez Ravine, where Dodger stadium now sat, to East Los Angeles. Home of Peace was now owned by a national cemetery and mortuary chain. Few such chains were under Jewish management.

Southern California's best-known Jewish cemetery was Hillside Memorial Park, he decided, after learning that many of the region's most illustrious Jews were buried there. Milton Berle, Jack Benny, Al Jolson—no surprises. But baseball slugger Hank Greenberg—and singer Nell Carter?

Both slept beneath Hillside's gently rolling turf. Hillside's Website said the facility was owned by Temple Israel of Hollywood.

Ben called American Jewish University, a small but highly regarded Conservative Judaism institution that trained rabbis and prepared professionals for careers in Jewish institutions of many kinds. After threading his way through several department secretaries, he made an appointment with a professor there.

By early afternoon he sat across the desk from a plump, pleasant, graying woman, an adjunct professor who taught a class on Jewish burials and funerary issues.

She explained that although Hillside was owned by a synagogue, it was operated by contractors; the temple leadership had little to do with day-to-day operations.

Over the next hour, Ben filled several notebook pages. He learned that many older U.S. cemeteries were subsidized by local taxes, but Jewish cemeteries, not open to the general public, almost never receive taxpayer money.

Starting a new cemetery, explained the professor, began with buying raw land, developing the site, landscaping, building a chapel and perhaps a mortuary, then selling grave plots. The price of each plot included a percentage that went into an endowment for so-called perpetual care—watering and cutting grass, maintaining access roads, repairs to facilities, a directory service to help visitors find specific graves, etc. And for security—even in America, Jewish cemeteries were desecrated more often than others.

Cemeteries make money by subdividing acreage and selling plot-sized pieces for several times the cost of the land. In Southern California, however, land values have increased almost continuously for more than a hundred years, and cemetery plots have followed in lockstep. Land for a cemetery like Hillside, for example, purchased several decades earlier, cost a few thousand dollars an acre—much less than the current price of a single Hillside plot.

The price people were willing to pay for a particular plot could be increased by creating an aura of exclusivity with attractive shrubbery, fountains, sculpture, etc.

Cemeteries charged for opening and closing a grave and for grave liners, typically of concrete or plastic, to guard against sinkholes. Cemeteries often tried to sell elaborate liners, often at greatly inflated prices.

Cemeteries often include a mortuary, both for client convenience and as an additional profit center. Preparing a body for burial in accordance with ancient Jewish law, embalming services, and the sale of coffins all provided income streams.

By Jewish custom, a headstone is erected a year following burial, on the anniversary of the death, an observance believed to originate in Genesis, which noted that Jacob erected a monument at his wife Rachel's grave. Headstones provide yet another cemetery revenue stream, as do charges for engraving and installation.

A cemetery could be profitable for many years, Ben realized. As, inevitably, it began to fill, above-ground mausoleums could be erected, multiplying the number of remains kept on the space. Adjacent land could be purchased; if none was available, some operators, even in some Jewish cemeteries, moved the oldest graves to smaller plots in less desirable areas.

Long before they reached capacity, however, owners of for-profit cemeteries usually sold or transferred them to local governments or to companies with the resources for further development. Too often such sales provided opportunities for either buyer or seller to loot the perpetual care endowment through a variety of accounting schemes.

When Ben asked about Shabbat Tamid, the professor pulled a face. "An East coast company bought it several years ago. I'm not sure they ever turned a profit. Then there was a scandal—the endowment fund had somehow come to be invested in stocks worth almost nothing. And their accounting records were a mess—nobody could figure out where the money went or when.

"There was an investigation, a lot of angry talk and finger-pointing from families with loved ones buried there, but nobody went to jail. A few months ago the cemetery was purchased by a company I've never heard of. They still hold funerals, but they're not selling plots."

She pursed her lips, her voice dripping disdain. "Now they're expanding the mortuary to refocus their business."

Ben said, "And you don't think much of that idea?"

"It's very competitive. They'll have to do a lot of marketing and find some gimmick or pricing formula that's more attractive than the established mortuaries. I'm really not sure why anybody would buy that particular cemetery now."

Very, very interesting, Ben thought, on the drive back to his sublet.

There he went back online and used Google Earth to peer at satellite photos of Shabbat Tamid. It looked to be nearly full, with few unused grave sites. Adjacent land was covered with homes—further expansion seemed impossible.

Maybe, if Shabbat Tamid management was desperate for cash flow while their mortuary was closed for expansion, someone might have resorted to desperate measures, like selling plots they didn't own.

But who actually owned the cemetery?

He Googled the California Department of Corporations, which listed no corporate officers, not even a corporate name, only the "service agent"—the individual who would accept legal documents on behalf of its ownership. That turned out to be a Sacramento attorney.

Ben called the attorney's office and listened to a recorded message about how to serve documents. That led him to a second law office, this one in Los Angeles, and a second recorded message specifying that all documents were to be served by registered mail to a Burbank address.

Ben Googled the address and found that was a house on a cul-de-sac that ended at Shabbat Tamid.

It was almost time to visit the cemetery. Ben decided.

CHAPTER 14

That night Ben dined alone, reading musty Beit Joseph board minutes, often browning mimeographed pages with faded blue text, meanwhile tucking away toasted Muenster cheese and green olives on a fresh Noah's cracked pepper-potato bagel, and tomato soup.

He tried Bert's number again at eight, hoping to catch him before he went to bed, but again the call went to voicemail. How is it, he wondered, that everybody carries a cell phone and nobody ever answers?

This time he left a message.

To his surprise, Bert called back almost immediately.

"Ben! How're they hanging?"

"High and tight, as always."

They both laughed at the private joke.

"What's up, Bert?"

"First off, how are you? For that matter, *where* are you—I went by your apartment but your car's not there."

"I stored it in a garage—do you need to borrow it?"

"No, no. Just wondering."

"I'm in Burbank—near Los Angeles."

They made small talk for a few minutes. Finally Ben said, "So, what's so important?"

"We've had a breakthrough, Ben."

"A cure? You found a cure for me?"

"Not a cure. But maybe a path to one."

"Go on."

"You know, we've tried everything to eradicate the virus, and we're doing a pretty good job of killing or blocking it in the blood with drug therapies. In fact, we're getting closer to a vaccine than ever."

"But it's still in there, somewhere, waiting."

"Exactly. And now we know where it lurks: In marrow."

"In my bones?"

"Exactly.

"What does that mean for me?"

"It means that we may be able to stamp out the infection by replacing your marrow."

"A marrow transplant? How will you find marrow matches for everyone infected with HIV?"

"That's over half a million people, Ben, and the short answer is that we can't."

"Then what?"

"We already know how to treat leukemia by removing some of a patient's marrow, killing the cancerous cells, then using the cleaned marrow to replace the cancerous marrow. There's no risk of the patient's body rejecting donor marrow, so there's no need for immunosuppressors."

"So you might be able to clean *my* marrow?"

"It looks possible. We're writing grant proposals now, and if we get most of what we ask for we might be able to start trials as soon as next year."

"And how long before the trials are completed and evaluated?"

"Three to five years at the soonest. But Ben, you might be able to get into a trial. You're young, you're otherwise healthy, and you're in good physical condition."

"Something to think about."

"Yes, think about it. Marrow transplants are very hard on a patient's body. But it's worth considering."

"You bet I will. Thanks for the heads-up."

"You know I've got your back."

"I know, Bert. Thanks for calling."

Ben brushed his teeth and then, facing east, recited the *Sh'ma*, the seminal prayer drawn from Leviticus that is fundamental to all Jewish beliefs:

Sh'ma Yis'ra'eil Adonai Eloheinu Adonai echad.

Hear, O Israel, the Lord is our God, the Lord is One.

Barukh sheim k'vod malkhuto l'olam va'ed.

Blessed be the Name of His glorious kingdom for ever and ever.

Although it was still early, he undressed and lay down on the bed, unable to sleep, his mind churning with feverish thoughts about Bert's news, trying to resist the urge but feeling more and more that at long last, there might be hope for him.

He awoke before dawn, drenched in sweat, horrified at imagining the feel of pitiless invaders silently entering his body through his bleeding wounds as he knelt in the ruins of a Jerusalem café to save a life.

CHAPTER 15

MONDAY: MAY 17

Ben stepped into Beit Joseph's office down the hall from the conference room, where Rabbi Kimmelman awaited him. He wasn't alone.

Kimmelman said, "This is LaShonda Harris, our synagogue administrator. LaShonda, say hello to Rabbi Ben Maimon, a visiting scholar."

Ben turned to see a tall, shapely woman with clear café au lait skin and long, braided hair falling almost to her slender waist. She wore modest business attire that she nevertheless imbued with an aura of sensuality. To Ben's eyes, she might have been anywhere from thirty to fifty years old—he couldn't tell.

"Pleased to meet you, Ms. Harris."

"It's LaShonda."

They shook hands. Was it his imagination, or did her fingers brush the back of his hand ever so lightly?

Kimmelman said, "LaShonda is our glue—she holds this place together."

LaShonda smiled, displaying perfectly even, perfectly white teeth. "Think of me as the Tar Baby, rabbi."

Ben laughed, appreciating her wit no less than her beauty.

She said, "So what does a visiting scholar do?"

"I'm here from Boston researching a possible book, and Rabbi Kimmelman was kind enough to offer me a place to hang my hat, office space, a phone, a computer."

Kimmelman said, "And Rabbi Ben was kind enough to volunteer to do some teaching and work with our interns."

LaShonda bobbed her head up and down, braid shaking. "So when holy men get together, they wheel and deal too! Who knew?"

Ben smiled in spite of himself. LaShonda was forthright and uninhibited—unlike any synagogue supervisor he'd ever met. It occurred to him that she might hear things that neither Kimmelman nor the board were privy to. It could be fun finding out, he thought.

Ben had stopped at Beit Joseph primarily to get a list of Burbank-area synagogues and temples. he planned to call each to inquire about how many Shabbat Tamid plots they had or that had been purchased by members but were as yet unused.

But when he asked LaShonda to assemble the list, she volunteered to make the calls. That left Ben free to call Chang Rosenfeld, who invited him to his workshop.

Rosenwood, as Chang called his shop, was in an industrial section near a railroad spur, a collection of machine shops, plastic extruders, metal fabricators and assorted small manufacturers in older stucco buildings.

Ben found the curbs tight with parked trucks and trash dumpsters; he had to park down the street from Rosenwood. Walking back he saw three hard-faced, tattooed, teenaged Latinos smoking, idling and eying him from a truck's narrow shade.

Chang had repurposed an old-fashioned service station into an office, workshop and storage area. Near it was a second building, smaller, with shuttered windows and locked doors that made it seem almost abandoned.

A half dozen cars and pickups were parked inside Chang's chain-link fence. Ben found Chang in his office, sitting at a computer running 3-D design software.

After exchanging pleasantries, Ben unfolded a sheet of notebook paper and showed Chang a sketch.

"Can you make this for me?"

Ben had drawn a long, thin cylinder about five feet long and tapering from half an inch in diameter to a rounded, blunt end about a fourth of an inch wide.

"You want me to make you a pool cue?"

"Something thinner than that: A probe. I want to push it into the earth to look for buried objects."

"Like in a graveyard?"

"Or in a place that *might* be a graveyard."

"I'm happy to help."

"It needs to break down into four lengths of about eighteen inches that screw into each other for assembly."

"To carry without advertising your intentions?"

"Or just to fit in a briefcase."

"How soon do you need it?"

"The sooner the better, but don't lose any sleep over it or turn down any business."

"I'll have it by the end of the day."

"What will you charge me?"

"On the house, rabbi."

"I have expense money and if I don't spend it I'll just have to return it. I insist."

"Since you put it that way, how about forty bucks?"

"How about fifty?"

Chang laughed and clapped the smaller man on the back. "You gotta be the coolest rabbi I ever met."

***

On the drive back to Beit Joseph, Ben passed a notions store. On a whim he went around the block and pulled into the mini-mall, which also featured a Japanese restaurant. Suddenly hungry, he dashed into the notions emporium and bought needles, thread and a roll of adhesive-backed Velcro. Then he went next door and feasted on tuna *sashimi*, marveling at the freshness of the fish and the price—less than any place he knew in Boston.

I could get used to living here, he thought, then banished the idea. He had a job to do, and then on to the next. Or maybe he'd take a year off, try to get into that marrow trial. If he could finish here quickly, he could afford the time off.

Returning to his tiny synagogue office, Ben found a hand-written list on his desk. LaShonda had called fifteen area synagogues; between them they had six Shabbat Tamid plots, all singles, in widely scattered areas. As he suspected, the cemetery was virtually full.

Ben went down the hall and found LaShonda at her desk, nibbling on a homemade tuna sandwich.

Ben said, "That was fast. Thanks so much."

"Nothing to it! Somebody else's been calling around looking for those burial plots, so everybody I talked to knew right off where to find the information."

"Did anyone happen to mention who was looking?"

"I could call back and ask."

"No, that's okay. Listen, I really appreciate your help. You saved me a lot of time. Can I buy you dinner or something?"

"You're asking me out?"

"Not exactly. I'd just like to take you to dinner sometime."

"That's a date, honey. But I've never gone out with a rabbi—I don't know what to wear."

"It's just dinner, LaShonda. Not a date—okay?"

"That's how you do things in Boston, huh?"

Ben had to laugh.

"I guess. What's a good night for you?"

"A good night is when I get to take a sweet young thing like you home."

"C'mon."

"Then how 'bout tonight?"

LaShonda grabbed a pen from her desk, and scribbled on a Post-It. "That's where I live. Seven o'clock? That gives me time to get home and freshen up."

"I'll see you at seven."

Headed back to Chang's workshop, Ben realized that he was actually looking forward to seeing LaShonda. Maybe it really *is* a date. He pulled out his iPhone and called Mitch Katz in Chicago but again, frustratingly, the call went to voicemail. He's probably with a patient, thought Ben, deciding not to leave a message. I'll call him after the date, he thought.

Then he thought again and dialed Gary Burkin's office.

CHAPTER 16

Ben spent the afternoon in his apartment, where he used a razor blade to open the lining of his suit jacket at the wrist seams. He pressed Velcro on either side of the opening, creating a flap that could be opened or closed easily.

In late afternoon he returned to Rosenwood. Chang was in the workshop; Ben watched appreciatively as he guided a thick board through a ripsaw, sawdust caking on his apron and dusting his goggles. As he turned from the machine, Chang saw Ben in the doorway and beckoned him inside.

"You probe is ready—unless you need it varnished?"

"No, don't bother."

Ben looked around the room and spied an alcove where finished work was stacked. A bench, several cabinets, a long wooden box with an unmistakable shape.

Ben pointed. "A coffin?"

Chang smiled. "Every once in awhile I get a special order from a mortuary. Beats me why, but some people like to go out in style. Let me get your stick."

While he went to get it, the door to the supposedly - abandoned building opened and an attractive young couple in evening clothes—he in a tuxedo, she in a long gown— appeared. They drove off in a Lexus just as Chang returned.

Ben said, "Who are those people?"

"Welcome to La La Land, Rabbi. I rent that building out for photo shoots, TV commercials, whatever."

"That explains all the cars."

"I ought to charge for parking. Its ten minutes of musical cars every time a load of wood is delivered."

***

LaShonda's neat little townhome was in a low-slung complex on the setback from a well-trafficked street in Valley Village, a Los Angeles neighborhood a few miles northwest of Beit Joseph. Ben parked on the street and followed a curving walkway until he found her unit.

"Come on in," she trilled from somewhere behind a screen door and Ben stepped into a spotless, neat-as-a-pin room with gleaming wood floors and Danish Modern furniture.

"Ikea," she said, making a grand entrance in an elegant white dress hemmed to display long, slender, well-toned legs. "That's where all my money goes."

Ben tore his eyes from her legs and looked around. "You have exquisite taste."

LaShonda did a fake curtsy before spinning around to show off the dress. "Twelve bucks at "Out of The Closet"—what do you think?"

"I think you're wasting your time at Beit Joseph. You should be modeling swimsuits."

"Been there, done that, and Ben, honey, it ain't what it looks like. It's all nasty-mouth photographers and getting up at three o'dark to do makeup so you can be standing in cold water half an hour before the sun comes up. And everyone, and I do mean everyone, trying to get my panties off."

Ben laughed in spite of himself.

LaShonda took a framed photo from an end table and handed it to Ben, who saw a handsome, light-skinned black man in crisp Navy whites.

"Your father?"

"My *son*, Ricardo. He's nineteen and just started avionics school in Florida."

"You can't possibly be old enough to have a nineteen year old child."

"I was barely sixteen and stupid. Do the arithmetic."

"What about his father?"

"Enrique. 'Loco Henry.' Lucky guy who went to prison."

"That was lucky?"

"He's out, he's alive. Most all his homeys got shot or stabbed, OD'd, dead. Or life in prison. But who cares?"

"I'm sorry."

"Don't be. He's a pig. Got me pregnant, went around bragging on it like he was a prize bull, saw his baby once and then wouldn't hardly talk to me till Ricardo grew up."

Ben wasn't naïve. He knew such stories were common in America's black and Latino ghettos. But he knew few people from that world.

"I can see that even with all that on your back, you've made a life for yourself and your son."

"Got that right, rabbi. *I* made a life."

After an awkward pause, LaShonda took the photo from Ben and set it down. She took his arm.

"I'm starvvvvving! Where are you taking me?"

***

With help from LaShonda surfing the Web on his iPhone, Ben found The Milky Way, a dairy restaurant on Pico owned by the mother of a world-famous film director.

LaShonda inspected the menu, frowning. "I've never been in a kosher restaurant. What is all this stuff?"

"Jewish comfort food. Shall I order for both of us?"

"Good idea!"

Ben ordered cheese blintzes as appetizers, followed by an order of crisp *latkes* for himself and a mound of pistachio pasta for LaShonda, who ate every last noodle.

"I want to lick the plate," she said. "But how does that look for a black girl in this neighborhood."

Ben pointed at the table near her plate.

"I think you missed part of a pistachio."

Under the table, she rubbed his leg with a bare foot.

Later, strolling down Pico and drawing suspicious looks from passers-by whose dress identified them as Orthodox Jews, LaShonda took Ben's arm, bringing their bodies into contact. Ben tried not to think about the soft, firm mound of flesh resting against his biceps.

He said, "I like what I'm feeling but maybe this isn't such a good idea in this particular ghetto."

She giggled. "You think it'd be better in South Central?"

As if on cue, a tall, bearded, bulky man appeared on the sidewalk before them. He was a head taller than Ben.

"Are you a Jew?" the man said in Yiddish.

"My Yiddish isn't good," Ben replied, in Hebrew.

"Why do you bring your *schwartzer* harlot here to shame decent people?" the man said in halting Hebrew.

Probably a Russian émigré who spent a few years in Israel, Ben thought.

"She's a respectable woman who works for a synagogue."

LaShonda touched Ben's shoulder. "What's he saying?"

"He said you're a black whore who has no right to come here and parade your wickedness before the decent people of our community," said a deeper voice from behind LaShonda, in thickly-accented English.

Ben whirled to confront a bearded man in the black suit favored by Hassidic Jews, an ultra-orthodox group that sought to emulate the strict mores and dress codes of earlier centuries. He was even taller and heavier than the first man.

LaShonda turned to face him. "You watch your mouth!"

Ben said, "Do not wrong the stranger or oppress him, for *you* were strangers in the land of Egypt."

"The Torah also says that harlots are to be stoned. In *Mea Shearim* we would stone you both."

"This is America, and we go where we please. If you can produce two witnesses to harlotry, we will convene a *beit din*, a rabbinical court."

"Go now before we break your bones," said the first man, reverting to Yiddish.

"We came in peace, but if it's war you want, let it begin now."

The bigger man laughed, then swung a massive fist at Ben. With blinding speed Ben intercepted the punch with both hands, seizing his assailant's right arm above the elbow and at the wrist. Using the man's momentum, in one smooth motion Ben jerked the arm back with one hand while pushing hard with the other.

The arm gave way with a sickening crunch and the big Hassid screamed, staggering away, his arm dangling uselessly.

Ben whirled to confront the other man, who held out open palms and backed away.

"Take your friend to a hospital."

"And learn some manners," LaShonda said.

***

LaShonda took Ben's arm but remained silent until they turned the corner and saw Ben's parked car.

"I didn't know there were Jews like those guys."

"It's only a handful. Most of the Orthodox are peaceful and honorable. These guys are dangerous because they think they're righteous. There have always been such fanatics among us. That's why, on Yom Kippur, we ask forgiveness for 'being zealots for bad causes.'"

"What if he calls the police?"

"Then he must tell them that I was six-feet six and 300 pounds."

LaShonda giggled. "I had no idea you were some kind of Kung Fu warrior. Where on earth did you learn how to fight like that?"

"A year of rabbinical school was in Israel. The IDF—Israeli Defense Forces—gave classes in self-defense. What they call *Krav Maga*, which means contact fighting."

Ben neglected to add that his grandfather, noting Ben's puny adolescent physique, had sent him to YMHA martial arts classes. Over a year each of Aikido, Taekwondo and Karate, he developed a degree of self confidence rare in teenagers, a quality that transcended physicality.

"So I guess those IDF dudes gave you an 'A.'"

"An aleph," he said, taking out his keys.

As LaShonda tugged on her seatbelt she turned to Ben.

"Why did you ask me to dinner? I mean, really, what's this about?"

"Rabbi Kimmelman asked me to help him with something, and I thought, as synagogue administrator, you might have heard or seen something that could be useful."

"This is about those phone calls I made for you?"

"Why would you think that?"

"Because I just remembered that Mr. Seddaca was all pissed about something he found at that cemetery, Shabbat..."

"Shabbat Tamid."

"Same as the one you asked me to call about."

"What do you know about what Seddaca found?"

"Something in a grave that wasn't supposed to be there. I don't know what he meant. I mean, he didn't go and dig up no graves, did he?"

"I'm sure he didn't. But actually, I wanted to ask you about something else."

"Then why did you want to know about the plots?"

"Part of my research is on the economic viability of Jewish cemeteries. I'm looking at Shabbat Tamid because it appears nearly full and I hoped to get a sense for how long it would be before they stopped having funerals."

"Oh. So then what did you want to talk about?"

"Are any Beit Joseph members having marriage troubles? Or getting a divorce?"

"Well, there's Mr. Burkin, of course. He and Mrs. Burkin—Susan—are separated."

"Anybody else? Or somebody maybe doing something that could lead to a divorce?"

"Like putting a move on me?"

"That would be one thing, if he got caught out."

"Then you need to go talk to *Mrs.* Feingelt, because I never liked the way *Mr.* Feingelt looks at me."

"Has he ever asked you out?"

"He never says anything much at all. But a girl knows when she's getting hit on."

"Was I hitting on you?"

"No, sugar. I was hitting on the Kung Fu rabbi."

***

LaShonda rested her hand lightly on Ben's arm as they drove. Neither spoke for a long time.

"LaShonda—"

"Ben. Before we take this much further, I got to know where we're headed."

"I don't know. It's all very sudden."

"Then let's just leave it at dinner. Next week, if you like, I'll make *you* dinner."

"Deal."

"But Ben—I don't play all those games, understand?"

Ben eased the Honda to a halt in front of LaShonda's building. Before he could move she was kissing him.

She tasted like strawberries, and when her hand caressed his groin he almost exploded.

Then she was gone, heels clicking on the concrete.

A little later, undressing for bed, Ben was shocked to find that his shorts were stained.

Ben parked at the far edge of the parking lot and joined a line entering the Shabbat Tamid chapel. Like the other men, he wore funeral garb: dark suit, conservative tie, white shirt. His head was crowned by a simple, black yarmulke. Inside he took a seat at the rear and listened to tearful eulogies delivered by family and friends of the late Shmuel Toeplitz, Holocaust survivor, businessman, humanitarian, father, grandfather and great-grandfather.

The Toeplitz clan, now known as Teplits, was numerous and seemingly affluent. They paid little attention to Ben, who waited patiently until the eulogies and prayers concluded and mourners queued up to file past an elaborate wooden coffin. As at all Jewish funerals, it was closed, the better to recall the departed as he had been in life.

Ben found the chapel restrooms at the end of a hallway, went into the mens room for a quick look at the windows, then joined the crowd milling around the parking lot waiting for the pallbearers. In a few minutes they appeared with the coffin and ceremoniously stowed it in a shiny black hearse. As the hearse slowly moved off, the mourners formed a loose procession and strolled after it toward the grave site.

Ben followed at a distance, noting the faces of the funeral director and two assistants. As mourners assembled at the open grave for more prayers, he slipped away.

He walked deeper into the grounds to where, consulting Seddaca's hand-drawn map, he found the grave of Solomon Seddaca. He undid the Velcro inside first one sleeve and then the next and the four sections slid out. Kneeling behind a tombstone, he assembled Chang's probe, screwing each section into the next.

The ground in front of the tombstones was covered with neatly trimmed turf. To the right of the Seddaca grave was a row of seven empty spaces—lumpy, uneven earth with new grass shoots poking through the soil.

Ben moved to the nearest grave and after a quick look around to see that no one was watching, firmly pushed the pointed end of the probe down through the earth. The first two sections, about thirty inches, went in easily. He pushed harder and the probe hit something hard and stopped midway in the third section. Ben pulled the probe out and tried again, two feet farther up the plot. Same result.

Ben probed the next plot and encountered the same impenetrable object three and a half feet down. The third plot yielded identical results; the next four appeared empty. He went back to the first plot and pushed the probe back into the original hole, then tugged it back and forth, enlarging the hole, before withdrawing it. From a pocket Ben took a powerful magnet on a length of string, and lowered it into the hole. Halfway down, it leapt from his fingers to fasten itself to the bottom of the excavation.

No Jewish coffin is made of anything but wood, thought Ben. Either it isn't a coffin or it isn't a *Jewish* coffin.

He returned the magnet to his pocket, then scooped up a handful of soil from the side of the hole and tucked it in a small plastic bag. Then he pushed dirt back into the hole. After breaking down his probe and stowing it in his sleeves, Ben walked back toward the chapel, taking his time, noting the wide drive-on entrance between the chapel and the mortuary, a side gate for heavy vehicles, a small, fenced area where earth moving equipment and two battered blue pickups were parked, and, hidden behind a row of majestic Lombardi poplars, a wrought-iron pedestrian gate. Ben had failed to notice it approaching the cemetery, and suspected that its far side was also screened by foliage.

On the wind came the distinctive chant of Mourner's Kaddish, amplified by a hundred voices. The service was almost over. Ben slipped behind the trees to approach the gate, where he bent to peer at the lock.

It was a Slage, its brass faceplate still bright and smooth. A *new* lock—that was interesting, he thought.

"Can I help you?" a man said. Ben thought it held a faint trace of the South—Alabama, maybe, or Tennessee.

He turned to find a tall, solidly-built man in an-off-the-rack suit with a funeral director's nametag: Cone. The fabric below his shoulder bulged out slightly. A phone? Did funeral directors pack heat? Ben wondered.

"Isn't there a restroom around here somewhere?" Ben asked, making eye contact.

"Back that way," Cone said. "Behind the chapel."

"Thanks."

Ben turned and strolled purposefully toward the chapel, feeling Cone's eyes boring into his back.

Ben locked the restroom door behind him and looked around. Urinal, toilet stall, sink. By the look of these fixtures, this was a recent addition to the chapel. Ben knew a little about the building trades. It's cheaper and easier to attach pipes in an add-on room to existing plumbing in the main structure. So, he reasoned, the pipes from this room were likely plugged into pipes on the other side of the wall—inside the chapel.

If the room on the other side had plumbing, then it was probably a bathroom or kitchen. But there was no reason to have a kitchen in a funeral chapel, and the chapel's public restrooms were on the opposite side of the building. So the room behind the wall was probably a private bathroom, and that was probably in the director's office.

Ben looked up. Above the toilet stall a hollow square of wooden baseboard covered an expanse of wallboard that seemed slightly paler than the wall. Probably the entrance to a crawl space, he thought. If he wanted to get into the chapel and couldn't use the front door, this bathroom might offer a route

He washed his hands, and then flushed the toilet before leaving the room.

Hidden in deep shadow beneath the trees, Cone watched Ben close the restroom door behind him and stroll toward the parking lot.

CHAPTER 18

Back in his sublet apartment, Ben took a shower, all the while trying to sort through the blizzard of thoughts and emotions raging within him.

He was sure that something was buried in three Beit Joseph plots. A corpse, perhaps—but only the most expensive caskets were of steel or nickel, metals that attract a magnet. Whatever it was had been put there recently, just long enough for grass seed to sprout.

No one buries anything but a coffin in a cemetery unless they're trying to keep it secret.

So whatever it was, Ben, decided, it wasn't kosher.

Should he tell his Beit Joseph clients? Turn it over to police?

Toweling himself dry, Ben examined his options. If he told Beit Joseph that there was probably something illegal on their property and they confronted cemetery management—assuming he could pierce the corporate veil to discover Shabbat Tamid's true owners—that could lead to a protracted legal proceeding. But if Beit Joseph's leadership knew that something illegal was concealed in their own cemetery property and failed to notify authorities, both the synagogue and its directors were potentially exposed to criminal penalties.

Then he recalled what the American Jewish University professor said: Shabbat Tamid was expanding its mortuary facility and phasing out burials. If there were no funerals, there would be no need for most staff and equipment operators. That would save a lot of money. And that gave Ben an idea.

Wearing a navy blazer, khaki pants, blue shirt and conservative necktie, head covered with a black Fedora—what he thought of as his "rabbi outfit," Ben rented a two-year-old Buick LaCrosse from a small, family-owned agency in nearby Glendale; the proprietor, Aram Takarian, insisted that Ben accept a discount "because your people, like mine, have known the suffering of a holocaust."

Half an hour later Ben parked the Buick at Shabbat Tamid and strode purposefully toward the chapel.

The door was locked, and there was no response to his knock. Ben looked around and saw a workman carrying a bag of cement toward the construction site behind the mortuary, and hurried after him.

As he half-ran down the sidewalk a door opened behind him in the side of the mortuary and a man in coveralls hailed him.

"Can I help you, Rabbi?"

Ben turned to face the man, who approached him, wiping his brow with a handkerchief. He appeared to be about forty, with dark hair, an expanding waistline and a receding hairline.

"I'm looking for the... I don't know what to call him. Whoever is in charge of this cemetery?"

"That would be me."

Ben peered closely at the man's face and realized that it was the funeral director who had presided over the previous day's funeral.

"I'm Rabbi Ben Maimon, from Congregation Beit Joseph."

"Lawrence Mint, executive funeral director."

"Mr. Mint, our congregation owns several burial plots here, and I'd like to talk to you about them."

"What about them?"

"This could take more than a few minutes. Is there some place inside where we could discuss this?"

"Certainly. I'll get the keys. Meet me across the street at the chapel—the side door."

A few minutes later the man returned carrying a ring of keys. The coveralls were gone and he wore dark slacks and a short-sleeved shirt with a green floral pattern.

Ben followed him down a hall that he recalled led from the chapel sanctuary past the bathrooms. Mint unlocked a door at the end and they continued down the corridor to an office, a dark, windowless room. Mint flipped on the lights and gestured to a chair.

"Have a seat, Rabbi."

Mint sat behind the desk, which held only a low stack of manila file folders and a small computer.

"Now, what can I do for you?"

"As I said, we own several burial plots here. We're starting a capital campaign to redevelop our campus, and our board has been looking at synagogue assets to decide which to keep and which to dispose of."

"Go on."

"Checking with our members, we find that most have advance arrangements at other cemeteries. We offered our plots to several other synagogues. They're interested in taking one or two, but no one wants to take them all. So we'd like to know if you'd be interested in buying them back."

Mint turned in his chair to look at the computer. He clicked the mouse a few times, and then looked back at Ben.

"That was B-E-I-T J-O-S-E-P-H?"

"Yes, Beit Joseph."

"That's nine plots, total, right?"

"Correct."

"What are you asking for them?"

"We're aware of their individual market value, and we also know that having seven together potentially adds value. That's why we're reluctant to break up the set, as it were. But we'd consider any reasonable offer."

"As it happens, we're planning to phase out burials soon. We may be able to accommodate you. I'll have to call corporate headquarters."

"Where is that?"

"Back east."

"Back east in New York? Florida?"

"Thanks for coming by, Rabbi. Is there anything else?"

"I don't think so. Thanks for your understanding."

It was all very polite, but beneath Mint's façade of civility, Ben felt something else. He wasn't quite sure what it was, but it made him slightly uneasy, as though he were dealing with a wild animal that might turn on him in the blink of an eye.

CHAPTER 19

Tova glared across the Starbucks table at Rabbi Kimmelman.

"We're paying him a king's ransom! And what does he do with our money? He's wining and dining and *shtupping* the help! And he's supposed to be a rabbi!"

Kimmelman sighed.

"Calm down, Tova. What are you talking about?"

"On Monday he went out with LaShonda. And now she thinks she's in love with him or something!"

Clutching a steaming paper cup, Burkin set his heavy briefcase on the floor and sat down.

"Who's in love with *shtupping* the help?"

"Ben—Rabbi Ben! And now LaShonda thinks he might stay in California and that he loves her!"

Burkin and Kimmelman exchanged amused glances.

Burkin said, "Tova, relax. He took LaShonda to dinner at a kosher dairy restaurant, and he pumped her—"

"I knew it!" Tova exploded.

"—pumped her for information. Then he took her home. That's it."

"That's his story? I don't believe it!"

Burkin said, "He told me in advance that he was taking her to dinner, and I suggested the Milky Way because I knew it would give them time to talk on the drive in to Pico-Robertson. And it turns out that she did know something was wrong at the cemetery, because she overheard Manny Seddaca yelling about it to Rabbi Kimmelman."

Tova remained silent for a long moment.

"There's gotta be more to it than that. LaShonda is literally bursting with happiness!"

Kimmelman said, "And when you saw that, the bursting, you called 911?"

Burkin chuckled. "What makes you angrier Tova, that she's younger than you, or that she's black?"

"That's beneath you, Gary. I never realized what a male chauvinist you've become. Is that why Susan left you?"

Kimmelman said, "Both of you, stop. This is ridiculous, childish behavior. Gary, you should apologize to Tova. And Tova, you're way out of line, too."

Tova and Gary glared at each other across the table.

Tova said, "'Blessed be the peacemakers.'"

Kimmelman frowned. "You're quoting Saint Matthew to me? Is that a Jewish thing now?"

Burkin said, "Matthew—or whatever his real name was—was an apostate Jew, but that doesn't mean he lacked wisdom or compassion."

Kimmelman smiled. "Better to quote Hillel, 'Be of the disciples of Aaron, lover of peace and pursuer of peace, one who loves mankind and draws them nearer to the Torah.'"

Burkin said, "Tova, I apologize. I should not have accused you of being jealous or a racist."

Tova said, "Thank you, Gary."

"That's it—that's your apology?"

"And I'm sorry for what I said about Susan."

Kimmelman smiled. "Now that that's settled, let me tell you what Rabbi Ben Maimon told me this morning."

**

Ben had said nothing to Kimmelman about the metallic objects buried in Beit Joseph plots. He had instead shared his conversation with Lawrence Mint, omitting only the vague sense of danger that he'd felt in his presence.

Then Ben called another M.I.T. classmate, now teaching forensic chemistry at Stanford University, and asked him to analyze the soil he'd taken from Shabbat Tamid. With the understanding that it might take several days, Ben sent it via FedEx to his friend's Palo Alto lab.

Then he called the California Cemetery and Funeral Bureau, a regulating agency, and confirmed that Lawrence Mint was a licensed funeral director. He also learned that Shabbat Tamid was controlled by a company named Bliss Enterprises. The company was registered in Delaware, but its headquarters were in Nassau, the Bahamas.

Back east, indeed, thought Ben. If he was right, the inquiries to other synagogues about Shabbat Tamid plots had originated with Mint, or someone in his employ. If so, they were probably getting ready to make offers to buy back unsold plots. Ben had merely taken the initiative on something that fit with their corporate plans. He was pretty sure that Mint would make an offer that Beit Joseph would not refuse.

But what the hell was in those graves?

CHAPTER 20

TUESDAY: MAY 24

Seddaca shook his head in amazement. "My oldest boy, he's an engineer. Computer software. This, this is what he would call an 'elegant solution.'"

Kimmelman nodded agreement.

"Elegant, indeed."

Burkin cleared his throat importantly.

"If Tova agrees, I believe we can close this matter out."

Tova shook her head, her bosoms quivering.

"There are other things to consider."

Ferguson held up the check that Shabbat Tamid had sent by messenger, along with legal documents for Burkin's signature.

"We have to accept this. I say the only question now is what do we do with the money? I think we should put it in the capital campaign fund. Every dime."

Tova said, "Wait. Are we really ready to say that Rabbi Ben has completed the job we hired him for?"

Burkin said, "Tova's right. We hired him to find out who was using our bank account. Are we satisfied that his work is now completed? What do you think, Rabbi?"

Kimmelman said. "It would be nice if he found out what happened, but as it turned out the mystery deposits came and went. And I understand that Gary closed that account?"

Gary nodded.

"Moved the funds to Bank of America."

Kimmelman said, "So what's left? We hired him because we wanted to find a way to keep that mystery money for our capital campaign. Well, that ship sailed without us. But this is a very nice consolation prize. If we announce that one hundred ten thousand dollars from the sale of excess burial plots was deposited in the building fund—that would be a fabulous way to kick off the campaign."

Ferguson said, "Let's do it."

Tova said, "Okay."

Kimmelman said, "And don't forget, Ben is going to donate ten percent of his fee to that fund as well."

Tova said, "So he's going back to Boston?"

Kimmelman said, "I imagine so. I don't see why he needs to stay here much longer."

Tova said, "But what about LaShonda? She thinks she's in love with him!"

***

LaShonda had felt the chemistry between herself and Ben, the smoldering flame of sexual attraction, and yet she also knew that he had a raft of reasons for backing away: He was highly educated, a clergyman, and, not least, lived on the other side of the country. She was black, she wasn't Jewish, and she had little schooling. She'd kept expectations low, tried to damp down her desire, but she couldn't control her feelings: Any mention of his name, any reference to the visiting rabbi brought warmth to her groin area, a feeling of moisture mixed with yearning.

Ben had made up his mind to put an end to their brief relationship. When LaShonda came into his little cubicle and renewed her offer to cook him dinner, he frowned.

"I'm very particular about food. I'm really not comfortable eating in a home that I know isn't kosher."

"Paper plates. Plastic forks and knives."

"I won't eat meat unless it's kosher."

"LaShonda's plantation shack cheese blintzes. Aunt Jemima's latkes with George Washington Carver apple sauce. Uncle Remus Smoked white fish."

Ben giggled in spite of himself. "Eight o'clock?"

"You're way too easy. Bring flowers."

***

Walking through Beit Joseph's crowded parking lot toward his car, Ben was surprised to see Chang Rosenfeld get out of a big, brown step van that looked like it had once been used to deliver packages. He wore coveralls and carried a heavy tool box.

Chang said, "How's it going, Rabbi? How did that pool-cue thing I made for you work out? The probe thingy?"

"I tried pushing it into soil and it seems to be strong enough."

"Cool."

"You're here to install the new ark?"

"I've got a couple of hours free, so I thought I'd do some prep work. Tear out the old one, for starters."

"Yasher *Koach*. Beit Joseph is lucky to have you as a member."

"The privilege is mine, Rabbi. Coming to my shofar class?"

"I'll try to do that."

Ben got into his Honda and drove away. He headed for the Bank of B. Cohen again. Two blocks away he realized that it was past noon and they were closed.

CHAPTER 21

"I'll do the dishes," Ben said, and LaShonda giggled, then watched, hands on hips, as he shoveled everything from the table—paper plates, plastic cups from their Baron Herzog—strictly kosher!—zinfandel, plastic cutlery and a paper table cloth into a plastic trash bag.

"All done!" he announced.

"Take that out to the trash and *then* you're all done."

Ben dutifully trooped outside and found the covered trash bin. When he returned the kitchen lights were off and three scented candles cast a soft glow and filled the small apartment with the smell of fresh pine needles.

"LaShonda," Ben said. "We have to talk."

She patted the sofa next to her.

"Come over here and tell me all about it. C'mon now."

He sat down, trying but failing to keep his thigh from touching hers. Her warmth seeped through the thin fabric of his trousers and seemed to invade his loins. He felt himself growing hard, and willed himself to stand.

"LaShonda, I can't have sex with you."

"Boy, you sure don't put no gravy on your greens. What's going on here? Am I too black for you?"

"You are 'black but comely... Like the tents of Kedar, like the curtains of Solomon. Behold, you are comely, my beloved; your eyes are like doves. Your lips are like a scarlet thread, your breasts are like two fawns, the twins of a gazelle, who graze among the roses.'"

LaShonda threw back her head and roared.

"Ben, you are so full of it!"

"Wait, there's more. 'Your lips drip flowing honey, honey and milk are under your tongue, and the fragrance of your garments is like the scent of Lebanon.'"

"That's all from the Bible?"

"The Song of Songs. But seriously. I can't get involved with you. Or anyone. My life is in Boston. And there's so much you don't know about me."

"And just as much you don't know about me. What makes you so damn sure I want to jump your holy bones anyway?"

"Please, let me talk. It's not what you think."

He sat back down, keeping a small distance between them. "You are a gorgeous, intelligent, sexy, industrious woman. I'd be lucky to be allowed into your life, let alone into your bed. It has nothing to do with who you are. And everything to do with me. I am not what you think I am."

"So you're actually a Catholic priest? You're celibate?"

As much as Ben wanted to have a serious conversation, he couldn't help laughing.

"I am, really, a rabbi. I'm also a sort of Jewish paladin. Do you know the word?"

"Didn't there used to be like a TV show, in the Sixties?"

"It was called 'Have Gun, Will Travel.' From way before our time, but I've seen re-runs on cable."

LaShonda said, "And there's a kind of character in Dungeons & Dragons called a paladin—I think."

"You play Dungeons & Dragons?"

"Not really. But I had this boyfriend once, and for about two years that's pretty much all he did besides get high and spend my grocery money on weed."

"I'm sorry for that."

"This ain't a pity party! Just tell me your story. And this better be good, Mr. Paladin rabbi."

"In French mythology—no, wait—King Arthur and the Knights of the Round Table, does that mean anything to you?"

"You're really confusing me."

"In medieval times, the French and later the Italians had their own version of the Arthurian fables, the Paladins of Charlemagne. Knights in service to France's most revered king. When the king died, the knights continued to serve their people. They were in a bunch of early adventure stories: Holy knights who rescued maidens, slew villains and dragons, searched for the Holy Grail. Each knight was a paragon of virtue and goodness who performed good deeds—"

"You're saying that you *did* take a vow of chastity?"

"No. Wait. Let me tell it, please."

LaShonda sat back, her beautiful face skeptical.

"I am a rabbi, and I would dearly love to set down roots in one community with my own pulpit. I'd like get to know and serve the spiritual needs of a congregation. Instead, I travel from synagogue to synagogue, across the country. Even to Canada, once."

"That's what they call a visiting scholar?"

"No. A visiting scholar is something else. That was my cover story. I came to help Beit Joseph out of a jam. And I'm very sorry, but I can't tell you what it is or what I did. That's part of the deal I made with the synagogue."

"So now you be done with Burbank and you goin' back East."

Ben noticed that LaShonda had lapsed into an argot that some, unkindly, call "Ebonics." He ignored it.

"Soon. The synagogue leadership is happy, but I have some loose ends to tie up. And I've paid rent for a few more weeks, so I may as well stay a little longer.

"But that's not why we can't have sex."

"Then what?"

"I'm a nomad, roaming the country, rarely in one place more than a few months. I'm rarely home even that long. To me, and the way I was raised, and what I believe is proper conduct for a rabbi, sexual relationships grow out of intimacy, out of closeness, as an expression of total commitment, body and soul, between two people. They don't grow out of casual encounters, and they don't prosper in long-distance relationships."

"So you a virgin? That what you sayin'?"

Ben laughed. "Sorry, no. I didn't mean to give you the wrong impression. LaShonda, I like sex. Like it a lot. And when I was married, I wanted to have sex almost every time I was alone with my wife."

"So she divorced you for being a sex-maniac?"

Again Ben laughed. Then he grew sober. "My wife was killed. In Israel, eight years ago, by a bomb. She was seven months pregnant."

"Oh Lord! Ben, I am so sorry for that. Please don't be mad for what I said."

"I'm not. And this isn't, as you said, a pity party. What I am telling you, is that I won't be here, in California, long enough for a real friendship, the real intimacy that I know leads to the only kind of sex that I want to have, sex as an expression of unconditional love and mutual commitment."

LaShonda could only stare at Ben.

"Are you okay?" Ben asked.

LaShonda stood up and shook herself, like a dog emerging from a pond. Ben felt himself growing hard.

"I'm going to make tea," she said.

"Tea?

"Don't you even think about leaving. We're not done."

Ben stretched, and then sat back on the couch.

Five minutes ticked by, an eternity. Ben began to wish that he had not been quite so forthright. Maybe he shouldn't have shared so many details of his occupation.

He was lost in thought when LaShonda reappeared. She wore only a filmy robe that revealed more of her body than it hid.

She knelt before him.

"How long has it been, Rabbi?"

"Don't do this, please."

"How long since the last time you were with a woman?"

Ben sighed, feeling desire building, unable to resist his body's demands. "Six years. Almost seven."

"That is way, way, too long."

LaShonda unbuckled Ben's belt and slid his trousers off. Then his shorts. From somewhere appeared a flask of baby oil and a small white towel. She tugged on his shorts.

"Oh my! So that's what you've been hiding!"

Ben sighed. He had to decide, and now.

"Just leave everything to me," she said, and poured a few drops of oil on her hands.

Ben got to his feet, awkwardly pulling his pants up.

"I'm sorry. As much as I would like to, as much as I appreciate what you've offered, and the spirit in which it is offered, I just can't."

LaShonda shook her head helplessly.

"Then let me put this stuff away and we'll just cuddle for a while. You *do* cuddle?"

"Not in a very long time. And thank you."

An hour later Ben and LaShonda emerged from her home to walk arm-in-arm to Ben's car, she still clad in the sheer robe. After a lingering kiss, Ben drove off.

Across the street, in the cramped back seat of her car, Tova sat up, returned her opera glasses to her purse and opened a fresh pack of cigarettes.

CHAPTER 22

TUESDAY: MAY 25

Ben twisted the cold water handle and felt the fine, stinging droplets pelting his head, chest and shoulders get hotter and hotter. He endured the heat as long as he could, then abruptly rotated the control ninety degrees and gasped under the shower's icy shock. He emerged, minutes later shivering, feeling better than he had in years.

LaShonda was an incredible woman, he thought, so selfless, so giving. He had little hope for a future together, but clearly they had established a connection.

The distinctive warble of a cell phone ringtone ended his musings. Who but LaShonda could be calling at this hour, he thought, and grabbed his phone.

"Hi!"

"Ben—this is Rudy Estrin in Palo Alto."

"Rudy?—I was expecting someone else."

"Apologies—I really thought this would go to voicemail. Sorry for calling so late, but between teaching, committee service and trying to finish my book, I don't have much free time to putter around the lab."

Ben said, "If I'd known you were so busy, I'd have asked someone else."

"No, it's okay, really."

"And how is Graciella?"

"Thanks for asking. She's great with child! Next month, we hope. That's why I've been working overtime—to get the book done before the baby comes."

"Congratulations! Mazel Tov!"

"Thanks, Ben. Tell me, where did you get that soil?"

"I dug it out of a cemetery."

"A cemetery! That's amazing."

"What's in it, Rudy?"

"It's mostly organic compounds that I'd expect to find in any garden, plus trace amounts of sodium borohydride, red phosphorus, lithium, methylamine hydrochloride, THC, benzoylmethylecgonine and several other chemical compounds."

"What should I know about them?"

"Benzoylmethylecgonine is a form of cocaine. THC is the principal psychoactive component of cannabis. The other compounds, only trace amounts, include opiates and the precursors and ingredients of methamphetamine."

"Methamphetamine?"

"Sometimes called meth. It's an—"

"Illegal drug. Like heroin, cocaine and cannabis."

"So now what, Ben? Shall I send you a report?"

"That'd be great. Can you put it on university letterhead and sign it?"

"My pleasure. Do I need to send a bill, too?"

"By all means, send me a bill. Glad to pay it."

"I was joking, Ben."

"Are you sure? I'm happy to pay for your expertise."

"Never, pal. Aside from all this, how's the rabbi business? How's life treating you?"

"Better than it has in a long, long, time."

After Rudy hung up, Ben sat thinking for several minutes. He had speculated about what might be hidden beneath the soil of Shabbat Tamid, but never had he considered that it might be illegal drugs. On the other hand, Ben realized, he should have asked Rudy if any of those chemicals might also be used in mortuaries.

He made a mental note to call back in the morning. In the meantime he was left to wonder how that soil got into a grave plot and who put it there.

***

Ben said, "As agreed," and handed his personal check to Gary Burkin, who glanced at it and passed it around the conference table.

Kimmelman said, "That's too much."

"I just rounded it up to the nearest thousand."

Seddaca said, "That's very generous of you."

Kimmelman said, "If you don't mind my asking, how on earth did you convince them to buy back the plots?"

"I had a good look around and I realized that there were probably less than twenty unoccupied plots, and except for your nine, the others were singles scattered around the grounds. From the size of the new building going up, it's obvious that their expanding mortuary capability. If they got out of the burial business they could save a lot of money on staff and equipment.

"So I told them that we knew our plots had value, and that we would consider any reasonable offer. I'm guessing they'll try to buy back the other plots as well."

Seddaca said, "But you didn't find out what was buried in those graves?"

"I can't be sure what it is without digging it up. It might have something to do with landscaping—maybe the sprinkler system. But the good news is that whatever it is, it's no longer Beit Joseph's problem."

Burkin said, "Exactly. And we're grateful to you for a quick and painless resolution."

"Thanks. And I've got an idea about how to resolve that other matter, as well. I'll get right on that now that the more serious issue is behind us."

Burkin frowned. "What other matter?"

"The mysterious deposits in the synagogue account."

"Oh, that. We're not worried about that any more."

Ferguson said, "I don't know, Gary. I'd sleep a little sounder if I knew how that happened."

Burkin shrugged, "Whatever. It does no harm, but at this point it's probably a waste of your time."

"I won't go overboard, then."

Tova said, "So then you'll head back to Boston?"

Ben shook his head. "My rent is paid until July, and I have a few old friends in the area who I haven't seen in years. I might hang around for a few weeks."

Ferguson said, "That's wonderful. Enjoy yourself."

Tova's eyes narrowed to slits. "This has something to do with LaShonda, doesn't it?"

Ben smiled. "She's a fine person, and we've become friends. I hope I'll get to spend a little time with her."

"You're *shtupping* her, aren't you!"

Kimmelman said, "That's really none of our business."

Burkin said, "And it's really rude of you to ask."

Ben said, "Tova, I'm not *shtupping* LaShonda, or anyone else."

"I don't believe you!"

Kimmelman said, "I'd like you to apologize to Rabbi Ben Maimon, Tova. You're embarrassing yourself and this congregation."

"He's lying, and you know what—he didn't do much to earn his fee. I think he should give back *half* our money!"

Ben said, "Tova, I understand that you feel hurt and maybe jealous, but listen to yourself. You don't have all the facts—actually you don't have *any* facts. You can think whatever you like, but I ask to you to keep your private feelings out of this. My relationship with your congregation is professional, and if it had turned out that, as you so crudely put it, I was *shtupping* LaShonda, that is none of your business. As for refunding half my fee, recall that I found a solution to a serious problem that leaves Beit Joseph considerably better off than it was. And, not least, you and your committee agreed in advance that my fee was nonrefundable."

"You're a liar! Tova shrieked, grabbing her purse as she fled the room.

Burkin said, "Please forgive her, Rabbi."

Ben nodded, slowly. "I do. And I feel bad because she's unhappy. Is there anything I can do to make her feel better?"

Seddaca said, "Not unless you're prepared to give her a ring and spend the rest of your life kissing her *tuchus.*"

Everyone howled except Ben, who allowed himself only a tiny smile.

Ben said, "One more thing. I believe that the Shabbat Tamid payment came with a bunch of paperwork attached— cemetery plot sales are considered real estate transactions. If it's all signed and ready to go, I'd be happy to bring it back to the cemetery."

Burkin said, "We were going to mail it, but if you want to hand-carry it, fine."

"Thanks. Oh, and one more thing. Do you happen to know someone who does family law? I've got a matter that I'd like to discuss with an expert."

Burkin said, "My expertise is really in criminal law and personal liability. But perhaps one of my associates—"

Seddaca interrupted, "What about Sandy?"

Burkin said, "That's our member Sanford Feingelt, Rabbi Ben. He handles estates. I don't think he does family law."

Kimmelman said, "I'll be happy to ask around for someone."

Seddaca said, "Why do you need a lawyer? Tova wants a prenuptial agreement?"

This time Ben joined in the laughter.

Still, he was worried about Tova. She was acting irrationally, and she could make trouble for LaShonda.

CHAPTER 23

THURSDAY: MAY 27

Wearing his black Fedora, a summer-weight suit and a conservative tie, Ben turned into Shalom Tamid's access road and stopped, his way blocked by a high gate. He pulled to the right side, and then made a three-point turn so that the rented Buick faced away from the gate. Then he took out his cell and punched in Shabbat Tamid's number.

A tinny-sounding recorded message said:

"Shalom, you have reached Shabbat Tamid, a Jewish cemetery at 2700 Heaton Road, Burbank.

"We no longer accept new burials. To serve you better in the future, our mortuary is closed for renovation and expansion. Due to safety requirements during construction, viewing hours are temporarily limited. If you wish to visit the grave of a loved one, we are open between eleven a.m. and one p.m., Monday through Friday, or from nine a.m. to four p.m. on Sunday. Shabbat Tamid is closed on Saturday.

"We're sorry for any inconvenience this may cause.

"For further information, please leave your name and a daytime phone number, including area code.

"Thank you for thinking of Shabbat Tamid."

Now that is strange indeed, Ben thought. A thread of logic ran though it, of course, but he had never heard of a Jewish cemetery being open only during the lunch hour.

Ben shut off the engine and got out of his car. He walked to the gate, where he recalled seeing a bell. It took him a few minutes to find it, almost hidden beneath the drooping, vine-like stems of a potted plant strategically placed on the wall above the bell button.

Ben listened carefully; no sound came from the grounds. He pushed the button and heard the distant sound of a buzzer. Nothing happened. After several minutes he tried again. As before, the distant buzzer sounded.

There was no response.

Ben checked his watch. It was almost eleven. He got back in the Buick and waited. At ten past the hour he got out and tried the buzzer again. Nothing stirred inside.

Ben returned to the Buick and drove away, thinking.

Half an hour later he found the Burbank City Planning offices in a low-slung building just off the Golden State Freeway. He used a lobby computer terminal to find the legal location description from the cemetery address, and then filled out a short form to request the plans.

Twenty minutes went by before a clerk beckoned him to the counter.

"Thanks for your patience, Rabbi. You can look at them over there. You're free to take notes. If you want copies, that takes three working days."

"I understand. Thanks."

Ben sat at the table, opened an oversized manila envelope and slid out the permit application and plans for the mortuary expansion. He read the project description, and then unrolled the plans. It was to be a long building with beefed up plumbing and electrical capacity, far bigger than the present structure. The old structure would be converted to administrative purposes, with offices, a showroom, presumably for coffins, and reception and viewing areas.

The addition was to have a low-ceilinged mezzanine above the main floor. A half-dozen operatories, each with water and sewer connections, would be available to "process human remains," as the plan description put it.

The walls and roofs were to be soundproofed and hermetically sealed. A central compressor would provide positive air pressure in each operatory, which would be equipped with safety doors. That must be to contain infectious microbes from a corpse, Ben thought. Very forward looking. And very impressive—this project would cost millions to build.

At a quarter to one he turned onto the cemetery road and was not surprised to find the gate still closed.

He tried the buzzer again, and as before he heard it ring somewhere inside. There was no sign that anyone inside the fence was alive.

Before returning to his apartment, he drove completely around the cemetery, which required navigating a series of curving residential streets, each of which ended in a cul-de-sac next to foliage screening the cemetery's high, ivy-covered wall. On the first of these streets he saw the partial outline of a gate through Eucalyptus trees and realized it was the one behind the chapel that he'd seen a week earlier.

The next street, Ivy Avenue, also ended in a cul-de-sac backed by leafy trees and the wall, but after turning around he noticed a small playground with a tiny parking lot.

On the way home he stopped at the post office to mail Beit Joseph's documents. Around the corner, at a 99 Cent store, he bought a big wooden spoon and a package of baggies.

SIX YEARS EARLIER

Seventeen months after losing Rachel, at a time when his faith in the God of Abraham, Isaac and Jacob was buffeted by loss and injury, Ben was ordained a rabbi in the United Synagogue of Conservative Judaism and flew down to Miami for his first job interview.

Baruch Barthmann, Congregation Rodef Shalom's retiring rabbi, who would remain as Rabbi Emeritus, was yet another former Yeshiva student of his grandfather.

Ben was made to feel welcome; Rabbi Barthmann all but promised him the job. All that was required was a pro forma interview with the synagogue president and the board, and then he would be asked to spend a Shabbat with congregants, presiding over evening and day services, delivering a *drash*—a sermon or Torah lesson—and in general allowing congregants an opportunity to take his temperature. Unless some member raised a serious objection, the president would offer him the position. A pre-employment physical exam was required because the position involved teaching day school students.

No one objected to Ben and he received a formal offer of employment, with a salary commensurate with his experience, a housing allowance, and health insurance. The details would take a few days to arrange; in the interim, a wealthy congregant invited Ben to stay, free of charge, in his small, exclusive beachfront hotel.

Ben could have gone back to New York; the paperwork handled by mail or FedEx. His possessions were few and easily packed and shipped. But Ben was still healing inside, and he had never been to South Florida. He decided to stay, find an apartment, get the lay of the land, and enjoy his first vacation in years.

His host, Mordechai Allen, had been born Alón Mordechaiovsky. Ben didn't know it at the time, but for seven years in the Sixties and Seventies Alón was South

Florida's infamous White Puma, a cat burglar seemingly able to walk through walls, a high-risk thief specializing in looting the impregnable homes of the rich and powerful of cash, jewelry, coin and stamp collections—anything small and valuable. By the end of his criminal career, however. Mordechaiovsky was so drunk with power that his burglaries had become less about enriching himself and more about taking absurd risks, defying every convention of the successful burglar to feed his sense of invulnerability.

He was almost begging to be caught.

When, finally, he was apprehended, tried, sentenced and imprisoned, it came almost as a relief.

Then, although it might have shaved years from his sentence, he refused to name his former associates, served eleven years hard time, and left prison with no enemies but a deep conviction that he must change or die, and that he wanted to live.

He began by changing his name.

In time he found a rabbi who wouldn't be conned, who confronted Mordechai's evasions, who forced him to take responsibility for who he was and what he had become, for the damage his actions had inflicted. Slowly, in small steps that took years, he began living an observant life, adopted kosher eating habits, and in time created a Jewish home. He found work selling jewelry, about which he knew a great deal, then opened his own shop, then invested the profits in real estate. By age sixty he was wealthy. And over the years all this took he studied Torah, Talmud and other Jewish literature, became a pillar of his congregation, and lived an exemplary life.

When Ben accepted Alón's hospitality, he knew his host only as a respected member of the Jewish community.

Ben took his required physical on the day he moved into Mordechai's hotel. Two days later his blood test came back and Ben learned that he had been infected with HIV. The only way it could have happened was in the bombing, when he was covered with not only his own blood but that of other victims.

That evening, after a contentious but secret board meeting, Rodef Shalom confirmed its obligation to pay Ben's travel expenses but withdrew its offer of employment.

Crushed, Ben didn't know what to do: He couldn't return to New York after telling all his friends that he'd been hired by one of Florida's largest congregations.

At Mordechai's urging. He remained in Miami for over a month. Empathizing with Ben's pain, the pain of rejection and the anger of betrayal, the older man befriended him. Gradually he shared details of his youthful life of crime, and allowed Ben to talk out his bitterness, to examine his beliefs. They discussed God's nature and the deity's relationship with mankind. Ben felt that he learned more about God from this reformed thief than he had in rabbinical school. By the time he was ready to leave, Ben felt very close to Mordechai—and to the Master of the Universe. They stayed in touch.

Five years later, long after shelving ambitions for a congregation and a pulpit and reshaping himself for a new profession, Ben had encountered a situation that he was powerless to resolve: A stolen video tape that might free an innocent man convicted of murder was locked in a Cincinnati penthouse, and every ruse Ben had attempted to get inside that home had failed.

Ben had called Mordechai, who invited him to Miami for a crash course in lock-picking, security alarms, safe-cracking and the art of residential burglary. After a month of intensive instruction, Ben went back to Cincinnati, gained entry to the penthouse and retrieved the video.

***

THURSDAY: MAY 27

When Ben returned to his apartment from the 99 Cent Store, he pulled a suitcase from the closet. From a hidden pocket in the lining he retrieved a tiny set of lock picks.

CHAPTER 24

Ben had planned an early dinner with LaShonda in the San Gabriel Valley east of Los Angeles. She had told him that its small cities, once largely Latino, were now filled with Asians and offered a great variety of dining experiences, including excellent vegetarian fare.

He had rented the Buick for a week; since it was more comfortable than his Honda, he decided to take it instead. As twilight fell Ben climbed into the Buick and headed west along Magnolia Boulevard. After a few blocks he noticed a beat-up gray pickup truck that seemed to be following him. To confirm this, Ben signaled, and then turned into a supermarket parking lot, threading his way through parked cars and shoppers with carts laden with groceries, until he emerged onto a side street. As he turned back onto Magnolia he saw the pickup idling in a bus stop zone behind him. In his mirror he glimpsed a driver in sun glasses and a dark brimmed hat pulled low.

The pickup pulled away from the curb behind him.

He drove a half mile past LaShonda's home, with the pickup keeping pace. Abruptly turning into an alley, he sped down the narrow pavement until, just before the street, he saw a vacant carport behind an apartment building, braked hard and turned in. Ducked down, he heard the pickup shoot by at high speed.

Ben waited ten minutes before taking side streets to LaShonda's building. He parked behind it in the alley.

He told LaShonda that he didn't yet feel comfortable navigating rush hour freeways; she immediately volunteered to drive. Ten minutes later, as they left in her Toyota SUV, Ben saw the pickup parked on Magnolia, in a spot with a good view of LaShonda's townhome. He had been followed, and by someone who knew or had guessed his destination.

Ben wondered if Shabbat Tamid had a hidden security camera trained on its entrance area.

***

LaShonda reached across the table and took Ben's hand.

"Ben, I've been thinking."

"So have I. This isn't going to work out, is it?"

"You <u>do</u> read minds!"

"Not at all. I'll make it easy for you: I loved your offer of a hand job, and I loved cuddling. But you need someone who can give you a lot more than I can. You need a husband that's as fine a man as you are a woman."

She regarded him across a table of dirty dishes.

"I guess I do. But Ben, we're going to be friends from now, right?"

"Of course."

"I mean, *real* friends. Who talk to each other, tell the truth, watch each other's back."

"Such friends are rare. Hard to find. But sign me up."

LaShonda's eyes filled.

"Oh, Ben. You don't deserve to be alone always. Do something nice for yourself, just once."

Ben, too, began to weep.

"Not yet. I just can't," he sobbed.

***

Early the next morning Mitch Katz called from Chicago and Ben told him about his brief romance with LaShonda.

Mitch said, "How do you feel now?"

"I feel sad. Kind of empty. Like I've lost something."

"Good. That's normal. You'll feel better soon."

"Right now I don't want to feel better."

"You're thinking about—what's her name, Shayna?"

"LaShonda. Yes, I'm feeling a sense of loss, and that I somehow disappointed her. Let her down."

"So right now, you're not thinking about Rachel?"

"No."

"So, that's good, isn't it?"

"Then why do I feel so bad?"

"Ben. We've talked about this. It's a process. And you just did something very important for yourself. You've taken another big step toward healing."

"If you say so. But what about LaShonda?"

"You were honest with her?"

"Always."

"Then let LaShonda worry about LaShonda."

"Easier said than done, Mitch."

Mitch said, "Gotta get off now, my first patient is here. But stay in touch. And keep looking. You're going to be just fine, I know it."

Ben lay back in bed thinking about what his life might have been, about the roads he'd passed up, the choices he hadn't made, and drifted into an uneasy, half-waking sleep.

CHAPTER 25

SUNDAY: MAY 30

A half moon slunk behind low clouds as Ben left his apartment half an hour before midnight. He wore a black hoodie, black jogging pants, black shoes and black socks, his face dark with flat black camouflage paste. In the underground garage he climbed into the old Honda, then drove east, past Shabbat Tamid's entrance to Ivy Street, the second cul-de-sac beyond the main cemetery gate.

He left the car in the playground lot and walked down the middle of the pavement toward the cemetery wall, hoping that the street's canine residents would ignore him.

At the cul-de-sac he slipped through shrubbery and behind a screen of eucalypti, and then made his way along the wall to the side gate. There he stopped to listen for several minutes, hearing nothing but the distant hum of traffic, the muffled barking of a dog, and the wind rustling through foliage.

Ben took out a tiny flashlight and in its red-filtered beam slowly probed the top and side of the wall, looking for a video camera. Finding none, he knelt before the door and peered at the lock. Satisfied, he tucked the flashlight away and took out his picks. As Mordechai, the Seventies terror of Miami's Gold Coast high-rise condominium dwellers had taught him, such thirty-dollar locks usually yield to deft picks in seconds. But this was only the second time he had tried it in the field and it took more than a minute.

He put tape across the latch plate to keep the door from locking behind him and cautiously stepped inside.

The cemetery was silent, but lights burned in the interior of the old mortuary. A car and a hearse were parked nearby. Ben skirted the area, sticking to the rows of graves. Moving away from the mortuary toward the rear of the cemetery, he stopped at every fourth or fifth row. Clearing away grass and leaves he dug a shallow hole with the wooden spoon, then took a little soil. When he had filled a dozen bags from graves on randomly-selected rows, he unfolded a small draw-string bag of dull black cloth and tucked bags and spoon inside.

As he moved back toward the side gate he heard a door open. Mint, the funeral director, and Cone, the assistant who had stopped him near the gate a week earlier, emerged from the mortuary wearing coveralls. A bright light high on a nearby pole, perhaps triggered by a motion detector, flicked on. As Cone headed for the gate, Mint opened the back of the hearse. A roll-up door opened and two more coverall-clad men wheeled a coffin on a cart. They pushed it to the end of the hearse, and then slid the big box inside.

That's odd, thought Ben. The phone message said the mortuary is closed. And why put a coffin in a hearse? And then he understood why: Because they no longer performed burials.

The two men climbed into the hearse as Mint pushed the cart inside and closed the roll-up door. Cone unlocked and pushed open the main gate.

Ben expected Mint to get into the car and follow the hearse through the gate, then stop for Cone to lock the gate behind him. Instead they left both vehicles. Cone closed and locked the gate and both men headed for the side gate.

If they reach it before I do, Ben thought, they'd find the tape he'd left blocking the latch plate. But even running full speed, he'd never beat them there.

As the pole light winked out. Ben dashed forward to the first row of graves. A couple of big pebbles rested atop a large headstone, undoubtedly left by a recent visitor. Ben grabbed one and threw it hard at the parked car. It missed, but the pole light came back on.

He took the second pebble, and cocked his arm.

131

From the corner of his eye he saw the inscription on the tombstone: Mark Thompson Glass.

He froze: That was *his* name!

It had also been his father's name.

CHAPTER 26

MONDAY: MAY 31

Ben cocked his arm again and threw the second pebble, striking the car door and triggering the alarm.

As Mint and Cone appeared, Ben took off through the tombstones, running hard but not full out, being careful where he stepped. In a minute he was at the side gate, then through it. He ripped the tape off, and then backed away from the entrance, hiding in the dark shrubbery past the trees.

The car alarm stopped.

A few minutes went by, and as Ben's heart slowed and the pounding in his ears receded, he heard Cone and Mint approaching. At the gate, one man fumbled with keys, unlocked the gate, and then relocked it from outside.

Flashlights probed the foliage, twin beams splitting the night in both directions. Prone behind a big tree, Ben was all but invisible.

Conversing inaudibly, Mint and Cone walked away. Ben followed, remaining between trees and fence, until he saw the dark outlines of both men. They left the trees at the first cul-de-sac from the main gate, and then entered the nearest house by its front door. Lights went on inside.

Ben waited several minutes, and then moved carefully between trees and wall until he reached Ivy Street. Again he stuck to the center of the pavement until he reached the playground, where he retrieved his Honda.

Lights out, he drove slowly away from the cemetery until he reached a cross street, then switched on low-beams and drove north, away from his apartment. He got on Interstate

Five and sped four exits north, changing lanes twice, then got off and headed east into Glendale before turning south onto a side street for a mile.

He parked on a darkened street and waited ten minutes.

Satisfied that he wasn't followed, Ben returned to his apartment, where he left the Honda in underground parking.

He undressed, showered, brushed his teeth and climbed into bed. But he could not sleep. Was the Mark Thompson Glass buried in Shabbat Tamid his father—the man he had always believed was a gentile and so could not have been buried in a Jewish cemetery? The father who supposedly perished overseas in a mysterious plane crash when Ben was a toddler? Did the pebbles on the headstone mean that someone had recently visited the grave?

Was everything that his mother and grandparents had told him about his father's death a lie?

***

Ben awoke at nine, stiff from having slept in an awkward position. His mind racing over the implications of the tombstone, he stretched for fifteen minutes, then put on running clothes and hit the streets, putting in his regular five miles and one more good measure.

After a shower and coffee, Ben decided that as tempting as it was to pursue the issues raised by that tombstone, they could wait. He'd been thinking about the unauthorized deposits in Beit Joseph's account, the ostensible reason that Beit Joseph had hired him. Burkin and the others had seemed desperate to find a way to keep that money. Then it vanished as mysteriously as it arrived, and now they were uninterested. It didn't add up.

In his mind, Ben had begun to sketch out the outlines of a theory about them. But first, the cemetery soil. He fired up his computer and after logging on, Googled an independent soil analysis lab in Bakersfield, a hundred miles north. He telephoned to arrange sending them his samples for testing.

Then he got back on the computer and Googled public records depositories in Los Angeles County. Divorce proceedings are civil suits. With rare exceptions, in most states they are public records. Cases that had been adjudicated were available online, but those still pending were not. That meant a trip to downtown Los Angeles.

At noon Ben stopped at a FedEx Office to send the samples, and then got on the freeway. He found the County Hall of Records, suffering the heat and the downtown traffic until he gave up on finding street parking and pulled into an outrageously expensive lot. He walked back to the records repositories, pausing along the way at a vendor's cart to nibble a soft pretzel and drink a bottle of water.

The records center was cool and dark. Ben was looking for Burkin v. Burkin, a divorce case. At a lobby computer he typed in the names, found the case number, and got in line to see a clerk. Half an hour went by before he stood at the counter. The clerk looked at the number, typed something into a computer terminal, and directed Ben to a waiting room filled with library tables. A pair of clerks consulted a computer, and then disappeared into a vast, dimly-lit archive. After a time they re-appeared with a file, called the name of the case, and one of those waiting claimed it. An hour passed before Ben was called.

"Do not write in the file," the clerk, a gray-haired Latino, recited mechanically. "If you need copies of a document, list the page on this"—he handed Ben a form—"and we'll make copies. Fifty cents a page."

Ben took the file to a table, sat down and began to read. Susan Burkin, Gary's wife, was represented by Sanford Feingelt. Gary was represented by Manheim Maldonado, of Burkin, Turner and Overstreet. That was Gary's firm, Ben recalled.

By all outward signs, this was a friendly divorce.

Divorce in California is "no fault," meaning the plaintiff, in this case Susan, need not show cause for requesting a divorce. The only issue to be decided before the court was the division of communally owned property.

In Burkin v. Burkin, Susan had been granted an "interlocutory" decree, meaning divorce was granted upon expiration of a state-mandated six-month waiting period. That was to give the couple an opportunity to reconcile before the split was finalized. In slightly over four months the Burkin divorce would be final.

The decree listed the division of property. Susan kept their primary residence and its art and furnishings, while Gary retained their Palm Springs condo and its art and furnishings, along with a Colorado time-share. Susan kept her three-year-old Mercedes, which was paid for, and a five-year-old minivan, also paid for.

The Burkin also owned other cars: a three-year-old Volvo wagon, a two-year-old VW convertible and a 1965 Mustang. Gary got all three, which Ben suspected were driven by their college-age children. Owning them meant paying for their insurance.

Ben continued reading. Susan kept the coin collection, Gary got the sports memorabilia. Ben skipped through the minutia to the stock, cash and other valuables.

Jointly they owned stocks, bonds and certificates of deposit worth just over a million dollars, which the court split evenly between them. They also owned investment property: a half-interest in a mini-mall partnership and one-third interest in an eight-unit apartment partnership. Both carried mortgages but generated positive cash flows. These properties would remain jointly owned by the couple.

Finally, Gary was to pay all Susan's divorce expenses, including attorneys fees, and eight thousand five hundred dollars monthly alimony for five years, unless she re-married before then.

Attached to this ruling was a sheaf of papers that included the real-estate partnership agreements, brokerage and bank statements—all the details upon which the financial settlement rested. Ben skimmed through them.

All in all, Ben decided, it didn't look terrible for either Susan or Gary. But something about the settlement nagged at Ben. Something that didn't seem quite right.

At twenty to five Ben was crawling in Golden State Freeway traffic when he was struck by a thought. There was one thing about the Bank of B. Cohen account that he'd forgotten to check, and he'd have to do that at Beit Joseph. But the office closed at five o'clock. Mindful of California's prohibition against cell phone use while driving, Ben pulled onto the freeway shoulder and stopped before taking out his iPhone.

LaShonda answered on the first ring. "Shalom, Congregation Beit Joseph."

Ben thought her voice sounded cheerful.

"Shalom, LaShonda. This is Ben. Can you do me a favor?"

"Of course!"

"I'm stuck in traffic but I'll be there in an hour or so. Can you find the Cheder Halakha scholarship fund records, all of them, and leave a note on your desk telling me where they are?"

"Sure. It won't take a minute. You have the office key, right?"

"I do. And thanks, LaShonda."

By the time Ben had fought his way through late afternoon traffic to the synagogue it was after six. The parking lot was empty except for LaShonda's car. The classrooms were dark. Oddly, the front door was open. He walked down the cool, dark hallway to the office.

LaShonda lay crumpled on the bloodied carpet, her beautiful face smashed into a torn, twisted horror mask of mangled flesh and broken teeth.

Fighting panic, Ben grabbed the phone and dialed 911.

"Put the phone down and show me your hands," said a voice and Ben turned to find the barrel of a big pistol pointed at his head. Behind the gun was a uniformed cop.

CHAPTER 27

TUESDAY: JUNE 1

Just after midnight Ben was escorted into a brightly lit room where two rumpled men with five o'clock shadows waited. The older, a heavy-set black detective, said, "Sit there."

He sat at the table, glancing around at vomit-green walls and a mirror—behind it, he knew, his every move and gesture was studied, his every word and inflection parsed.

Since finding LaShonda's body, Ben had been in a holding cell, fighting shock and sorrow, praying for LaShonda's soul. His last food had been a noontime pretzel. He was hungry and thirsty and sure the police knew it. You've done nothing wrong, he told himself. It's no worse than a Yom Kippur fast. You can get through this. And he thought, Master of The Universe, be with me now.

The second cop, a wiry Latino in his late thirties, set a can of Coca-Cola next to Ben. He ignored it.

The wiry man said, "I'm Detective Mendoza. This is Detective Harris. We're going to ask you some questions."

Mendoza then read Ben his Miranda rights.

Harris said, "Do you understand these rights?"

Ben said, "Yes. Excuse me Detective Harris, but were you related to LaShonda?"

Mendoza said, "*We* ask questions. You answer them."

Harris said, "We don't get many like you in here."

Mendoza said, "People who hide behind their religion to steal, abuse, and murder."

Ben said, "I don't know what you're talking about."

Harris said, "You've been running around the whole country ripping off your own people. The Jews. You killed LaShonda Harris—I bet she wasn't your first. Now you belong to us, and we're gonna make sure you pay for it."

Ben said, "You are mistaken. I've harmed no one."

"You swindled that temple—Beit Joseph—out of over a hundred thousand dollars."

"Not true."

"Bullshit. It was a con, a wrinkle on the old pigeon drop. Same kind of scam you used on a temple in Allentown, Pennsylvania, and a Jewish school in Trenton, New Jersey."

"You know very well that isn't true."

"You used LaShonda to get in with Beit Joseph. She found out what you were up to, so you killed her."

"*That's* your theory of the crime? Total nonsense."

"We've got a witness who can put you at the temple a few minutes before Ms. Harris was murdered."

"Excuse me, Detective. I know that you're allowed to lie to a suspect if you think it might help solve a crime. But you have no witness, because I committed no crime. And if you want my DNA and fingerprints, don't put a Coke can in front of me. Just ask me. By the way, soda with high fructose corn syrup only increases thirst. I'll wait for water. And, one more time, I didn't kill LaShonda."

Mendoza said, "That's not what Doctor Levine says."

It took Ben a moment to realize that he meant Tova.

"She can say what she likes. I didn't kill anyone and I didn't swindle Beit Joseph."

Mendoza said, "What exactly do you do at the temple?"

"I'm a visiting scholar researching twentieth century burial societies. Ask Rabbi Kimmelman or Gary Burkin."

"Were they in on it, too?"

"You're embarrassing yourself."

Harris said, "You were dating LaShonda Harris."

"We went to dinner a few times. That's not a crime."

"You spent the night at her apartment. Twice."

"Not true. Even if I did, that's no crime either."

"You had sex with her."

"I *never* had sex with her."

"She was raped. We'll find your DNA in her. You're gonna get a needle, Rabbi. If you really are a rabbi."

"Really, I'm a rabbi. And you won't find my DNA in her or in anybody else. I haven't slept with a woman in years."

"So you're a faggot!"

Mendoza said, "Yeah, that fits. She found out you were gay so you had to kill her."

Harris said, "Tell me, Mark, do you find Mendoza attractive? Or am I more your type?"

Ben said, "I've never had sex with a man and never wanted to. I choose to be celibate. But since you asked, I find Mendoza the far more attractive detective. He'd look good in a slouch hat and a trench coat. Very sleuthish."

Mendoza leaned closer. "You're scum—a miserable excuse for a human being. You make my skin crawl."

Ben sat back in his chair. "If you really want to find LaShonda's killer—and I very much hope that you do—then

I might be able to help. But if all you're going to do is call me names, then you're wasting the taxpayers' money."

Mendoza sat down and opened a file folder.

"Mark Thompson Glass, aka Moshe Benyamin Maimon. Which is it? Are you Glass or Maimon?"

"Moshe Benyamin Maimon is my Hebrew name."

Mendoza said, "All Jews have a Hebrew name *and* one in English?"

"Mexican Jews have a Hebrew name and a *Spanish* name."

"Nobody likes a smart-ass."

Harris put on reading glasses and picked up the file.

"Mark Thompson Glass, aka Marty Thompson, aka Marcus Thompson, aka Martin Glass, aka Thomas Glass, aka Tom Marcus, aka Rabbi Glass, aka Rabbi Marcus, aka Rabbi Tomashevsky. Assault, extortion, fraud, grand theft, arson, attempted murder, robbery, witness tampering, bribery—you've been a busy, busy boy, you worthless fuck."

Ben said, "You forgot my speeding ticket on the New England Turnpike. Right outside of Barnard's Cross—

"I just thought of something. LaShonda had been dead an hour or more by the time I arrived."

Harris looked up. "How do you know that?"

"I saw her wounds. She bled a lot. But now I recall that almost all the blood had soaked into the carpet."

"So you killed her at five, and then came back?"

"No, at five I met with my sleeper cell. We want to take over Burbank and make it into a Baha'i theocracy. So I have an alibi."

Mendoza said. "You're a member of a sleeper cell?"

"No, but why should you guys get to have all the fun? I want to make up stories too."

Mendoza said, "You're some piece of work! Jerking us off while your girlfriend lies on a slab in the morgue."

"I'll mourn her in my own way at the right time. Right now, I'm trying to help you catch her killer. But instead of listening to me, you want to play games."

Mendoza leaned in until his nose was almost touching Ben's forehead. "Fourteen arrests, no convictions. But we got you now, shithead. Your life of crime is O-V-E-R."

Ben said, "I get it. This is one of those reality shows! The camera is behind the mirror! I'm supposed to panic when you read that fairy tale. Get some union writers—not cheap, but they'll do much better for you."

"Dr. Levine saw you go into Beit Joseph this afternoon. You were carrying something in a shopping bag, something very heavy."

Harris said, "Something like the rock you used to smash that poor girl's face into hamburger."

Ben shook his head. "You're misinformed or lying. I went into the temple a little after *six*. Evening, not afternoon. LaShonda was dead on the office floor. When I saw her I dialed 911. Then a police officer walked in."

Harris said, "Too bad we don't have the electric chair any more. I'd really enjoy watching you fry."

Ben said, "Do you want to catch her killer or not?"

Mendoza said. "We already have. You did it. We have a witness. We have your fingerprints on the murder weapon. You raped that girl and we have your DNA to prove it."

Harris said, "Was it a lover's quarrel? You didn't mean to kill her? We can understand that. But we can't help you if you don't tell us what happened."

"Help me? Helping me is *not* your job. *Your* job is catching the killer. So *do* your job! Stop threatening and insulting me and listen to what I have to tell you."

Mendoza slammed his fist on the table, hard. "You cocky little prick. I ought to split your face open, like you did to that girl."

Harris said, "Hold on, Mike. Let's hear what the man has to say."

Mendoza said, "Okay. Let's hear your bullshit."

"Not bullshit. Last week LaShonda and I had dinner at a restaurant on Pico. Then we took a walk. Many Orthodox Jews live in that neighborhood; two of them, two Hassidic men, called LaShonda a whore. Then one threw a punch, so I had to stop him. I dislocated his shoulder."

Mendoza looked skeptical. "You broke his arm?"

Ben said, "I dislocated his shoulder. Not the same thing. I just wanted to put him out of action before he could cause real damage."

Harris said, "Stand up."

Ben got to his feet.

Mendoza said, "Five-eight, a hundred fifty-five."

Ben said, "Close enough."

Harris said, "Sit down. This guy's arm you broke, what did he look like?"

"Heavy-set, curly dark beard going a little gray."

"How tall?"

"It was dark, but I'm guessing six-three or a little more. Big around the middle—I'd say he went two sixty, two seventy, something like that."

Harris said, "And you broke his arm?"

"I *dislocated his shoulder.*"

"So you're some kind of martial-arts expert?"

Ben sighed. "He swung at me. If we'd traded punches I could have lost an eye, broke my nose or worse. So I stopped him."

Mendoza said, "You're full of shit. You didn't break anybody's arm, you little punk."

"Listen to me! Before he attacked me, he said that LaShonda was a whore who should be stoned. I told them she was a respectable woman who worked in a synagogue."

Harris said, "So what?"

"They threatened to *stone* her! Maybe they found out where she worked and killed her with a big rock."

Mendoza said, "If you're a martial arts expert, maybe you didn't need a rock. Maybe you just beat her to death with kicks and punches."

Ben held out his hands. "And I did that without leaving a single mark on my hands?"

Mendoza smiled. "So you wore gloves?"

"I never laid a finger on LaShonda. She was my friend."

Harris said, "Wait. Hold on—we never said the murder weapon was a big rock. How did you know that?"

"*You* said a rock. I saw poor LaShonda's face. She wasn't mangled with a *small* rock."

Mendoza said, "So you used a *big* rock to kill her?"

"Detective! *You* said a witness saw me enter the building carrying a shopping bag with something very heavy in it. A *small* rock wouldn't have been very heavy."

"So you carried that rock into the synagogue."

"No. But, *if* you actually have a witness, and *if* this witness actually saw *someone* carrying a shopping bag with *something* very heavy in it, and *if* it was a rock, then it would certainly have been a *big* rock."

Mendoza said, "You got an answer for everything."

Ben said, "You should find the man who attacked me. I have nothing more to say. I'd like to call my attorney."

"You're going to booking. *Then* you get a phone call."

Harris said, "I'll bet a night in jail improves your attitude."

"Ten minutes ago I was a master criminal with a long arrest record. Now a night in jail is supposed to scare me? Are you guys *really* homicide detectives?"

Harris said, "Stand up. Hands behind your back."

CHAPTER 28

Escorted by Mendoza, Ben entered the station's booking area to find Gary Burkin and Captain Bruce Henderson, a trim, balding, uniformed man of about fifty.

Burkin said, "Rabbi Ben, are you okay?"

"I'm fine. What are you doing here?"

"I thought you needed an attorney. Now, it seems that you don't."

Henderson said, "You're free to go, Rabbi."

Mendoza said, "Cap, are you sure?"

"The Levine woman says you misunderstood her. He didn't swindle the temple and he wasn't the guy carrying a shopping bag into the building about five."

"Misunderstood? We've got her signed statement."

Henderson said, "I apologize for detaining you for so long, Rabbi. Just doing our job."

"I wish your detectives were better at it. Maybe they could cut back on watching "Law & Order" and spend some time reading the Laws of Evidence."

Henderson frowned. "I'll take that under advisement."

"Captain. I gave them a description of two men who threatened to stone LaShonda. They might know who killed her. I hope you'll follow up on this lead aggressively."

"We'll look into it."

"If you don't, I will."

Burkin shot Ben a cautionary look.

Mendoza said, "Police business. We don't need help from vigilantes."

"If you'd listened to me seven hours ago, when I was arrested, you might have them in custody now."

Henderson said, "Thanks for your cooperation, Rabbi."

Burkin said, "I'll drive you home."

***

Burkin watched, amused, as Ben wolfed down a green salad followed by four hard-boiled eggs, a baked potato with sour cream and two servings of cottage cheese. They were the only patrons in the Lankershim Boulevard diner.

"It's hard keeping kosher, isn't it Rabbi Ben?"

Ben swallowed, and then signaled the waitress. "Peach cobbler with vanilla ice cream, please."

As the waitress left, Ben drank some water and looked at Burkin for a long moment. "I suppose you mean that a cheeseburger and a milkshake would have been a lot tastier. Of course they would—but that's not possible for me.

"Did you pass the bar on your first try, Gary?"

Burkin shook his head. "Third time was the charm."

"Mastering what you needed to become a successful lawyer—that wasn't easy, was it?"

"You're right. Anything worth doing well comes hard."

"I believe that if being a Jew was easy, there might be more Jews but they wouldn't be better people and it wouldn't be as worthwhile being a Jew. We would not be as engaged in *tikkun olam*, healing the world."

"I never thought of it that way."

"That's why you're a millionaire and I'm a rabbi."

"I think you'd make a helluva lawyer. I really admire the way you handled yourself at the police station."

"How did I go from Public Enemy Number One to 'sorry we had to detain you'?"

"When the police found LaShonda, they called Rabbi Kimmelman, me, and Tova—we were all on the emergency contact list on LaShonda's desk.

"Tova got there first, then Rabbi Kimmelman, then me. Those detectives—"

"Mendoza and Harris."

"They interviewed each of us separately. Tova was really upset—she and LaShonda were close—and she said some crazy things. But I didn't see her statement until just before you went into the interview room.

"While you were in the holding cell, Henderson read all three statements and re-interviewed Kimmelman and me about Tova's allegations. When he went back to Tova, she turned around, said she was upset and hadn't been speaking rationally. The police have no physical evidence—nothing to link you to the murder except your presence in the room. But there was no blood on you, no murder weapon was found, there was no nothing to indicate that you were the killer.

"By the way, you were absolutely correct about the time it took blood to soak into that carpet. The crime scene squad put that in their report."

"That's good to know, but my God, we're talking about a human being. LaShonda was—I'm having trouble thinking of her in the past tense. She was a wonderful person."

"Yes. Very warm and caring and good at her job."

"You were saying?'

"By the time they got around to putting you in the interview room, the coroner had determined that she'd been dead an hour or more before you were arrested. The arresting officer touched the hood of your car—it was hot. They found a parking stub from downtown L.A. with a time stamp in your car. So they knew you got to Beit Joseph after LaShonda was murdered."

"How did they know to come to Beit Joseph?"

"Anonymous 911 call at about six p.m."

"Just when I arrived."

"Yeah. So they pretty much had to let you go."

"But they interrogated me anyway?"

"Harris was convinced that you killed LaShonda, that you're some kind of Rasputin who hypnotized Tova. That you killed her, left, then called 911 and came back so the police would find you and it would look like you just got there."

"Is Harris related to LaShonda?"

"According to Henderson, they're some kind of cousins. Not very close. So he gave him a shot at getting a confession. And then he saw how well that went."

"You know Henderson well?"

"Friendly enemies. He's the Harlem Globetrotters and I'm the New York Nationals—his team wins almost all the games."

"You watched that interrogation?"

"I did."

"What was all that nonsense that about my criminal record? All those crimes and aliases?"

"They make stuff up as they go. For example, LaShonda *wasn't* raped. They wanted you to deny raping her, which might be construed as an implicit murder confession."

"So their only imperative is closing cases?"

"Pretty much. These two guys are all right, but some don't care if they get the right guy or not. They think, if he isn't guilty of this one, then surely he's guilty of something else. It evens out in the end. And they want credit for closing a case."

The waitress put a plate of cobbler and ice cream in front of Ben. He ate it slowly, savoring every bite.

When he looked up from his empty plate, Burkin was laughing. "I guess you were hungry."

"Now I want a shower and a bed."

"Sure. Say, did you really break that guy's arm?"

"I dislocated it. Torn tissue, not broken bones."

"Why?"

"All things being equal, big guy fights little guy, the big guy wins. That's why boxing has weight classes. A street fight—no rules. The longer a fight between mismatched fighters goes, the more likely the little guy will get hurt. His best shot is to end the fight quickly."

"So, how did you do it? Kung Fu? Jiu-Jitsu?"

"In New York, when a short Jewish guy doesn't have a father, a big brother or a gang behind him, he either becomes a talker or a fighter. I needed to be both, so I took classes at the 92nd Street YMHA. Aikido, Karate, Taekwondo. And, later, an IDF self-defense course."

"Could you show me a few moves sometime?"

"Sure, but then I'd have to whip your ass."

They both laughed.

Ben said, "Seriously, do you think the Burbank cops will look for those Hassids?"

"Maybe, but Harris still sort of thinks you did it. So they'll call a few hospital ERs asking about big, bearded Jews with dislocated shoulders, and maybe send an inquiry to LAPD, and meanwhile they'll search LaShonda's apartment for clues and maybe look at the hate groups. And they'll watch you."

"You *don't* think they'll find her killer."

It was a statement, not a question, and Burkin considered his answer carefully. "They don't get many major crimes in Burbank. They don't have the expertise or manpower to do a really thorough investigation. Do you think the Hassids killed her?"

"I'm too tired to think straight. But I'll bet it won't take me more than a few days to find those guys."

CHAPTER 29

WEDNESDAY: JUNE 2

Tova came out of UCLA's Bunche Hall and half-way down the stairs looked up to see Ben on the sidewalk below.

Ben said, "Tova, we need to talk."

Tova said, "I have nothing to say to you."

"You followed me. You saw me with LaShonda and you—"

"—you're going to kill me, too?"

"You followed me to her home and you saw what you expected to see."

"Exactly. I saw that you were *shtupping* her."

"You saw what you *expected* to see, but what you *thought* you saw was not what really happened. You drew a false conclusion because you had incomplete information."

"I know what I saw."

"Tova, listen to me. You saw a woman in a négligée kissing a fully-clothed man, and you decided that we had just had sex. Well, we didn't. Not that she didn't offer, and not that I didn't want to accept. But I didn't."

"You were *shtupping*. I'm sure of it."

"I've been celibate for six years."

A trio of pretty co-eds carrying bulging backpacks passed, looking at Ben and giggling.

Tova's face turned red.

"I don't believe you. And you killed LaShonda."

"I can't control what you think. But if you're so sure of that, why did you retract your police statement?"

"Because I wasn't actually at Beit Joseph when the police say LaShonda died. I left before five. Maybe you didn't actually beat her to death, but you're responsible just the same."

Tova turned and started back up the Bunche Hall steps.

"I agree with your last sentence."

Tova stopped and craned her neck to stare at Ben.

Ben said, "And I'd like your help finding her killer."

***

Tova said, "The guy you beat up killed LaShonda?"

"The police don't believe that I was even in a fight. Why do you?"

"Because LaShonda told me about it. She was really impressed with the way you defended her honor."

Ben shook his head. "I was just trying to keep him from hurting us. And in 'defending her honor,' I made the mistake of saying that she worked at a synagogue. I should have known that any half-wit racist zealot could have found her in a couple of days. But that was only a week ago. I doubt that a man with a dislocated shoulder could have beaten her to death. But he was with a friend that night, and maybe they have other friends. So they might know something. Maybe. The police haven't found them. I don't think they're even looking very hard."

"What do you want me to do?"

"Just one thing," Ben said, and explained.

***

Four hours later, at two in the afternoon, Tova began walking west on Pico Boulevard from the dairy restaurant where Ben and LaShonda ate dinner several evenings earlier.

Wearing an ankle-length skirt, a long-sleeved blouse and a dark blue head scarf, she moved slowly down the south side of the street looking at each shop.

Ben had recalled that he and LaShonda had passed several stores offering a variety of merchandise and services—a dry cleaner, a picture-framing shop, a vacuum repair store, a "glatt kosher" sandwich deli, a dentist's office and a tiny Orthodox synagogue. All closed. Only a chain-store pharmacy and shop selling floor coverings were open that night. Ben thought his assailants might have come out of the latter establishment. It was equally possible that they were merely passers-by.

Tova had decided to ask at each store if anyone had seen "a fist-fight" she'd witnessed from "across the street" several nights earlier. She wondered if anyone had been hurt, and if the neighborhood was still "safe" for respectable people. She started in the sandwich deli.

The teenaged girl behind the counter listened, regarding Tova with a mixture of amusement and contempt. "So now the police send little old ladies to make trouble for Jews?" she said, in an Israeli accent.

"Who are you calling *old*?" Tova shrieked.

"Then you admit it, you're police."

"I'm not police! And I'm not old!"

"Then you only come to make trouble for Jews!"

"I *am* a Jew, you insolent ignoramus."

"Okay. So what kind of sandwich do you want today?"

Tova stormed out of the shop, ready to quit her quest, only to see a tall, bearded man in a dark coat going into All Floors, the floor-covering store.

Entering the store Tova was greeted by a dumpling-shaped woman of perhaps sixty in a blonde *sheitel,* a wig that some Orthodox women use to cover their shaved head.

"Shalom, shalom,"

"Shalom," Tova replied.

"What can I help you with today? Maybe some nice tiles for the kitchen? An area rug for the living room? You have a house, dear, or are you renting?"

"A house, kind of a fixer-upper."

"A fixer upper! For that you need to bring your husband to come in also."

"Excuse me?"

"It's going to be a major purchase, he'll want to know where his money's going."

"I'm a widow. My husband—Ben died last year. Rectal cancer—it was horrible."

"I'm sorry for your loss. *Olav hashalom.*"

"Thank you. Listen, I was walking the other night, maybe a week ago, across the street. Nine o'clock or a little before, and I saw a fight, right in front of your store."

"You saw those *schwartzer mamzers* beat my Avi?"

" *That* was your husband?"

"My son! They broke his arm, and they got in their car and drove away, all six of them."

"He's all right, your Avi?"

"His arm is broken, I just told you. And his brother, Yakov, they punched him and kicked him, too. But you saw it!"

"I didn't really see anyone, just shadows. And there was a woman—a black girl. Your Avi, he's a smaller man, maybe average height?"

"No, no. He's very tall, very strong—but there were six or maybe seven of them. And the girl, a whore, Avi said. They had knives. One had a gun! You didn't see their faces, from across the street?"

"No, it was too dark."

"But you'll talk to the police?"

"Of course I will, mother."

The woman reached beneath the counter and produced pad and pen. "Please, to write your name and telephone."

Thinking furiously, Tova wrote 'Sara Kagan,' and made up a number, omitting the area code.

"Thank you so much, Mrs. Kagan. I am Mrs. Feigenbaum. You can call me Gitel. Now, can I show you some samples?"

For the next half hour, Tova listened to the virtues of ceramic floor tile compared to laminate or wood, accepting several samples and eventually, pleading another appointment, excusing herself with a promise to return as soon as she made up her mind.

The shopkeeper held the door open for Tova. "And you'll tell the police what you saw?"

"Of course. But as I said, I didn't see any faces."

"You saw the fight, it's enough. Now Avi can collect the Workman's Compensation, because he threw them out of the store and then they attacked him on the sidewalk."

"Of course, of course. Shalom, goodbye."

Not until Tova was back in her Prius did she allow herself to laugh. Six or seven black men! With a whore! Knives and a gun! And they all escaped by jumping into *one* car!

Tova couldn't wait to tell Ben.

CHAPTER 30

THURSDAY: JUNE 3

At first Mendoza and Harris insisted that Tova remain in the LAPD's West Los Angeles station. But after Ben explained that she had located the Feigenbaum brothers, Detective Einhorn, the LAPD liaison, agreed to let her come along if she remained in his car.

Einhorn parked on Pico, half a block west of All Floors, got out and approached the store. Not until then did Tova discover that she was locked inside an unmarked Crown Victoria.

Tall and lanky, Einhorn wore jeans, a denim work shirt and paint-spattered safety shoes. He entered All Floors and asked the burly, bearded Yakov if he could look at tile. Yakov, engrossed in a catalog, pointed to the tile section. Meanwhile Harris slipped into the alley to wait near the store's loading dock. A few minutes later Mendoza, also in working man's attire, went inside and pretended interest in rolls of industrial carpet.

Down the block, Ben, wearing jogging shoes, jeans, a polo shirt and a Red Sox cap, went into the sandwich shop and ordered a kosher sub: soy Swiss, roast beef, pickles, tomatoes, lettuce and peppers. As he took his first bite his cell phone rang.

"Rabbi Maimon," he answered, still chewing.

"I think I've found what you need," Mendoza said on the phone. "Come right over to the tile section."

Ben dropped the sandwich.

A minute later he entered All Floors and headed straight for Mendoza. At the counter behind Ben, Yakov looked up from the catalog—then looked again.

"You son-of-a-bitch!" he yelled in Yiddish.

Avi, his right arm in a sling, stuck his head out of the office in the rear of the store.

Still in Yiddish, Yakov said. "You got a lot of nerve, coming here! Where is your black whore?"

In English, Ben said, "Calm down. I just want to talk to you."

Yakov turned back to the counter, reached deep inside and came out with an old Remington pump shotgun.

Mendoza yelled, "Gun!" and reached for the snub-nosed Colt under his shirt.

Einhorn yelled, "Gun" and went for the Glock holstered in the small of his back.

Yakov pumped the slide that put a cartridge in the chamber, dervish. A dervish on tiptoe, Ben whirled across the room and with a taekwondo kick sent the shotgun flying.

Pivoting in a tight circle, Ben's second kick, to Yakov's solar plexus, sent him sprawling backward atop the counter.

Einhorn said, "Police! Freeze!" Holding an automatic in one hand and his badge with the other, he ran over to Yakov, who writhed atop the counter, gasping for breath.

Avi rushed forward but was restrained by Mendoza, also holding his badge aloft.

Avi said, "That man broke my arm! Last week he assaulted me and my brother! Arrest him!"

Einhorn said, "You're sure it was *him*?" He pointed at Ben. "This guy right here?"

"Yes! That's him! He was with some black whore! They jumped us out on the sidewalk!"

Ben said, "Good to see you again, Avi. I hope you're feeling better soon."

Einhorn said, "That's very strange, Avi. Three days ago you and your brother came to the West L.A. station and under penalty of perjury swore that six black men with knives and guns came into this store, and when you told them to leave they beat you up and broke your arm."

Avi said, "I am mistake. Not good the English, me. This one, gang leader. They beat us. He give them orders."

Ben said, "Nice, Avi. I don't think they'll buy it."

The front door opened and Gitel Feigenbaum entered.

"What is going on here?"

Einhorn held out his badge. "Detective Einhorn, LAPD." He pointed to Ben. "This man dislocated your son's shoulder."

Gitel shook her head, frowning. "No. Avi said it was a gang of black men. *Schwartzers.* Not this nice young man."

Einhorn said, "I've heard enough. Avigdor Feigenbaum, you're under arrest. Yakov Feigenbaum, you are also under arrest."

Gripping his Smith & Wesson in both hands, Harris stepped into the store from the back entrance.

Mendoza said, "You missed all the excitement, Len. The little rabbi dude just put a Kobe Bryant Kung Fu move on the big bearded guy like I've never seen."

***

Everyone in Los Angeles knows a cop car, even when it isn't a black-and-white with a city logo on its doors and a bubble-gum machine on the roof. Seething with indignation, Tova sat in Einhorn's backseat, enduring the stares of curious passers-by until she saw the detective emerge from All Floors carrying a long, odd-shaped package wrapped in brown paper and tied with string—the shotgun.

Ben followed him out and after a brief conversation waved to Tova, then headed the other way toward his car and the sandwich he hoped was still waiting for him.

Out of Tova's view, behind the store, Mendoza and Harris led the Feigenbaums, handcuffed to each other, to their own squad car.

With Tova pounding furiously on the window, Einhorn stowed the shotgun in the trunk before slipping into the front seat. He turned the ignition key and pressed a button, and Tova heard the doors unlock.

Einhorn said, "Come up here in front, if you like."

Still seething, Tova climbed out onto the sidewalk, and then got into the front seat.

Tova yelled, "You locked me in!"

"For your own safety. No way that we could protect you in that store if there was gunplay. And there was."

"But you could protect Ben—the rabbi?"

"I'd say he doesn't need much protection. More like the other way around."

"What? What happened in there? Is he all right?"

Einhorn started the engine and, glancing in the mirror, flicked his siren on and off as he and pulled a U-turn to head west on Pico. Then he told Tova what had happened in the store.

Tova said, "Wow! I wish I could have seen that!"

"Your boyfriend probably saved my life—I was right behind him in the line of fire. If he hadn't moved just when he did, hadn't kicked the gun away, neither Mendoza nor I would have had an aimed shot before Yakov fired."

"Ben is not my boyfriend."

"Coulda fooled me. The way you look at him. The way he sticks up for you."

"You're jumping to conclusions. We're just friends."

"If you say so."

"What about Avi and Yakov? You didn't arrest them?"

"My Burbank colleagues are bringing them to West L.A., where we'll book them for felony ADW—assault with a deadly weapon—and perjury. Then we'll turn them over to Burbank on suspicion of murder."

CHAPTER 31

Ben said, "I don't think they know anything about LaShonda's murder."

Tova and Ben watched through the one-way glass as Avi and Yakov were unshackled in the interview room.

"Of course they do. They probably paid someone to find her and kill her."

On the other side of the glass Mendoza set a cold Coke in front of each man and took a seat across the table.

Ben shook his head. "I don't think so. They committed themselves to a story about being mugged by a gang, then filed Workman's Comp claims to pay medical expenses and what they'll claim is lost wages."

"They tried to commit fraud. So what?"

"So they can't very well admit they made that story up. That's what they'd have to do to get someone to stone LaShonda to death—admit that they got beat by one man. They'd also have to convince an observant Jew to commit murder. I don't buy it."

"But they could have gone five miles east and found some Salvadoran or Mexican or Columbian to kill LaShonda for a few dollars."

"They don't like dealing with outsiders, and especially with *goyim*—gentiles. But say they did. What gangbanger is going to bash a girl's face in when he could just shoot her and be done? Now that I think about it, that suggests a crime of passion. I'm sure the Feigenbaum brothers didn't have anything to do with her murder."

Tova said, "You're very sure of yourself."

"Look, they're bullies. They've always gotten their way and they're used to pushing people around. They're totally invested in their personas—the big, tough guys that nobody wants to mess with. Then someone did mess with them. They're ashamed to let anyone know what really happened—it goes to their core, their sense of self. Maybe, in time, they'd have realized how wrong they were to accost LaShonda and me in the first place."

"But they're Hassids! They think Jews should act like they were living in eighteenth-century Poland."

"I really don't have a problem with what they believe. It's when they try to force me to live by their rules, their values, that I draw the line.

"Anyway, I don't think it was about religious convictions. More about being able to throw their weight around. Bullies often feel a sense of superiority over others, that they're entitled."

"Sociopaths?"

"To a degree. A lack of compassion. Poor social skills. No impulse control."

"Now you're an expert on bullying?"

"Not really. But... 'Know thy enemy'—a good rule. Growing up, undersized, I was often bullied. You can take it or you can do something about it."

"You're saying Avi and Yakov get their jollies by being cruel?"

"Yes. Religious piety is just a convenient excuse for venting anger and frustration on weaker people."

"So instead of eating a whole box of cookies at one sitting, they beat somebody up?"

"Or instead of running five miles when they're pissed off at themselves."

"Is that what *you* do, Ben? Run five miles?"

"Six. And *then* I eat a box of cookies."

Tova laughed in spite of herself.

Ben reached up and turned on the speaker, then sat back as Harris read Avi and Yakov their Miranda rights.

***

Ninety minutes later the door to the observation room opened and Captain Henderson stepped inside.

"Rabbi, Dr. Levine. For now, I'm going to send these two back to LAPD. They were both working in their store when Ms. Harris was killed and we can't connect them to the murder. We still need to run their financials and their phones. It takes a few days. Unless we turn up something there, some link to murder-for-hire, we can't make a case."

Tova said, "But you'll keep looking for her killers?"

"Of course. And we'll have a couple of officers at her funeral taking pictures of people and license plates. Just in case the killer turns up to watch her buried."

Tova started to weep. "That poor girl. She didn't deserve to die that way."

Ben said, "Nobody does."

MONDAY: JUNE 7

Although the funeral had been delayed until LaShonda's son could get emergency leave and fly in from Pensacola, LaShonda's family was represented only by Ricardo, LaShonda's aged aunt, and her wheelchair-bound mother.

Ben tried to speak with the older woman but the waved him away.

Mendoza and Harris observed the proceedings from the shade of a giant Italian stone pine while two plainclothes officers photographed mourners and car license plates.

From Beit Joseph came Ben, Kimmelman, Gary Burkin and the entire board of directors, two dozen other members, along with the Hebrew school teachers and other synagogue employees. Kimmelman also invited several rabbinical colleagues; including Ben and Kimmelman, eleven male and two female rabbis assembled, a pond of dark hats, dark suits and long beards. Less accustomed to attending funerals than to presiding over one, the rabbinical contingent looked vaguely uncomfortable in a Christian burial ground listening to the stylized oration of the Reverend Dumachus Wilson, an elderly yet vigorous Baptist.

Although it is not a Christian custom, at the conclusion of prayers the Jewish mourners lined up to take turns performing the mitzvah of helping to bury the dead. LaShonda's coffin was lowered into the earth; then each Jew in turn took a spade and shoveled a little dirt atop it.

After a hasty, whispered conference with the Reverend Wilson, Kimmelman led the Jewish grievers in Mourners Kaddish, the traditional prayer for the dead.

Later most of the mourners went to Kimmelman's back yard where his wife had covered a table with kosher food.

Ben was eying a bagel when a young black man tapped him on the shoulder. Ben turned and stuck out his hand. After a moment's hesitation, Ricardo shook it.

"You're LaShonda's son, Ricardo?"

"Yes sir. And you're that Kung Fu rabbi she was seeing."

"Mixed martial arts. Call me Rabbi Ben, or just Ben."

"So were you seeing my moms for a long time?"

"No. No, I'm sorry to say I only met her about three weeks ago. We went to dinner a few times, and then—"

"—then somebody bashed her head in."

"She was a wonderful person. I'm truly sorry for your loss. I'll do everything in my power to find her killer."

"That's good, Rabbi. My moms told me about you, how you were just getting to know each other. But I could tell she thought you was pretty special. Not just the Kung—the martial arts stuff."

"That's very kind of you to say."

"But I'm sorta confused. You're a rabbi, but you were dating? Isn't that, well, kind of against the rules?"

Ben stifled a laugh. "Not at all. We're not priests. Rabbi means teacher—that's what we do. We study Jewish law and customs and we teach our communities about them."

"But I thought Jewish people were different."

"We're different in *some* ways. Rabbis get married and divorced. I was married once. My wife was killed."

"You got really bad luck with women, huh?"

"Not at all, Ricardo. I wouldn't trade the three years I had with Rachel, the woman I married, for anything. And knowing your mother, even for only a short time—I feel blessed."

"Rabbi, I got ten days leave. Could we kind of hang out some time before I have to go back to Pensacola?"

"Tomorrow good?"

"Naw, gotta spend some time with my grams and stuff."

"Day after, then? Start at six in the morning?"

"Oh-six hundred? There's nothing open that early."

"Did you bring your running shoes, Ricardo?"

"Old ones, at my mom's house."

"I'll see you right outside her door at six. And do your stretches before I get there."

"You a hard man to be such a little runt, Rabbi Ben!"

CHAPTER 32

WEDNESDAY: JUNE 9

"You ready, Ricardo?"

"Ready as I'll ever be, Rabbi Ben."

"You stretch for fifteen minutes?"

"That's for old guys. Five is all I ever need."

"We'll see. One thing, this is when I usually say my morning prayer. Give me a minute?"

"Do your thing, yo."

Ben said, *"Modeh ani lefaneicha melech chai v'kayam shehechezarta bi nishmati bechemlah - rabbah emunatecha."*

"Let's go." With Ricardo beside him Ben followed the curving sidewalk out to Magnolia Boulevard.

Running abreast facing the sparse morning traffic, the low sun was warm on their backs. Ben set the pace.

After a few minutes Ricardo said, "Rabbi Ben, can I ask you a question?"

"Any time."

"What was that you said, that prayer? And what language is that, Jewish?"

"Hebrew. It means, 'I offer thanks to you, my eternal King, for your compassion in returning my soul to me - your faithfulness knows no limit.' Something like that."

"Jewish people believe that God takes your soul while you sleep, is that it?"

"That's the literal meaning. But so much of prayer and scripture is metaphor, simile or symbolism. Think of it as poetry—that's a better way to understand it."

"Jewish pray all the time? All day long?"

"The pious pray three times daily. Saying a prayer first thing reminds us that God is always present in our lives, and that our duty is to fulfill God's will."

"It was God's will that somebody kill my moms?"

"I can't believe in that God, Ricardo. I know there are people who do, but not me. Did God know what was going to happen to your mother? That's a different question. If you believe God sees all, knows all, looks into everyone's heart and mind and understands their intentions—that *is* my notion of God, for now."

"So God knew that somebody was gonna kill my moms?"

"I believe that. But I don't know *when* God knew it."

"So, God could have saved her, but he didn't?"

"That's the mystery: Why does a loving being allow bad things to happen. Is God in fact all-powerful? Are their limits to God's power? Rabbis have been debating that for more than two thousand years. For as long as there have been rabbis."

"But why? Why would God let somebody kill my moms?"

"We could talk about this for hours. The Cliff Notes version: God granted us the power of free will. Somebody decided to kill her, God didn't interfere."

"What does that mean, free will?"

"Each of us gets to decide how we live our lives. Do we hurt people? Do we help each other out when needed? Are we concerned only with ourselves, or do we look around and try to make the world better?"

"I rob some dude, yo, I get his money. What do I get if I help somebody out, give them some money or something?"

"Virtue is its own reward. You get to know that you did the right thing, that you behaved as God wants you to."

"This is some heavy stuff. I'm not sure I get it all."

"Me neither, Ricardo. I'm still learning. But I do believe that God knows that I will do everything I can to find out why your mom was killed and to bring her murderer to justice. I believe God has the power to help me. But I believe there are there things that humans can't grasp. Does God have a plan? Does making a killer pay for his crime fit with that plan? We'll see about that."

"I want to help."

"You're going back to Pensacola next week, right?"

"Damn straight. The Navy is way cool. I'm learning aircraft weapons systems, command and control avionics—all that stuff. That's gonna be my ticket to a good job. Or I might even stay in the Navy—it's not so bad, after boot camp."

"Glad to hear it."

"But I know something about my moms that you don't."

"I bet you know a lot about her."

"Hey, how far are we going today?"

"Tired already?"

"Naw. Just want to pace myself."

"How far do they run you down in Pensacola?"

"I guess about three miles or so."

The runners passed into the darkness under the low, curving arch of a freeway, then seconds later burst back into daylight. A major intersection appeared ahead.

Ben said, "That traffic light up there—"

"Laurel Canyon."

"—is three miles from our start. Want to go back?"

"How far was you planning to go?"

"Coldwater Canyon and back"

"So like six miles, yo?"

"I usually only do five, but I'm thinking, hey, the Navy is in port, can't let 'em down."

"Then let's do Coldwater. How 'bout I set the pace back?"

"Fair enough."

They ran on in silence until Coldwater Canyon Boulevard came into view. Ben pointed to the traffic signal, just turning red against them, then led a sprint to the crosswalk and then across the street.

Ben said, "Lay on, Mac Duff."

Ricardo said, "Huh?"

"Take the lead, press the attack, run the show."

The younger man, a head taller, immediately lengthened his stride, forcing Ben to increase his own. As they approached Laurel Canyon, Ricardo showed signs of tiring. Ben pressed him, made him dig deeper into his energy reserves. After another half mile, Ricardo pulled up short.

"Cramp!"

"Stretch it out, then walk it off."

Hopping on one leg to the sidewalk, Ricardo put both hands against a wall and stood on his left leg, slowly putting weight back on the right, stretching the calf muscle.

After a few minutes, looking sheepish, Ricardo signaled that he was ready and they set off at a slow jog.

"You run every day?"

"Except Shabbat—Saturday. If I have to miss, I'll make it up, run extra the next few days."

They walked the last quarter mile, where Ben led Ricardo to the shade of the parking structure to stretch. With a key from a buttoned pocket he opened the Honda's trunk and grabbed two multiple-use water bottles, passing one to Ricardo before twisting the other open.

Ben said, "You had something to share about your mom?"

"Not sure if it means anything."

"Try me."

"'Bout four months ago, when I finished boot camp, I got a leave en route to Pensacola. Ten days."

Ben nodded to show he'd heard, and then took another sip.

"So I go to see my best boot camp buddy, Jesus."

He pronounced it the Spanish way, "hay-soos."

"We're pretty tight; Jesus invites me to a party his folks had to celebrate his graduating from boot camp."

"Where does Jesus live?"

"Over in Pacoima."

"So you went to the party?"

"Yeah. See, my moms grew up in that neighborhood, till she had me. Then she moved to Glendale, and then Burbank. My grams still lives there. In Pacoima."

"Something happened at the party?"

"This guy Federico comes up to me and says we're cousins. He's a Mexican, my dad is a Mexican, but I never met my dad. He split when I was born."

"Go on."

"So Federico goes, 'My uncle Enrique is your dad, you should come over and say hello, give him respect, and he goes on like that. We have a couple beers, and I think, okay, *now* what I do?"

"You asked your mom, right?"

"Yeah. How'd you know?"

"That's what a good son does in that situation."

"I guess. So my moms goes, 'You're a grown-up now. You finished boot camp. You're not a little boy no more. Do what you think is right.'"

"You went to see him."

"Yeah. Scary looking dude, all them prison tats. But he acted like he was glad to see me 'n all. Said he was sorry he'd missed my growing up, sorry that he didn't send my moms any support money—all like that. Said he wanted to, but he was doing hard time."

"But now he wants to make it up to you?"

"Something like that. Wants me to meet his other kids. Asked if he could come by and say hello to my moms.

"I said I didn't know if she was up for that. But he musta followed me home, 'cause the next night he just shows up.

Mom freaks. Told him to stay away—don't want him coming around, ever. But she said that if I wanted to hang with my father, that was my business, but she never wanted to see him again."

"Hold on a minute. Let's go back to him following you. How did you get to your buddy's place in Pacoima?"

"Moms let me use her car. She stays home most nights during the week."

Ben looked at Ricardo and saw he was blinking back tears. "Take it easy, man. And if you gotta cry, then let it out. Nothing to be ashamed of—we only get one mother."

Ricardo turned his back and leaned against the wall, his body shaking with grief as the tears flowed.

Ben was thinking. If Enrique spent years in prison, chances were that he was part of California's Mexican Mafia, a prison-based gang whose tentacles reached into every corner of the Latino community. They often had girlfriends or relatives with no criminal records apply for clerical jobs in state agencies. These insiders were then able to feed the gang information. If Enrique was connected, LaShonda's license plate number was enough for an associate at the Department of Motor Vehicles to get her address. He didn't have to follow Ricardo.

Ricardo turned around. "Sorry, man. I just couldn't—"

"It's fine, Ricardo."

"Call me Ricky. What all my Navy buds call me."

"Ricky Ricardo?" Ben couldn't help but smile.

Then he had a sudden thought. "Does your father—Enrique—have a nickname too?"

Ricardo stiffened. "They call him Loco Henry."

"Anything else you remember about that visit?"

"Said he was gonna get me a ride. Had this Ninety-one Ram he was rebuilding, and he'd paint it any way I wanted."

"He paints cars?"

"He and some guys own one of them garages—you know what it means to pimp a ride? Like trick it out special?"

"Like the cable TV show. Customized body work."

"Word. They do that. He even showed me the truck."

"What color was it?"

"He didn't paint it yet. Just primer."

"Red primer?"

"Gray."

"He showed you a gray pick-up truck?"

"Yeah. Just for now. Said he'd paint it any way I wanted, any color, flames—whatever."

"What did you say about that?"

"I said I appreciated the thought, but I was in the Navy. Can't have a car at Pensacola and after that I'll be on a carrier, probably, for a couple years. Won't need wheels for a long time."

"How did he take that?"

"I think he was kind of pissed, yo, but he didn't let it show. Then he was doing Tequila shooters and he got mad. Asked me was it true, what my boot camp bud Jesus said."

"Which was what?"

"We used to hang out a lot, Jesus and me. Just buddies, but some of the other guys decided we were queer."

"Queer as in gay? Homosexual?"

Ricardo nodded, yes.

"Some Mexican dudes in our platoon started calling us the Maricón twins, 'Little Ricky and Hung Hay-soos.'"

"How did you handle that?"

"Jesus wanted to whip their ass. And that felt pretty good, but then I got to thinking that maybe we do that, fighting and all, they kick us out of boot camp. Not worth it, so we just played along, held hands and waggled our butts, and after a couple times, when they saw they couldn't get to us, they just stopped."

"That was pretty smart."

"Tell the truth, it was my moms' idea. I called her and told her what was going on, and she said, 'Give 'em a little show, shut 'em up.' So we did."

This is an extraordinary young man, Ben thought, and then he remembered LaShonda as he'd last seen her, mangled and bloody. Tears filled his eyes and he turned away.

CHAPTER 33

Ben said, "The police need to hear your story, Ricky."

"The police?"

"Listen. Two or three times, I'm driving over to your mom's place, and I was followed by somebody in an old gray pickup."

"A '91 Dodge Ram hemi?"

"I don't know pickups that well. Could just as well have been a Ford, a Chevy or a Toyota. But a pickup. Guy driving it had sunglasses and a big straw hat, like I've seen gardeners wear out here. Couldn't tell how old he was."

"So what?"

"It might not mean anything, but you said Enrique had a gray pickup he wanted to give you but you wouldn't take it. That he got drunk and called you a queer. Then someone bashes your mother's face in. Seems more like a crime of passion than a murder for hire. Maybe Enrique got pissed off because the first time he tried to do something nice you rejected him. Maybe he decided that you *were* gay, and to a Latino gangbanger, that's unforgiveable. So he kills LaShonda, because of course if you're gay, it has to be *her* fault, not his, because *he's* not gay."

Ricardo said, "Neither am I."

"Of course not. Maybe there's nothing to it. Maybe there's no connection. But the police need to know."

"Hold on, Rabbi Ben. The police hear my own father thinks I'm gay, they gonna tell the Navy about it?"

"I can't think why the police would need to contact the Navy except to confirm that you were in Pensacola when your mother was killed."

"But what if they did anyway?"

"What if they did?"

"Then they could kick me out of the Navy for being gay."

"You just said that you're *not* gay."

"How do you prove you're *not* something? What if my boot camp buddies tell about me and Jesus holding hands and wagging our butts in their face? What happens then?"

"The Navy would really do that?"

"No telling. They could do whatever they damn well want to do, and if they think I might or could be gay, or Jesus is, they could kick us out. That's 'Don't Ask, Don't Tell.' They might think that our little show, Jesus and me, that was 'telling.' And then I'm out of the Navy."

"You've got a point. Ricky—you talked to me because you were sad from your mother's death and I'm a rabbi. Someone who will listen to you and try to offer spiritual comfort and advice. Is that right?"

"That, and my moms said you was a righteous guy, and one very cool dude."

Ben laughed. "A cool dude. She really said that?"

"Yeah. After you whupped that big, bearded dude."

"Okay. So you're protected—our conversation is privileged. I tell the cops what I know but not how I know it. They'll never hear gay or queer or *maricón* from me."

***

Captain Henderson said, "We didn't see a gray pickup at the funeral. But there *was* a pickup there, seems like I remember an old Dodge. When we ran the plate it didn't belong to that vehicle. It was off a '99 Ford Taurus."

Ben said, "What color was the pickup?"

Henderson sat down at his desk and brought up the file. He typed "DODGE" in the search window and waited.

"It was a '91 to '93 Dodge, candy-apple red, and there was some etching work on both fenders, like they were going to paint something in later."

"Flames?"

"Could be. Officer took a picture but it's too hard to see. I keep telling them to use higher resolution, and they keep asking for bigger memory sticks or something."

"So if LaShonda said Enrique, her ex, had an old gray pickup, this could be it?"

"You got a last name on Enrique, Rabbi?"

"Salazar. Her son's last name. He goes by Loco Henry."

"A banger?"

"She said that. Lived in Pacoima, wherever that is. Shot somebody or got shot by somebody. Went to prison. Don't know when, but a while back."

"I'll have our Intel sergeant run this."

"One more thing, Captain. I'm pretty sure that twice I was followed by a man in a gray pickup on my way to LaShonda's house. Twice that I noticed,"

"We'll check it out, Rabbi. Thanks for coming in."

Henderson watched Ben leave the building. A minute later Detective Harris came into the office.

"What do you think, Harris?"

"I think he ain't telling all he knows, what I think."

"Go see Intel, and we'll maybe bring him back in."

Ben said, "That's privileged information, Detective."

Mendoza said, "You're hiding something."

"Of course I am! I'm clergy. Conversations that are part of my pastoral duties are privileged communication. You might check sections 1030 through 1034 of the California Evidence Code. It says I may refuse to disclose names and what was discussed."

"Then why did you come forward at all? Why not just keep your mouth shut?"

"Because I have both a personal and a religious obligation to seek justice for LaShonda Harris's killer. So when I say that I learned certain facts about a man whom I have never met, you should attempt to verify these facts and see if they have any relevance to solving this crime."

Mendoza took a file from his desktop and opened it. "Enrique Salazar, a.k.a. Loco Henry, age 38, manslaughter, attempted murder, extortion, assault with intent, simple possession, possession with intent to distribute, grand theft auto, robbery, burglary... Out of prison, this time, two years six months. Member of Pacoima High Times Familia. Suspect in at least six unsolved gang murders. A bad-ass!

"Allegedly offed two guys using a baseball bat—so that's a point. Okay—he *could* have killed her. But why?"

"Because he and LaShonda had a son together. Until a few months ago, Henry hadn't seen him since infancy. Then he reached out to this son, Ricardo. The son rejected him. He turned up at LaShonda's place. She told him to get lost. Maybe he was following me, too. LaShonda was bludgeoned to death—suggesting a crime of passion. Loco Henry <u>has</u> to be a suspect."

"We'll look into it. Thanks for sharing what you know. Or *some* of what you know."

"One more thing. You had an officer photographing everyone at the funeral. And the cars in the parking lot. You found a suspicious truck there. What about Loco Henry himself? Was he at the funeral?"

"We'll check the pictures again. Anything else?"

***

SUNDAY: JUNE 13

Ben stepped out of the restroom, not seeing the woman in the bulky black burkha until she turned to face him. Just before the bomb exploded, he realized it was LaShonda.

He leapt from his bed, covered with sweat, his heart racing. He looked around his dark apartment, disoriented, the dying echoes of a car engine's backfire melding into the squeal of over-stressed rubber.

As the hotrod sped into the night Ben took long gulps of cool air into his lungs, cooling his body, clearing his head. He found his glasses and looked at the digital readout on the microwave, the only clock visible in the darkened apartment.

It was a little after two in the morning.

He took a shower, then made coffee and heated a day-old onion bagel in the microwave. There was neither cream cheese, butter nor margarine in his fridge, so he ate it with a dash of salt, a small piece at a time, savoring the flavor, downing two cups of coffee, suddenly glad again to be alive while simultaneously thinking that for the next few days, until he regained his footing in the world, he must focus on things other than LaShonda's murder. Cognitive dissonance, or I have a split personality, he thought, and smiled at his own joke.

A few hours before LaShonda's murder, as he left the Hall of Records, an idea had suddenly popped into Ben's mind: The money that mysteriously appeared in and then disappeared from a little-used account in an obscure bank. And the more he wrestled with this, the more it bothered him. Anyone who *knew* of a particular account's existence, Ben reasoned, could deposit money. But unless they were an account signatory, moving it out would take some covert connection to the bank or to a signatory. The thought then struck him: Why does the person who put the money *in* the account have to be the one taking it out? What if there were two people working this scam, whatever it was?

So he'd asked LaShonda to pull the records of the cheder account. Maybe the mysterious deposits that caught Ferguson's eye were not the first time that had occurred. After all, the account got only cursory attention, always focused on the bottom line, the disposable funds converted to student scholarships.

He had keys to the building and to the office and he knew the alarm code. Unless her assistant had re-filed them, the Cheder Halakha files should still be on LaShonda's desk. He would look at every monthly statement.

Two hours later, after running five miles, taking another shower and driving to Beit Joseph, he discovered that he was wrong. There was nothing on LaShonda's desk at all, and when he unlocked the lower drawer of the filing cabinet where older records were stored, he found the Cheder Halakha section empty.

CHAPTER 35

Mendoza said, "Cap, come look at this photo."

Henderson left his office and leaned over Mendoza's squad room desk, peering at an image on a computer monitor. "One of them rabbis at the girl's funeral?"

"That was the idea. Now look at his neck. Look close."

Henderson pulled his glasses up and moved in till his head was a few inches from the screen.

"My, my. Rabbi, what lovely gang tats you have."

Mendoza said, "Gotcha, Loco Henry."

Adjusting his trousers belt and tucking his shirt in, Harris entered the squad room. "Hey, what's going on?"

Henderson said, "We got LaShonda's ex at the funeral disguised as a rabbi. Take a look."

Harris leaned in, studying the image.

Henderson said, "So he puts on one of them rabbi hats and the whole rabbi getup. Gets somebody to give him a phony beard. But he forgot his neck tats."

Harris broke out a crooked grin and shook his head. "Whoda thunk a Cholo punk like that was smart enough to pull off something like *this*?"

Mendoza said, "So now you gotta wonder *why.*"

Harris said, "Speaking of rabbis, your favorite is outside waiting to see you, Cap."

Mendoza and Henderson looked up and saw Ben through the doorway. He was carrying a tray of four Starbucks cups and a paper bag. He waved.

Henderson said, "Sign him in, Mike."

Minutes later, studying the computer image, Ben frowned. "I don't remember him at the funeral."

Henderson said, "He came late. While you were doing that Jewish thing, taking turns with the shovel."

Harris said, "That's right! I remember now, he came up out of the parking lot and joined the back of the line."

Ben said, "So does that make him a suspect?"

Henderson said, "We'll pick him up."

Mendoza said, "On the other hand, Loco Henry might have come merely out of feelings for his ex. We still have to tie him to the killing."

Ben said, "A better question is, why come dressed as a rabbi? Is he smart enough to know that because she worked for a synagogue, some rabbis would be at her funeral? Or does he think all Jews dress like that, with the hat, the coat and the beard? Why bother with a disguise at all?"

Henderson said, "Maybe someone told him that the Beit Joseph people invited a bunch of rabbis. Maybe he didn't want to have to explain who he was."

Ben said, "Maybe his son, Ricardo, invited him. I don't know if they've been in touch since the murder."

Mendoza said, "You gonna drink all that coffee yourself?"

Ben laughed and held out the cardboard tray. "These are for you."

With his chin, Harris pointed at the bag, "Doughnuts?"

Ben said, "Bagels."

Harris frowned, "Don't know too much about cop cuisine, do you?"

Ben said, "Captain Henderson, the reason I'm here today is to find out what your crime scene guys took off LaShonda's desk."

Henderson looked at Harris, who shrugged. "They boxed up everything but the computer and the phone. We went through it. Looking for something in particular, rabbi?"

"The synagogue needs to hire someone to replace LaShonda. There were a few things that are usually on her desk that we couldn't find—they might be elsewhere in the office, or her killer might have taken them. But because I have such a special relationship with Burbank Homicide—"

Harris snorted.

"—I came to see what you guys took."

Mendoza said, "We went through the crime scene take but there was nothing out of the ordinary. I guess it wouldn't hurt to let you see the inventory. Cap?

Henderson nodded. "Sure. Let him see it."

Mendoza said, "Finish your coffee, Rabbi, and I'll find it for you."

Ten minutes later Mendoza handed Ben a property form. Each handwritten item was on a separate line.

Ben scanned the list: Desk calendar, two coffee cups, pencils, pens, synagogue phone directory, dictionary, two music CDs, a computer flash drive, an empty flower vase, and the current month's statement from the Cheder Halacha Scholarship account. Below that item a notation: "blood."

Ben pointed to the list. "What does that mean, 'blood'?"

Mendoza said, "For the bank statement?"

"Right."

"There was blood on it—I think only a few drops, likely from the victim. Won't know for sure until we hear from the lab."

"Okay, thanks."

Henderson said, "Did you need a copy of that, Rabbi?"

"No, we can get a copy from the bank if we need it. And the rest of it—nothing important. I suspect those music CDs were LaShonda's private property. We don't share the synagogue directory with the public, but the only reason we might need *that* copy is if LaShonda was using it to update the master list. But she'd probably do that on the computer. We can let you know."

"Thanks for coming in, Rabbi."

"What about Loco Henry?"

"Like I said, we'll bring him in."

***

Ben climbed into the Honda and drove off, his mind churning furiously. If blood was on the statement, then probably it had lain open atop the desk when LaShonda was murdered. The other cheder statements, going back fifteen years, were missing. Did the killer take them, leaving the one that had his victim's blood on it?

The realization hit Ben like a volcanic explosion. Overcome with shame and guilt, his lungs seemed to fill with fire. His heart raced, beating faster and faster. His body temperature soared; perspiration flowed from every pore. In moments his clothes were soaked in sweat that stung his eyes until he could barely see.

Ben pulled to the side of the road to think and calm himself. As his heart slowed he realized that he had been foolish—no, reckless. He had asked LaShonda to put the bank records on her desk for him to pick up after closing time. If the person depositing and withdrawing money was a synagogue member, he might know about his own brief romance with LaShonda. If he saw the statements on LaShonda's desk, he could easily assume that she was helping Ben unravel the mystery. That was why he killed her.

So the key to the puzzle was in those old statements.

Ben loathed himself. He was a rabbi, ordained to show his people the ways of righteous behavior, help them to heal the world, and lead them in service to God. He had come to California to help a synagogue, a holy congregation, but had allowed his judgment to be clouded by sexual desire—lust. Putting his needs before his duty to serve God, was surrendering to the evil impulses that forever beguile mankind. This he could and would repent in both word and deed; with proper penitence he could square his account with the Master of the Universe. But his actions had cost LaShonda her life, and that was beyond repentance. She was gone. Her death left a void in the world that could never be healed. It almost too much for Ben to bear.

When he was calm again, Ben pulled back into traffic. Distracted and distraught, he failed to notice the gray pickup following him.

CHAPTER 36

Ben headed for home, a shower and dry clothes at the top of his priorities. After that, he thought, he'd go back to Beit Joseph. To save the minutes required to get in and out of underground parking, he stopped at the curb near the complex's pedestrian entrance.

He pushed open the door; as his feet hit the pavement a blur of movement, the rising snarl of accelerating engine and a rush of warm air sent him falling backward and sideways just as something big and fast flew by to take off the door. Ben landed awkwardly, his side striking the parking brake; a few seconds passed before he pulled himself erect. By then whatever had hit his car was gone.

A Latino man in an immaculate, cream-colored linen suit, gripping the leash of a large, mixed-breed dog, appeared on the sidewalk. Ben recognized him as a neighbor, although they had never spoken.

"Are you hurt?"

Gingerly touching the sore spot on his waist, Ben shook his head.

"No, no. Just a bruise, I'm sure."

Across the street an elderly Asian woman in a pantsuit parked her car and got out. She hurried across toward Ben.

"I'm okay," he said, anticipating her question.

"I saw the whole thing. He tried to kill you."

"What did you see?"

"A man driving a pickup truck. He slowed down when he saw you and when you opened your door he sped up and hit your car!"

It was a fiercely hot day, but Ben felt cold and lightheaded. Shock, he thought. Carefully, he sat behind the wheel, feet on the asphalt.

The Latino man produced a cell phone. "You're very pale. I'm calling the paramedics."

"I'm okay. Give me a few minutes."

The Asian woman looked confused. "He didn't hit you?"

"No. Please, write down the license number of that..."

"Truck. It was covered with paint. Gray paint. There was some on the windows, too."

Ben tried to think, but was unable to focus.

"Call the police," he said, just before passing out.

***

He heard distant voices. Emerging into fuzzy consciousness Ben listened intently but couldn't understand what they were saying. He opened first one eye and then the other. The world was a hazy white. Then, slowly, the glare dimmed and things swam into focus: a ceiling, a light.

"I'm Doctor Yuan," said a woman's voice. Ben tried to turn his head but couldn't.

A pleasant, middle-aged Asian woman with a stethoscope arranged around her neck came into his field of view. Behind her a second figure, indistinct but somehow familiar.

Yuan said, "You shouldn't try to move your head."

"Is my neck broken?"

"It's just a precaution. You hit your head."

"Where am I?"

"Saint Joseph's."

"You mean *Beit* Joseph."

"No, Saint Joseph Providence Medical Center."

"Okay. A hospital."

"Can you tell me your name?"

"Yes."

Somewhere close by a woman tittered.

"Please tell me your name."

"Ben Maimon. Rabbi Ben Maimon."

"Thank you. Can you tell me what day it is?"

"No."

"Do you have any idea what day it is?"

"I passed out on a Monday. I don't know how long I was unconscious. Ergo, I can't tell what day it is now."

A familiar woman's voice said, "He's okay!"

Ben said, "The truck didn't hit me. Why am I here?"

Dr. Yuan said, "You hit your head when you fell. And you must have fallen across something hard because your kidney is bruised. And you were dehydrated."

"My kidney?"

"You'll probably pass some blood for a day or two. We're going to take you downstairs for an MRI now, just to make sure your neck is okay."

"All right."

"Your wife is here. Would you like a few minutes?"

"My wife?"

Tova leaned in. "Hello, sweetie."

"Doctor, how long was I unconscious?"

CHAPTER 37

The orderly pushed Ben's gurney against the corridor wall and stopped. "Right back," he said, and went through a swinging door marked "Imaging."

Tova leaned in to whisper in Ben's ear.

"Don't be mad. I had to tell them I was a relative or they wouldn't let me see you."

"When I get out of here we'll need a *get*," he said, referring to the document produced in a rabbinical divorce.

Tova giggled. "I didn't know you were so funny."

"Everybody's funny on painkillers."

The orderly returned with a technician, a robust man of perhaps forty. The hospital ID badge pinned to his lab coat read "M.B. Rosen. "Shalom, Rabbi,"

"Shalom."

Rosen turned to Tova. "This will take about thirty minutes, Mrs. Maimon. Waiting room's around the corner."

Tova bent over and kissed Ben's forehead.

"See you in a little bit, dear."

Ben bit his lip to keep from laughing.

***

Trailed by Tova, Dr. Yuan entered Ben's room. "The MRI was negative," she said. "Your neck is normal."

"Mazel Tov."

Dr. Yuan smiled. "I know what that means. We'll keep you overnight for observation. Your kidney will ache for a few days, but you'll be fine. Just drink plenty of cranberry juice until you stop passing blood."

"How will I know if what I'm passing is blood or cranberry juice?"

Dr. Yuan giggled. "Some police officers want to speak with you. Are you okay with that?"

"Only if you take this neck brace off first."

"I'll get a nurse."

As Yuan left, Tova leaned in. "I'd better go hide or the cops will blow my cover," she murmured.

Ben giggled in spite of himself.

"Thanks for coming. I mean it."

Tova squeezed Ben's hand for a long moment before leaving.

***

A nurse raised the end of Ben's bed, moving him into a sitting position as Mendoza and Harris entered.

Mendoza said, "How big was he this time?"

Harris said, "So your Kung Fu routine didn't work this time?"

Ben said, "Thousands of stand-up comics out of work and they send you two?"

Mendoza said, "You get a look at the guy who hit you?"

Ben shook his head. "Just a flash, out of the corner of my eye. There was a witness—"

"Mrs. Tanaka. Yeah, she saw a gray pickup. Like the one you said was following you a couple of weeks ago."

Harris said, "We found your car door, down the block. Traces of gray paint, and traces of blue paint."

"The blue paint is on top of the gray?"

Mendoza nodded. "Yeah. Gray primer covering blue. That narrows it down to a half-million or so."

Ben said, "Anybody else see it?"

Mendoza said, "Your neighbor, Mr. Cupertino, out walking his dog. His back was turned, he heard it, but he didn't see anything but a tailgate scooting around the corner."

"So, no clues."

"Just the paint on your car," said Mendoza. "But there's a silver lining to this."

Ben said, "I don't like the sound of that."

Harris said, "The silver lining is, this time you got a real good alibi."

"Why do I need an alibi?"

"Because about the same time you were dodging traffic, someone nined Loco Henry."

"Enrique? He's dead?"

"Four to the head and chest."

"I'm sorry to hear that."

"If he killed LaShonda, you're still sorry?"

"Of course. Even if he killed others. The Talmud teaches that 'whoever destroys a single soul is as guilty as if he had destroyed a complete world; whoever preserves a single soul, it is as if he had preserved a whole world.'

"Anyway, we don't know that he killed LaShonda."

Harris said, "I see where you're coming from, but *this* world is a better place without guys like Loco Henry."

"What about his children? His wife? What will become of them now?"

Mendoza shook his head. "Not our problem."

"I guess not. Where was he killed? Witnesses?"

Harris smiled. "Henry was porking down a roach coach burrito inside his chop shop."

"Chop shop? I thought he did custom body work?"

"He calls the place 'La Vida,' but the custom car gig was mostly for fun. His bread and butter was cutting up high-end stolen cars and peddling the parts."

"If it was lunchtime somebody must have seen something?"

Mendoza said, "It was early evening. But it's not our case. Pacoima is LAPD and they're welcome to it—when the law comes around everybody in the *barrio* is deaf, dumb and blind."

Harris said, "Captain Henderson thinks the kid did it. Ricardo."

Ben's head swam. He felt empty, drained.

"Ricardo? Why?"

Harris said, "One, he told his grandmother that he thought Loco Henry had killed his mother.

"And two, he's AWOL from—"

"—sorry, but I have to close my eyes for a minute..."

CHAPTER 38

Ben awoke with a start. The detectives were gone. Tova sat near the bed, pen in hand, making notations on a typescript. Looking up, she frowned. And when she realized that Ben was watching her, she began to weep.

Ben said, "What's wrong?"

"I have something terrible to tell you."

"Please, not another murder."

"Worse."

"Just tell me."

"About an hour ago, Dr. Yuan asked if I'd had a blood test recently. I said, 'Why?' and she says that they tested your blood. She wouldn't say what they found, but she said it was a good idea to get my own blood tested.

"Ben, do you have AIDS?"

Ben tried not to smile. "Did you get tested yet?"

"Why should I?"

He chose his words carefully, leaving out one vital fact but otherwise speaking truth: "I *don't* have AIDS and you don't need a blood test. When I lived in Israel there was a café bombing. I got hit by flying glass and bled a lot. I tried to help a couple of guys—actually, I'm sure they both survived. One was choking on his tongue. The other, a doctor had me put my fingers into his wound and squeeze a torn artery until he could get him breathing again. I'm sure some of his blood got on me. Not to mention blood from others in the café. Since then, every time my blood is tested, it comes back as a false positive for Hep-C."

"Hepatitis?"

"Yes. A virus that infects the liver."

"You didn't worry about infecting LaShonda?"

"*False* positive. I *don't* have Hep-C. Or AIDS. Anyway, you can't spread it through kissing. And we never had sex."

"You spent the night at her house! She was crazy about you! You *must* have been *shtupping* her."

"Never. Twice I stayed late, talking, hugging, kissing. But that's all."

Tova stared at Ben. "You won't have sex with me, and you won't have sex with LaShonda. Are you gay? Or do you have a wife stashed somewhere? Which is it?"

A wife stashed somewhere! Ben flashed on Rachel; in his mind's eye her olive skin faded to a death pallor, her wedding dress became a shroud. He fought the urge to weep.

"Tova. I'm not gay. I have no wife. I'm abstaining from sex and its complications, until when and if I meet someone I want to be with for the rest of my life, a woman who feels equally committed to me. Because of the nature of my work, that might be a long time.

"There it is. I'm sort of tired of talking about it."

Tova looked at Ben for a long moment. "If it's that important to you—"

"It is."

"Then I will say no more about this."

"Thank you, Tova, And I really appreciate you being here for me."

***

TUESDAY: JUNE 15

Tova drove Ben to his apartment. He opened the door to find a notice on the floor: The police had impounded his Honda as evidence and would hold it seven to ten days. Insult added to injury, he thought.

Ben needed to think; usually that meant going for a run, but it was well over ninety degrees outside and he felt woozy. He told himself that in the morning, if he felt better, he'd do a mile or two at sunrise.

Ben made coffee, dug through his landlord's CD collection and put on "Ode To Joy."

Then, sipping black coffee, he sat down with a notebook and a pen to make a list of everything still on his Beit Joseph plate:

<u>LaShonda's killer</u>—Connected to <u>lost records</u> for mysterious bank deposits ??

Loco Henry's murder—not strictly my business**, but connected ?? to LaShonda's murder, Ricardo's disappearance?**

Funny business at cemetery—check <u>soil samples</u>.

Ben put the pen down. It had been days since he checked his email. He turned on the computer, logged on to Gmail and went down the list of waiting messages.

The most recent was from his landlord. Thailand was experiencing unrest in its cities and there was bad weather. The production was behind schedule—did Ben want to stay another month?

Ben wrote back that he did, then logged onto his bank account and transferred the funds to the exec's bank.

Another recent message was from the Bakersfield lab where he'd sent the second batch of cemetery soil samples.

He opened the attachment, a lab report. Each sample had been analyzed; proportions varied from one to another but all contained the same witches brew of sodium borohydride, red phosphorus, lithium, methylamine hydrochloride, THC and benzoylmethylecgonine, plus a new compound identified as didehydro-4,5-epoxy-17-methylmorphinan-3,6-diol diacetate.

On a hunch he Googled "opiates" and learned that the last compound was heroin. So he had that, and compounds that he knew to be associated with methamphetamine, cocaine, and marijuana—a pharmacopeia of illegal drugs.

Ben sat back to think. He had initially supposed that whatever was buried in Beit Joseph's plots might be leaking these compounds. Now he had to think that either the cemetery had been built on a contaminated site, or that when the land was graded, fill dirt dumped atop the rocky surface came from a contaminated area. Or something else, something more recent.

He turned it over in his mind. Fifty-odd years ago, when Shabbat Tamid was built, marijuana and heroin weren't hard to find in Los Angeles, but meth and cocaine were far less common. He wasn't sure if meth had even been invented that long ago. It was, he decided, unlikely that the chemicals had been there for many years.

Then it occurred to Ben that perhaps the cemetery's new owners were using the mortuary as a drug manufacturing lab. If so, then it was not hard to believe that some of these chemicals were found in nearby soil.

Ben thought about bringing what he had to the police. If he did that, he realized, he'd have to explain how and why he got the samples and that would lead to breaking his vow of privacy for Beit Joseph.

In a few days, Ben thought, when I'm feeling stronger, I'll go back to the cemetery, then decide how and when to get authorities involved.

CHAPTER 39

WEDNESDAY: JUNE 16

Ben's kidney was still a little sore, but after jogging a careful mile in the pre-dawn heat, showering and downing a leisurely breakfast of eggs and toast, he put on a summer suit and took a taxi to Community Rental Cars, the Glendale agency where he'd rented the Buick.

As the cab deposited him on the curb, Takarian, the owner, came out of the tiny office.

"Shalom, Rabbi!" he called as Ben approached.

"*Barev dzez,*" Ben replied. "Hello."

"You speak Armenian!"

"A few words."

"It is good to see you. You found your wallet?"

Ben frowned. "Why do you ask?"

"Last week, your friend, the other rabbi, said you lost your wallet, He looked for it in the car you rented. The Buick."

"And he didn't find it."

"I am very sorry."

"Mr. Takarian, this is important. Please tell me everything you remember about this man."

"He wasn't a rabbi?"

"I don't know. What did this man look like?"

"He was about forty or forty-five, I think."

"Tall, short, fair, dark?"

"White skin and dark hair. Getting bald. Mostly in front, his forehead is already high." Takarian patted his own narrow waist. "And a big belly."

"Was he tall?"

"The same as me, about."

"Anything else?"

Takarian looked worried. "Is there trouble?"

"I think someone's playing a joke on me. What else do you remember about this man?"

"Well, after he looked for the wallet, he asked for a copy of the rental receipt. He said you needed it for the taxes."

"And you gave it to him?"

"Of course."

"You've been very helpful."

Takarian scowled, and then turned to business.

"A car today?"

"Yes, for about a week."

"The Buick LaCrosse is not available until five."

Twenty minutes later Ben drove off in a three-year-old blue Camry, his mind churning with questions.

Who was the man Takarian described?

What did he really want?

Ben couldn't think of a Beit Joseph member who fit the description, but he hadn't met all of them. Who would want to know where he lived?

The answer came in a rush: The guy who'd tried to run him down three days earlier. But who would know about this particular rental agency and a car that he'd driven only a few times?

Ben pulled to the curb, got out and inspected the Camry's license plates. Both front and rear bore the rental agency name. Anyone who had seen him driving the Buick might have noted the plates. Like Shabbat Tamid's funeral director, Lawrence Mint, who matched Takarian's description. For that matter, it could also match the other man, Cone, the one who saw him inspecting the lock on the pedestrian gate.

Why would Cone or Mint want his home address?

Did they suspect that he'd entered the cemetery that night? Was his nocturnal walkabout captured by a security camera? Ben didn't see one, but he couldn't be sure. An infrared camera?

Mint knew that he worked at Beit Joseph. And Ben had used the Buick on both his forays to the cemetery.

Suddenly it made sense. Mint and Cone suspected that he saw them doing something they wanted to keep secret. It was after *that* night when he was followed by the gray pickup. While driving the Buick, not the Honda.

They didn't know, then, that he had the Honda.

If Mint got his home address but couldn't penetrate building security, he might have staked out its underground parking exit waiting for him leave. When he drove off in the Honda, they either followed him, or waited for his return and attacked when he parked. Whatever was going on in the mortuary was probably illegal. The soil sample report suggested drugs.

Or maybe not. Maybe it was something entirely different. Either way, Ben now assumed that he might be followed at any time. He would return to the cemetery; this time, he'd look for the gray pickup. Or a blue pickup covered with gray paint. And if he could, he'd take a stab at unmasking whatever was going down in the mortuary.

This entry would again be clandestine and require darkness. But first he must find another place to live.

CHAPTER 40

THURSDAY: JUNE 17

Rabbi Kimmelman seemed dumbstruck. Seconds ticked by as he struggled to find his voice.

"Someone...tried to *kill*...you?"

Ben said, "I think so."

"Who would do such a thing? And why?"

Ben wasn't ready to share all of his activities with anyone. Even Tova, in the absence of Ben offering information to the contrary, believed he was the victim of a simple hit-and-run traffic accident. So for Kimmelman he now sketched out the facts of his two trips to Shabbat Tamid, leaving out such details as picking locks and drug-laced soil samples but including the mysterious buried objects he'd probed and the odd late-night activities at the mortuary.

Kimmelman listened in silence, periodically fingering his beard. When Ben finished he shook his head.

"You should have told me all this *before* someone tried to kill you."

"Suppose I had. Then what?"

"Let the police handle it."

"But I have no real evidence. I don't know what's buried in those plots, and if I was to tell the police that I suspect something is going on, but I don't know what it is, and the Shabbat Tamid people know that I suspect and are trying to kill me, what do you think will happen?"

Kimmelman stared at Ben for a long moment.

"You're right. They won't dig up a grave, even a supposedly empty grave. They'll write you off as a crazy."

Ben said. "Anyway, the synagogue no longer has any link to the cemetery. My activities there are not Beit Joseph's responsibility."

"Perhaps not in a legal sense. Nevertheless I feel personally responsible—I found you, invited you to come here, got you involved in all this. Now tell me, what can I do to help?"

"A couple of things. First, the guys who tried to kill me know where I'm staying—my apartment isn't safe. I have a motel room for tonight, but I need a less public place. Temporarily, until I can sort this out.

"Second, I must ask you to keep this absolutely secret. Involving the police or anyone else would only complicate matters. Tova knows I was injured in a hit-and-run, but that's all. I'd like to keep it that way."

Kimmelman's eyes narrowed and his mouth tightened.

"You think someone at Beit Joseph might be involved."

"Can't rule it out. And there is the matter of LaShonda's murder."

"I thought the police had solved that—her former husband, that Mexican Mafia thug."

"I don't think they were ever married. He was the father of her child, but that was almost twenty years ago. The police think he *could* have killed her, but there's no evidence, no proof, as far as I know."

"You're saying it might have been someone here?"

"It's possible. The hit-and-run could be connected to the murder instead of to the cemetery."

Kimmelman looked thoughtful.

"I'll make some calls. Someone will have a guest room and keep a kosher kitchen."

"Thanks, Hank."

"There's something else, isn't there?"

"Yes. I want to visit LaShonda's mother. At the funeral the aunt kept me at arm's length. They didn't come to the gathering at your home afterward. It occurs to me that LaShonda might have listed her as an emergency contact. Do you have her address or phone number?"

"I think so—but why do want to see her mother?"

"Because Ricardo, LaShonda's son, is AWOL and the police think that he might have killed his father."

"One tragedy after another. Is there no end to this?"

***

Elayne Harris's home was a green stucco cottage on a street of decaying tract homes. It stood out from the others: fresh paint on the trim, flowers blooming in a tiny garden, and new, shutter-equipped vinyl windows sparkling in front of simple yet tasteful blinds.

Ikea, Ben thought. This was LaShonda's work.

Ben had decided against calling ahead. If Ricardo was hiding there, or if Mrs. Harris was avoiding him, he didn't want to spook them.

Clad in a lightweight suit, Ben got out of the Camry, planted his Fedora squarely on his head, and looked up and down the sun-baked street. It was all but deserted except for two black teenagers lounging against a light pole near the end of the block.

Why aren't those boys in school? Ben wondered before realizing that they were likely lookouts for a drug dealer.

Ben waved to them. They stared as he moved up the walkway to the porch. They were still staring when he rang the bell. There was no answer for several minutes.

He rang again.

A tinny female voice issued from a hidden speaker.

"Who is there?""

"Rabbi Ben Maimon, from Beit Joseph"

"Just a moment."

A door latch clicked.

"Come in, close the door, and walk straight ahead."

It was very warm inside, and much darker than he'd expected; he paused for a long moment, looking around until his eyes began to adjust, and then moved ahead until he came to a hallway.

"Over here!"

Ben turned to his left and through a half-open bedroom door saw a back-lit figure in a wheelchair.

Ben said, "Mrs. Harris?"

"Come in, please."

The wheelchair backed away from the doorway to admit Ben. He found himself in a cool, airy, well-lighted and nicely appointed room. A flat-screen television, sound muted, stood in a corner.

"Please shut that door—the air conditioning is on."

Ben did as he was asked, and then turned back to his host.

"You're that Rabbi that LaShonda worked for?"

"Call me Rabbi Ben."

"We're Southern Baptist, you know. But LaShonda always spoke highly of the Hebrews. You know, your synagogues have something in common with our churches."

"I think we have many things in common. We both believe in the Hebrew Bible, do we not?"

"Of course. But I was speaking of the churches, not their members. Each Baptist church decides on its own interpretation of scripture and its own liturgy. It doesn't answer to a bishop or to the Pope. LaShonda told me that it's the same way with your people."

"It is. And thank you for enlightening me about Southern Baptists."

Ben looked around the room. Several identical remotes were strategically placed, each secured by a heavy cord. Ben supposed that they operated the door, the air conditioner, and maybe the television.

"You seem quite comfortable here, Mrs. Harris."

"My daughter was very good to me. A few years ago she hired some workmen. They spent weeks making it easier for me to be alone all day. My sister works, you see, and she has her own children to look after. Now that LaShonda's gone..."

"I'm sure you miss her. And that's why I'm here."

"So much for small talk! What do want?"

"Mrs. Harris, the police told me that Ricardo has gone AWOL, and they suspect that he killed his father."

The old woman slumped back in her chair, sighing.

"They were here two days ago. I don't believe them. Ricardo received an excellent upbringing and is a very bright and honorable young man. He isn't capable of killing anyone, even that hoodlum Enrique. Or Loco Henry, whatever they call him now."

"Then why did he go AWOL?"

"I don't believe that either. He loved the Navy. From the time he was ten, that's all he ever talked about."

"Then what do you think could have happened to him?"

Pain creased her time-worn face.

"He had his airline ticket, and he was going to drive his mother's car to the airport and leave it in long-term parking for my daughter and her boy to pick up."

"What airport was that?"

"I think it was Bob Hope. The small one, in Burbank."

Ben thought for a long moment.

"If Ricardo left a car at the airport, then how could your sister, or her son, retrieve it? Wouldn't they need to show the parking ticket? And how would they even find it?"

"That's the thing, Reverend. He was supposed to leave the ticket in the car, then call his aunt and tell her where he left the car, what level and what row. That sort of thing. He never did. None of that."

"So you don't know where LaShonda's car is now?"

"I really don't, Reverend Ben. I hope Ricardo is still driving it. Do you think you could help find him?

Ben took the elderly woman's hand. He looked at her face and saw traces of LaShonda.

"I will try my best, Mrs. Harris."

Chapter 41

Captain Henderson did not seem pleased to see Ben.

"I told you Rabbi, if we get any new developments in the Harris murder, we'll call you."

Ben said, "Surely you must have the medical examiner's report by now?"

"That's not public."

"Can you tell me, if you know, what it was that killed LaShonda? The murder weapon?"

"That I *could* do. But the fact is, we don't know. The coroner said it could be anything from a rock or a brick to a tree branch—something heavy, with an uneven surface."

"If it was a rock, a brick or a branch, wouldn't he have found traces of it embedded in the wound?"

"Probably."

Ben tilted his head slightly and raised his eyebrows.

Sighing, Henderson took a file from his desk, then opened it and leafed through several pages before stopping to read silently for several seconds.

"The only foreign substance in the wound were mascara, eyeliner, foundation with glitter and traces of keratins, possibly from an organic fertilizer."

"So the murder weapon could have been something that was in the ground or laying on the ground?"

"Yeah. Like a tree branch, a rock, or a brick."

"What about the glitter?"

"That's the stuff in liquid make-up that looks like specks of silver or gold."

"Thank you, Captain. Now, anything new on Loco Henry, or Ricardo?"

"Henry is LAPD's case. They haven't told us squat. And if the kid is AWOL, that's the Army's problem."

"You mean, the Navy."

"Army, Navy, Air Force—if it's not a crime in the city of Burbank, it's not in our jurisdiction. Saves all kinds of aggravation when we remember that."

"You're right, of course. But there is one thing that does fall under your jurisdiction. LaShonda's mother told me that her daughter's car is missing from the airport."

"A stolen car?"

"She said Ricardo drove it to the airport and caught his flight to Florida. He left the car at Bob Hope for his aunt and cousin to pick up. But they can't find it."

"He never got to Florida, so maybe he didn't get to the airport."

"Maybe. But there might be something in her car that could be evidence in her murder."

"'Might be. Could be.' Pretty thin, Rabbi."

"Can you have someone check the airport lot to see if her car is there?"

Henderson sighed. "No, I don't think so. This is a very small department. But if you want to look for it, be my guest."

***

On a hunch, Ben decided to go to LaShonda's apartment first. His last time there was the day following her funeral, when he met Ricardo to go running. Now he wondered if Ricardo was simply hiding there. Or if he'd left some clue to his destination. Maybe LaShonda's car was still there. If so he might find something in it that would help find Ricardo.

Ben turned into the alley behind the building and found a white subcompact in LaShonda's parking spot.

Ben parked in a guest slot, then came back to inspect the white car. He circled it, noting the Avis logo on both license plate frames.

"Hello!"

Ben looked up to see a slim, beautiful young woman in shorts and a skimpy halter that accentuated her large, firm breasts. A sun visor topped her long blond hair.

Ben said, "Hello."

"Did I park in your spot?"

"This belonged to LaShonda Harris—"

"Was that the lady who got murdered?"

"Yes."

"Are you with the police?"

"Do you have something to tell me?"

"I don't live here, I'm visiting my brother."

Ben arranged his face to look quizzical.

"So, her apartment. It's like her TV or radio is on all the time and it's all like Spanish or something. Was she a Mex— I mean, a Latino?"

"Anything else?"

"The lights are on in the bedroom."

"How long has this been going on?"

"My brother says it's been days and days."

"When did he report it?"

"Oh, he didn't know that lady. He doesn't want to get involved with the police or anything."

"What's your name?"

"I don't live here."

"Where's home?"

"Provincetown. That's on Cape Cod."

"And when you're in Provincetown, on Cape Cod, what do people call you?"

The woman blushed. "You must think I'm so dumb!"

"No, I think you're reluctant to give me your name. But it doesn't matter."

Ben walked around to the front of her car, took out a tiny notebook and wrote down the license plate number.

"I'm sure Avis has all your information."

"I *am* stupid. My name is Roberta Towne."

"Thank you. And your brother's name is..."

"James John. He goes by J.J. J.J. Towne."

"And he smokes pot?"

"Oh God—am I in trouble? Is J.J. in trouble?"

"Not with me. But if you live with someone smoking pot or tobacco, it gets on your clothes and in your hair."

"This is so embarrassing."

"Do you know anyone who has a key to that apartment?"

"I could ask J.J.?"

"Thanks."

"You're sure he's not in trouble?"

"When the uniformed officers come it would be better if they didn't find any reason to arrest him."

While Roberta went to find her brother and a key, Ben went to LaShonda's door. He put an ear against the heavy wood and listened to the murmur of a radio or television set, unable to make out what language it was.

He twisted the doorknob and to his surprise the door swung inward. Now he heard an announcer's rapid-fire Spanish for an attorney offering immigration services.

Ben peered into the dim interior then took a few tentative steps inside, being careful to touch nothing.

Even in the semi-darkness, Ben could see the place had been thoroughly trashed: Every drawer in the living room and the tiny kitchen had been dumped. Even the refrigerator and freezer had been emptied.

Ben made his way to the bedroom and looked through the open door. It, too, was a mess of overturned drawers.

Someone had been here looking for something.

Ben looked at the rear entrance, a sliding glass door. It was secure. Likewise all the windows. Only the front door was unlocked, and Ben's close inspection of the lock found no indication that it had been tampered with. LaShonda's keys lay undisturbed on the kitchen counter.

Ben went to find Roberta, but her car was gone.

He thought about her. He was never close enough to smell her clothes or hair, but when he'd offered the idea, she'd promptly admitted smoking pot to someone who might be a cop. He had just seen LaShonda's bedroom window and it was covered by floor-to-ceiling drapes: From the outside there was no way to see a light burning inside.

Nor, Ben decided, could anyone outside the apartment have heard that the TV clearly enough to identify the language as Spanish. Roberta Towne, or whatever her real name was, had to have been <u>in</u> the apartment.

When the building manager told Ben that no one named J.J. Towne had ever lived in LaShonda's building, he was not surprised.

Ben's mind raced as he drove away. Who trashed LaShonda's apartment? What were they looking for?

If the person who searched the apartment, Ben thought, had killed LaShonda, then he—it had to be a man or an incredibly strong woman—was looking for something that either linked him to the murder or had something to do with why she was killed.

So many conflicting ideas chased each other through Ben's consciousness that he couldn't concentrate on driving. He pulled to the side of the road and parked.

There was no sign that the apartment had been broken into, so the intruder either had a key or someone had let him in. The building manager said he had seen or heard nothing out of the ordinary and had given no one a key. Ben didn't know if police had ever visited the apartment, but he found it hard to believe that they would have torn it apart.

Could Ricardo have done this to his mother's home?

Not likely, thought Ben. He had no reason to be in a hurry, and he had too much respect for LaShonda's neat-and-clean ways to trash the place.

But maybe Ricardo had been *in* the apartment. Maybe he had opened the door for the person who ransacked the place.

Who would Ricardo open the door for? Someone he knew, or someone who might have offered a convincing reason.

Perhaps a sexy blond masquerading as a neighbor. Perhaps she, or a confederate waiting outside, had overpowered the young man and kidnapped him?

But Ricardo had been missing for four days. If he let the blond into the apartment and she trashed it, why come back? To retrieve something inadvertently left behind?

Ben told himself to stop thinking about might-have-happened situations and concentrate, for the moment, on finding LaShonda's car.

Ben's iPhone browser showed him that parking at Bob Hope International was spread among several enormous, open-air lots and a four-story parking structure across from the main terminal. He thought about Ricardo and what he might do if he'd been driving his mother's car and intending to leave it for his family to pick up later.

He would have tried to leave it someplace easy to find, which probably ruled out the huge, sprawling open-air lots.

Ben drove past the terminal, noting the enormous AVIS sign on it, and into the parking structure. Before taking a ticket from the machine he craned his head until he saw one of the security cameras.

The most likely place to leave the car, Ben reasoned, was on the roof. Usually the last choice of time-pressed travelers or people concerned about sun damage to their cars, it would have the fewest cars and the most light. Ricardo would have been more likely to find a convenient parking place there.

Ben topped the ramp in his Camry and turned into the nearest row. There, straight ahead of him, against a low wall, was LaShonda's SUV, or its twin.

He parked and got out. The midday Valley sun reflected off white concrete made the roof an oven. Squinting, Ben approached the SUV. The rear hatch was locked but its lower right corner seemed slightly ajar. On tiptoe, Ben peered through a dirt-glazed window and saw white trouser legs caked with dried blood running diagonally across the cargo compartment.

Recoiling from the scene, Ben sought shade and found it in the stairwell. His head swam from the heat and the enormity of what he'd discovered.

He broke out his phone and called Henderson. Waiting for the police, Ben used his GPS app to find east, then stood, bathed in fierce sunlight, to say Kaddish for Ricardo.

Harris said, "Coffee, Rabbi?"

Ben shook his head. "No, thanks. But I'd love some water."

"Water it is," he said and went to get it.

Mendoza said, "How are you feeling?"

Ben forced himself to think. "As though God has turned his face away from me. Ricardo was only nineteen. He had his whole life ahead of him. And LaShonda..."

"God didn't kill those people."

Ben laughed, a bitter chortle. "Now *you* sound like a rabbi. But this isn't the best time to discuss theology. Let's talk about finding the beast who took that boy's life."

"That's what we're all about, Rabbi. And in spite of what you may think, we're really not so damn bad at it."

"I'd be thrilled to be proven wrong. In any case, please accept my apologies. You had your reasons for doing a number on me that night, and I wasn't too happy about it. But even if it was unnecessary, I understand that it wasn't personal."

"Apology accepted. We *were* doing a number on you. That's how we close cases. Now tell us how you knew where to find the car?"

Harris returned with a bottle of water, and Ben gulped down half before sharing his reasoning about where Ricardo might have left his mother's SUV.

Mendoza said, "You weren't even looking for the kid?"

"His grandmother asked me to find the car. I didn't have any reason to suspect that he'd be in it."

Harris said, "The body is at the coroner's and like always, County is backed up. Could be a couple days before we get the report."

Mendoza said, "That car got real hot, and it cooked the boy's body pretty good. The M-E is going to have a hard time establishing time of death. But we're pretty sure he died from the gunshot wound to his chest."

Harris said, "The doer left the gun next to his body, so maybe it's a throwaway and we won't trace it, or else it was meant to look like he'd shot himself."

"Shot himself and then slammed the hatch on his own foot?"

Harris shrugged, as if to say, "Killers can be stupid."

Ben said, "What kind of a gun?"

Mendoza said, "A Glock nine, like the one that killed his father."

Ben said, "You know what kind of gun killed Loco Henry?"

Harris said, "LAPD gave us that yesterday. A G26—same model that we found with the vic."

Ben said, "But not necessarily the same gun?"

Harris shook his head. "Too early for ballistics."

Ben said, "You think somebody wants us to think that Ricardo shot his father, then killed himself?"

Mendoza said, "I do. But it was amateurish. Wiped the car down and got rid of all fingerprints. Who cleans up his car and then shoots himself?"

Ben said, "Could Loco Henry's people have killed him?"

Harris shook his head. "They have their own rules. They off someone, either he disappears and you never find a body, or they want everyone to know they did it. And they wouldn't leave an expensive and perfectly good gun behind."

Ben said, "Where does that leave us?"

Harris said, "The girl you met is our only solid lead."

Mendoza said, "Describe her."

Anything to get his mind off what he'd seen in LaShonda's SUV, Ben thought.

"Early twenties, five-four or five, about a hundred fifteen pounds, long blond hair, slender build, good legs, big chest, clear skin, light tan, perfect teeth."

Harris said, "Eyes?"

"Blue, but maybe not really."

Mendoza said, "What does that mean?"

"They were *very* blue. Deep blue. Might have been tinted contacts."

Harris said, "So what about her hair? Natural blond?"

"Probably colored in an expensive salon."

"Because?"

"Streaks, highlights, three or four slightly different shades all blended together."

Mendoza said, "But it *could* have been natural?"

"Sure."

Harris said, "You said, 'big chest.' You mean big tits?"

"Yes."

"Real?"

"I'd have to squeeze them for a few hours to know for sure, but I think so."

Mendoza and Harris laughed.

Harris said, "Good thing you're keeping it celibate."

Ben smiled. "True."

Mendoza said, "What else can you tell us about her?"

"Poised, smart and educated. A natural actress, but maybe she's had training, too."

"Where you getting all that, Rabbi?"

"She thought I was a police officer, and I never denied it. When I suggested that her clothes and hair reeked of pot, she copped to it immediately. She knew the difference between a narc and a homicide officer and wasn't afraid to admit to a minor crime if it might disarm me.

"I asked her name and she vamped, stalling, thinking up a good answer. When I pressed, she called herself Roberta Towne. And she said her brother's name was J.J."

Mendoza said, "Why does that seem familiar?"

"Ever watched 'Chinatown'?"

"Only about a dozen times."

Harris said, "That's Roman Polanski, right?"

Ben said, "Polanksi directed it. But the script was written by *Robert* Towne. And Jack Nicholson's character was J.J. Gittes.

"Also, she said she was from Provincetown, but she had no trace of a Cape Cod accent. I've been out on the Cape a dozen times and you can pretty much tell the locals by their inflection. She had no accent—none at all. And now that I think of it, I'm pretty sure that another Robert Towne movie was set in Provincetown."

Harris said, "Which one?"

"I don't remember right off. We can look it up."

Mendoza said, "So you think she's a movie buff."

"More like maybe a film student. Or an actress. 'Chinatown' is a story where no one is who you think they are, and nothing is what it seems."

Harris said, "That's deep."

Ben said, "She was playing me for her own amusement. I'll bet she laughed her ass off when she drove away."

Mendoza said, "You want to look at the mug shot book?"

Ben said, "If you insist, but I think it's a waste of time. I'd rather look at headshots from talent agents."

Mendoza said, "I would too. So we call up a bunch of agents and say we're looking for a suspect in a murder case and we'd like photos of all your cute, young, blond clients?"

Harris said, "You could put a notice in *Backstage.*"

Ben said, "Or you could let me use one of your computers."

In an hour Ben created a website for a fictitious production company dubbed "187 Films," and posted a casting call for headshots of sexy, young blond types on several on-line websites. Meanwhile Mendoza walked down the street to rent a post office box. Digital headshots would come to a newly created account at Google Mail, while hard copies went to the box.

With Ben, the two detectives crowded into Henderson's office to update him on the case. He listened in silence, looked at the website Ben made, and then granted a rare smile.

"Nice work, all of you. Rabbi, your hunch on the Avis car the girl had was correct. They reported it stolen four days ago."

Ben said, "How do you steal a car from a rental agency?"

Henderson took a sheet from his inbox, glanced at it, handed it to Ben.

This is good, Ben thought. I'm part of their team now.

He read the paper and shook his head. "Somebody left it in front of baggage claim, keys in the ignition, motor running, while they went inside?"

Mendoza said, "So it wasn't planned. They saw an opportunity and took it."

Harris said, "How do we know the girl was part of the murder?"

Ben said, "We don't. She might not have had anything to do with it except going to LaShonda's that one time."

Henderson said, "Or she could be the brains behind the whole thing."

Ben said, "Or maybe this was something different. Maybe the girl picked Ricardo up in the terminal, convinced him to go back to his car, and then she or someone else shot him and took his keys. They get the address from the registration and go there to loot the place, but there's not much to take."

Mendoza said, "The owner of an apartment that's a recent homicide? Too much of a coincidence."

Ben said, "You're right. But still, we don't know."

Mendoza said, "Try it this way. The doer wants to get into that apartment because there's something in it that connects him to LaShonda's murder. But he doesn't want to attract attention or set off an alarm by breaking a window or forcing a lock. So he follows the kid from LaShonda's to the airport and sticks a gun in his face."

Ben said, "Better. It's simpler and it answers the question how the killer knew when and where he was going.

"After he kills Ricardo, he takes his house key, steals the rental and drives to LaShonda's apartment."

Harris said, "And days later the girl goes back? Why?"

Ben shrugged. "Maybe to retrieve something she left behind. Or whoever searched the place left. I show up and see the Avis car and the girl sees me through the kitchen window. So she rushes outside and pretends to be an out-of-town ditz."

Mendoza said, "Okay. Suppose that's the story. But why kill the kid in the first place?"

Henderson said, "The only thing that makes sense is they wanted his keys to get inside LaShonda's. Then he was a loose end."

Ben said, "Wait a minute. The SUV key was in the ignition. Why not just drive it back to LaShonda's? Why take a chance on stealing a car?"

Mendoza said, "Maybe amateurs don't like driving around with a dead body in the back."

Harris said, "And maybe they knew there are airport security cameras all over the place and didn't want to drive it out of the building."

Ben said, "No camera on the parking structure roof?"

Mendoza said, "Someone shot it with a paint ball gun."

Ben said, "Could that help establish time of death?"

Mendoza said, "Airport security is working that now. When they get the time stamp off the video they'll start checking the other tapes to see who went in or out ten minutes before and after."

Ben said, "And you think that would narrow it down to fifty cars or so?"

The detectives nodded, almost in unison.

Ben said, "What if they stole the Avis car first—to drive to LaShonda's apartment, wait for Ricardo to leave, then followed him back to the airport?"

Henderson said. "Good question. We'll check that angle. On your earlier question, don't forget that Ricardo was big, strong and smart. They don't want him struggling in the car while they're driving."

Ben said, "They went to the airport intending to kill him?"

The three detectives nodded again.

Ben said, "Was LaShonda's house key on the SUV key ring?"

Mendoza said, "I don't think so. Why?"

"I saw LaShonda's keys on her kitchen counter."

Henderson said, "So what?"

"Ricardo was going back to Pensacola. He was probably never going to see that apartment again. His aunt and grandmother would need access to the place to deal with LaShonda's belongings, family photos—all that stuff."

Mendoza said. "So Ricardo would have taken those keys and left them in the SUV for his aunt."

Ben said. "And his killer used them to get into the apartment, and again to get back in."

Mendoza said, "So maybe the girl's fingerprints are on those keys. We'll dust them."

Ben's phone rang and he pulled it out to see who was calling. It was Rabbi Kimmelman.

Ben let the call go to voicemail and stood up. "Gentlemen. If you don't need me any longer now, I've got an urgent matter to deal with at Beit Joseph."

CHAPTER 44

FRIDAY: JUNE 25

Gary Burkin was annoyed. It was not like Rabbi Kimmelman to call him at work. And it was even less like him to ask the president of the congregation to come to his synagogue office and then keep him waiting.

And meanwhile, Burkin fumed, just down the hall in the chapel, half a dozen members were abusing his ears with enthusiastically misplaced attempts at blowing the shofar.

Kimmelman hurried into the room. "Sorry! So sorry!"

Burkin snorted. "I thought Chang Rosenfeld taught the shofar class!"

"He was running a little late and called to ask if I could get them started on *shevarim-teruah*. It's a little tricky, you know. *Shevarim* is supposed to be three connected short blasts and *teruah* is nine very short notes in three disconnected sequences of three notes each."

Burkin sighed. "I hope you didn't get me out of a partners meeting just to talk Yom Kippur music."

"No, and again, I'm sorry. I asked you here because Rabbi Ben needs our help."

"And this you couldn't tell me on the phone?"

"Gary, someone tried to kill him!"

Burkin stared. Then he laughed. "Okay, you got me. Now, what's really wrong? Is the basement flooding again?"

"Our basement is fine. A few days ago somebody tried to run Ben over. A hit-and-run. He just got out of the hospital, and he needs a place to stay for a few days."

"Wait. Back up. He's out of the hospital and he's got a nice little sublet in a secure building, so why does he need a place to stay?"

"Because whoever tried to kill him knows where he lives."

"He can't take a motel room for a few days?"

"He has been living in one for almost a week. But it's not right that he spends another Shabbat in a motel where he can't even get a kosher meal. Last week he asked me to help find him a room, but everyone I called is going on summer vacation, or they have guests from out of town, or they don't think their house is kosher enough for a rabbi."

"Have you forgotten? Susan kept the house and I'm living in my girlfriend's condo. No spare room, and she doesn't keep kosher enough for me, let alone a rabbi."

"I haven't forgotten. Actually, I called Sandy Feingelt, who has a kosher chef, but he's hosting four couples for some kind of week-long havurah. He said he'd be glad if Ben wanted to drop in and participate, but he doesn't have a place for him to stay. *He* suggested that I ask you to call Susan."

"Call my soon-to-be ex-wife, who thinks I screwed her on the property settlement, and ask her for a favor?"

Kimmelman sighed. "You're right. I wasn't aware you still had issues, but I should have known that it would be awkward."

"It is. But I need to speak to her about something else anyway, and one thing I've learned in thirty years of negotiating is that if you ask someone to do you a favor, they actually feel better about you when they say yes."

"I didn't know that. Gary, thank you. Let's not tell anyone else about the attempt on Ben's life. And please let me know what Susan says as soon as possible."

Ben drove into the, terraced hills just east of Burbank, glancing now and then at his iPhone GPS until he arrived at a long, circular driveway. The pavement rose at a steep angle through immaculate topiary until the long, graceful lines of the Burkins' expansive two-story home appeared.

He couldn't be angry with Rabbi Kimmelman, but he was disappointed. He'd asked him to keep the attempt on his life secret, yet he'd told Gary Burkin, of all people.

Ben had spent the last week in a motel full of noisy tourists, subsisting on limp coffee-shop salad and overdone fish—kosher and marginally healthy, but not what he was craving. Tired but unable to sleep, almost every time he'd dozed off he'd started to dream of going to the rest room in a Jerusalem café and forced himself awake.

On successive mornings he'd called Mitch Katz in Skokie, hoping to catch the psychiatrist before he left for the office, but Mitch's phone didn't answer and the call went to voice mail twice before Ben recalled that Mitch and Marcia had left the sweltering Chicago suburb for a skiing vacation in New Zealand, where it was winter.

Each morning Ben had put on running gear for a half-hearted five miles, taking it easy, trying to focus on the moment, to stay in the present—a technique he had learned for letting his unconscious take a shot at steering each piece of a puzzle to its one and only proper destination.

Each morning, standing under the motel room's tepid shower, he'd tried again and again to assemble the puzzle. He slowly became convinced that LaShonda was murdered because the cheder file was on her desk—a file now missing. Then someone searched LaShonda's home and someone killed her son—probably the same person. It *must* have something to do with the mysterious deposits and withdrawals. Three people had died because of those statements; now he wondered, yet again, if the hit-and-run wasn't connected to the cemetery at all but to LaShonda's murder and the cheder account.

Now, arriving at Susan Burkin's home, he realized that Gary Burkin had been in the middle of everything.

Burkin had brought him in to solve the bank mystery, but perhaps his hand had been forced by Tova, Kimmelman, Seddaca and Ferguson. When the money vanished from the account as mysteriously as it had appeared, Burkin appeared to lose interest in the mystery. He'd all but ordered Ben to back off. Ben asked him to leave the cheder account at Bank of B. Cohen open; instead he closed it.

Then there was the matter of the Burkin divorce. Sifting through the settlement file, Ben had been troubled by something in the pages of the financial settlement, a fact or inference that he couldn't quite put his finger on. His conversation with Kimmelman about staying with Susan Burkin had included an invitation from Sanford Feingelt, and that had reminded him about his previous unease.

But as he inched up the Burkin driveway, Ben realized what had troubled him about the financial settlement: the records showed that Feingelt had handled Susan's divorce, including the property settlement—but Burkin had made a point of telling him that Feingelt *didn't* do family law.

Feingelt was also a partner in real estate properties with both Susan and Gary and had other dealings with Gary's law firm. Had he represented Susan as a favor? A favor, perhaps, to Gary?

Did he have more to gain by keeping Gary happy with the settlement than by getting Susan a fair share? Could Burkin have used the cheder account to hide cash from his wife during the divorce? Did Feingelt know or help?

Ben couldn't prove that Gary Burkin had anything to do with LaShonda's murder, the missing bank documents or the millions that had come and gone from the scholarship account, but he was an obvious suspect. So was Feingelt.

Ben parked near a helpful sign that said "guests." He set the parking brake and got out as Susan Burkin appeared on the portico of her grand house. She waved.

He had met Susan twice before, at Beit Joseph's Shabbat services. At fifty she was petite and still beautiful, with frosted blond hair, pale blue eyes, clear, lightly tanned skin and a figure that belied both her years and the effects of motherhood.

"Shalom, Rabbi!"

"Shalom, Mrs. Burkin," he replied, noting that her smile faded at these words.

"Call me Susan, please. I'm taking my maiden name back as soon as the divorce is final."

"Sorry if I offended you. You're very kind to offer me a room."

"I'm not offended. I just want to move on with my life. And Rabbi, my kids are all grown up and this house is far too large for one person. You're welcome to stay as long as you like."

"Thank you, but I really hope that it won't have to be more than a few days."

"Why don't you put your car in our garage? Then you won't have to wash it as often."

Ben smiled. The car was already dirty.

As Susan went inside to open the garage, Ben got into the Toyota and turned around, then pulled in next to a gleaming, perfectly restored 1965 Mustang. Susan closed the garage door and handed the remote to Ben.

Ben said, "Nice Mustang!"

"Gary had it done at some place in Pacoima. Two or three years ago. For what he spent on that car he could have bought two new ones."

Ben tried to conceal his surprise.

"So he doesn't drive it much?"

"Hardly ever. His girlfriend—excuse me, but may *she* rot in Hell—has no garage space, so he keeps it here for now. You know, I should charge him rent."

"I understand how you feel. Susan, do you happen to know *where* in Pacoima he got that work done?"

"There's a decal or something under the hood."

"Do you mind if I look?"

Susan shrugged. "Do you know how to open it?"

"I think so."

Ben fumbled beneath the dash for several seconds, and then looked up to see Susan suppressing laughter.

"Here, I'll show you."

Ben followed her to the front of the car, noticing the way she moved, the tight fabric moving over well-toned flesh of her hips. She bent to stick two fingers under the galloping Mustang emblem and tugged on a latch. The hood popped up an inch or two.

Ben said, "I'll take it from there."

Susan moved aside and Ben leaned in, stuck a flattened hand into the opening and pushed the latch up until it clicked.

He raised the hood and peered into the darkened interior.

The decal was silver and shaped like a pistol. In bold red letters it said "La Vida Custom Cars."

Ben's blood ran cold and his mind reeled. Gary Burkin's Mustang had been restored by Loco Henry.

CHAPTER 45

Susan said, "Rabbi Ben—are you all right?"

Ben steadied himself on the fender, than closed the hood and gently pushed until the latch locked.

"Whoa," he said, turning back to Susan. "I guess I'm not quite recovered from my accident."

"Gary said it was deliberate—someone tried to kill you!"

"Could have been. I didn't see him coming till the last moment, and eye-witnesses aren't always reliable. I'm sure the police will handle it. Thanks for your concern."

"Please come into the house."

The interior was cool and the epitome of tasteful contemporary Mediterranean design. Picture windows with thermal glaze to minimize heat displayed expansive, breathtaking views of Burbank and the San Fernando Valley beyond. The walls were adorned with just the right number of paintings, including the requisite Chagall and works by such Israeli masters as Ze'ev Raban, Anne Ticho and Ahuva Sherman. Near the front door a large print of Theodore Herzl by the Zionist photographer Ephraim Moses Lilien greeted visitors, and an intriguing Harry Baron sculpture dominated the dining room. Except for the Chagall, a Giclee print, he was looking at a couple of million dollars worth of art. It put the Burkins' property settlement in a different light.

Even as that thought occurred to Ben, he felt the enchantment of the room. "It's like an Israeli art museum!"

Susan smiled. "There's more upstairs."

"Surely you must be an art curator?"

Susan laughed. "No, my professional accomplishments run to curriculum design and grant evaluation. I work at AJU—American Jewish University. Part-time, for now."

"Gary selected these works?"

Susan shook her head, no. "All of this, every piece, was recommended by Rifka Feingelt."

"Sanford's wife?"

"*Ex*-wife. She also did their bank, which is really more a private art museum than a private bank."

A light dawned in Ben's mind. "That would be the Bank of B. Cohen?"

"Do you know it?"

"Not exactly. I've passed the building a few times. And I think Beit Joseph used to have an account there."

"Yes, the cheder scholarship fund. They moved it?"

"I think so. Gary mentioned it about a week ago."

"Forgive me, Rabbi. You must be tired. Can I fix you something to eat? Or would you like to take a nap?"

"You're very kind. I think I'll be fine for now, though I wouldn't mind a cup of coffee, if that's not too much trouble?"

"Not at all. Espresso? A latte? Or just regular coffee?"

"Espresso sounds great!"

Ben followed Susan into an expansive, skylight-lit kitchen with industrial-grade appliances. She fiddled with an expensive Delonghi Magnifica espresso machine until hissing noises issued from it. A minute later Susan put two cups of steaming espresso on the table.

"Sit down and relax, Rabbi."

"Listen, please don't feel like you need to entertain me. It's more than enough that you've taken me into your home. I hate to take your time, too."

"Oh, I don't really have all that much to do. And Tova tells me you're a fascinating conversationalist."

"What else does Tova tell you?"

"That you're a Kung Fu expert who broke the arms of two giant bullies who threatened LaShonda."

Ben smiled as he shook his head. "Not Kung Fu. And I dislocated, but did not break, one man's shoulder. The other one then threw in the towel."

Susan smiled, and a playful look painted her features. "Even if you're not a Kung Fu rabbi, according to Tova, you're some kind of super-duper fixer. A troubleshooter."

Ben took a small sip of his espresso.

So much for keeping secrets in a small congregation, he thought. By now everybody at Beit Joseph probably knew.

"That's confidential. Officially, I'm a visiting scholar."

"Tova told me something else, Rabbi."

"I'm almost afraid to ask."

"She says that you're either gay, or faithful to a mystery woman who might be married to someone else."

Ben threw back his head and roared.

Then he grew serious. "Susan, let me speak to you, for a moment, as a rabbi. This is what happens when people engage in *loshon hara*. A single innocent worm of truth becomes a serpent that swallows everything in its path."

"I called Tova and asked her what you were like, since I knew you were coming to stay. And she merely described things that she knew to be true. Maybe I misunderstood or embellished in my own mind."

"I understand. Do you know the story of Do'eig the Edomite?"

Her lovely face turned serious. Susan shook her head.

"It's in the first book of Samuel, I think. Well, this guy Do'eig—recall that the Edomites were descendants of Jacob's brother, Esau—saw a priest named Achimelekh give David bread and a sword. This was a completely innocent act—David was an important figure in King Saul's court, and David was hungry and needed a weapon for self-defense. If anyone had asked either David or Achimelekh, they would have had no reason not to admit to either giving or receiving the bread and the sword. It wasn't a secret.

"But then Do'eig reports what he saw to King Saul and Saul decides that this proves that Achimelekh is supporting David in a rebellion! Scared, he murders all but one of the *Kohanim.*

"Tragic, but true."

Big tears laden with mascara rolled silently down Susan's face. "I am so sorry, Rabbi."

"I forgive you. Let's not speak of it again."

Susan nodded, and then dried her eyes on a paper towel.

"One more thing, Susan. I'd appreciate it if you would not carry this conversation back to Tova. I'll speak with her after Shabbat, and I'll mention no names but I will remind her that she needs to be more circumspect."

"Of course. Let me show you your room."

The room was bright and airy, with its own picture window and three small but tasteful prints on the wall.

"This is wonderful! May I ask another favor of you?"

"Of course."

"Were you planning on a Shabbat dinner?"

"Yes, I was just about to put the chicken up."

"Wonderful. Here's the favor: I left my apartment in haste, and I've been staying in a motel. I need to get some clothes and things, but just in case somebody's watching, I want to go in and out at a specific time, and I don't want to go in my car."

"What time?"

"With Daylight Savings Time, we light Shabbat candles a little before eight. So about six, which is when many of my neighbors get home from work. If I lay down in the back seat until we're inside underground parking, I'll probably get in unseen. Then I'll need about ten minutes."

"It sounds like an adventure!"

"I have to be honest. There is a small chance that someone might see me—someone who wants me dead."

"I'll risk it."

"You are a good woman, Susan."

***

Susan said, "I haven't done anything this exciting since I hitchhiked through Europe!"

Prone on the back seat of Susan's Mercedes coupe, Ben sighed. This was risky and he hated himself for involving an innocent like Susan. But when he'd fled his sublet he'd grabbed only his computer, shaving kit and what he ironically described, in literary jest to the sons of every Jew's

Uncle Ishmael, as his hegira kit—a change of clothes plus socks, underwear and anti-retroviral drugs for a week.

The potential complications of missing even one day of his drug regimen were frightening. If Ben failed to get the rest of his pharmaceutical store on this expedition, he would have to immediately email a 24-hour pharmacy in Cambridge and ask them to overnight a supply to Susan's house. That would probably force an explanation of the contents of the package, which would bring a choice between lying about the drugs and telling her about his condition.

Not a good set of choices.

Using the radio remote that opened the underground garage, Susan drove into the parking structure. Ben sat up and directed her to follow the sign to visitor parking.

"If I'm not back in ten minutes, call Burbank P.D. and ask them to send a car and backup and to notify Captain Henderson or Detective Mendoza."

"Henderson or Mendoza. Got it."

Ben ran for the gate to the secure area, where he punched in the four-digit code that unlocked it. Entering an elevator or stairwell required a key. This triple layer of security—garage remote, combination-lock gate and key-lock elevator—made most residents feel secure.

But not a student of Mordechai Allen, the former terror of Miami's Gold Coast high-rise dwellers. Radio remotes can be cloned either by stealing one or by using a black-box device to capture their signal code. Key locks can be picked, and none of the cheap ones in this building or most other residential buildings would have stopped Ben for more than two minutes. That left the combination lock, which could be breached by remote observation—a hidden video camera trained on the lock, then retrieved—or more simply and effectively by social engineering. A good-looking, appropriately dressed person following a legitimate resident had only to call out, "hold the door, please." Few residents would challenge that.

And none but the curmudgeonliest would have failed to hold a door, security or otherwise, for the beautiful young woman Ben had met outside LaShonda's apartment.

Ben took the stairwell, climbing quickly but silently to the third floor. He looked around the floor and window sill near the door and noted three identical cigarette butts.

Ben knew none of his neighbors, but he had twice seen a man about his age leave his apartment, light a filter cigarette, and enter this stairwell.

He examined the three butts. One was dry, one a little damp and one bone dry. So, he concluded, they were smoked at different times, possibly by his neighbor.

And not by someone lurking in the stairwell.

He stepped out onto a third-floor balcony fifty feet from his own door and overlooking the central atrium.

Before leaving his apartment, as a routine precaution, he had taken a scrap of paper, a third the size of a postage stamp, and folded it three times. He'd jammed it, ankle high, partway into the crack between his door and the doorframe on the side opposite the knob.

He knelt in front of the door and felt for the paper.

It had fallen to the floor.

Someone had opened his apartment door.

CHAPTER 46

Silently, Ben rose and moved to the three-foot space between the window facing the atrium and the door to his unit. Keeping his body in that space, he slowly twisted the door knob.

Locked.

Ben squatted on his heels, thinking about what might happen if he used his key. The lock was a deadbolt connected through the door to a lever. Turning the key in the lock moved the bolt and turned the lever with it.

If someone had taped or wired, say, a shotgun, to a chair or table, aimed it at the door and tied a string to that lever, then twisting the lock would send a shotgun blast through the door, killing anyone behind it.

Even simpler, a string attached to the door knob could be used to trigger a bomb.

Or someone might be waiting in his apartment.

The smart thing to do, Ben knew, was call the police.

He thought about it. If, inside, nothing was awry, he'd spend two hours, if not more, explaining to a succession of beat cops, supervisors and detectives why he'd thought there might be. And if there *was* something inside, a bomb or booby trap, and police defeated it without harm, then it would be four or five hours explaining how he knew and why someone would try to kill him. And if, God forbid, someone got hurt, he would spend the rest of the night explaining.

That would be the end of his Shabbat. And Ben was very much in need of Shabbat. Of a day of peace and reflection.

He considered the alternatives, and then decided that he trusted himself to learn what was behind his door. Safely.

Reaching into his pant cuff, Ben withdrew a small screwdriver. Keeping most of his body behind the wall between door and window, he pried off the window screen and quietly moved it to one side. Then he put the flat of the screwdriver tip against the window lock and struck it sharply with the heel of his hand.

The window lock broke.

He waited, listening, and then slid the window open.

Across the courtyard a woman peered at him through the corner of a curtained window. Ben ignored her.

He waited. Counted to one hundred. Listened.

Still keeping his body against the wall, he picked up the screen with his left hand, tilted it until it could fit through the window, and pushed it against the drapes inside.

Nothing happened.

He laid the screen on the floor and then, rising, in one fluid motion went through the window, pushing the drapes aside to come up in a crouch.

Empty. As his eyes adjusted to the dim light streaming through the drapes, he turned his head to look around.

And froze. A thin filament—fishing line!—ran from the doorknob to a spot on the wall between the door and the window he'd just come through.

Ben bent slightly and saw a white tube held horizontally against the white wall by white duct tape. From three feet away it was almost invisible.

The tube was a tipoff to the type of device this was.

Looking for more wires, Ben walked slowly to the desk and slid the drawer open. He found a small flashlight and a scissors, the property of his landlord. He found a big metal paperclip and pulled it straight.

Then he moved back to the wall and shined the flashlight inside the tube. As he had expected, the line was tied to the top of a fragmentation grenade. The safety pin was out. The tube restrained the spring-loaded spoon—a thin, curved metal tab about two inches long.

It was simple, almost foolproof, and deadly. Open the door and the line pulled the grenade free, the spring forced the spoon upward, igniting the fuse. In three to five seconds, the grenade exploded.

Anyone within thirty feet would be cut to pieces.

Ben muttered a silent prayer, and then cut the line with the scissors. Nothing happened. He moved to the bathroom and returned wearing latex gloves, then put the paperclip between his lips. Gripping the tube with his hands blocking both ends, he pulled it from the wall.

He tipped the tube up with his left hand, letting the grenade slide slowly down into his right until his thumb could cover the spoon. He held it down and pulled the tube away until the grenade nestled in his right hand.

For an infinite instant he was back in the carnage of a Jerusalem café reeling under the screams of the dying. In his mind, his nostrils filled with the scent of blood and death.

He took a long breath, concentrating on the moment.

With his left hand he took the paperclip from his lips and stuck it into the hole from which the grenade's safety, a thick cotter pin, had been removed. He bent both ends of the paperclip down so it couldn't fall out.

Now the grenade was safe.

Probably.

It looked old. Different from the practice grenades he'd handled in an IDF class. But similar. Very similar.

Righty tighty, lefty loosey, he told himself.

Gripping the grenade in his left hand he twisted the fuse assembly counterclockwise with his right. Nothing.

He tried harder.

It wouldn't budge.

The fuse assembly was rusted to the body.

In the pantry he found a bottle of canola oil. He poured a little into a spoon and then into the fissure between fuse and body. He twisted with all his strength.

He felt it move.

He twisted again and it moved almost a quarter turn.

A few complete turns and it lifted out. He laid the fuse assembly in the sink and the grenade on the table.

Then as quickly as he could, Ben filled a small suitcase with his drug bottles and a big one with clothes, leaving little behind and nothing that he would miss.

***

Susan looked up to see Ben hurrying toward her.

"I was just about to call the police!"

"Sorry. The trunk?"

She opened the latch; he dropped both bags inside and closed the trunk, then got in beside her.

"Nice and easy. Don't draw any attention to yourself."

As the Mercedes approached the exit gate, Ben pushed the seat back, reclining until his head was below the door. He stayed that way until they were a few blocks away.

Sitting up, he looked around and pointed to a supermarket in the next block.

"Could you stop in the parking lot for a minute?"

Susan maneuvered between two parked cars and braked.

Ben got out. "Sorry, but I need to make a call."

He stepped away from the car, pulled out his phone and dialed Henderson's cell. It rang twice before he answered.

"Captain, this is Rabbi Ben—"

"Can this wait?" Henderson growled. "My son is about to blow out his birthday candles."

"Sorry. When you get a few minutes, please send an evidence team and the bomb squad to my apartment."

"The bomb squad?"

"Grenade booby trap. But no hurry. I defused it. I had to break the window lock. I used canola oil to loosen the fuse assembly. But maybe you'll turn up fingerprints or something."

"This better not be a joke."

"Say happy birthday to your boy. I'll see you Monday. You can call me after Shabbat—after sunset tomorrow."

Ben looked up to see Susan, mouth open, staring.

"You defused it? *DEFUSED* IT? My God, who are you?"

CHAPTER 47

Ben said, "There's nothing to worry about. The danger has passed. We need to light Shabbat candles in less than half an hour. We should probably get going."

"You just defused a bomb, so now you want to light candles?"

Ben smiled. "I guess it sounds silly. But don't make too much of the bomb. It was no big deal. And Shabbat is coming! We should go home and *bench licht*, light candles. Maybe have a good stiff drink before dinner.

"And then I'll tell you all about it."

"A bomb in your apartment? Who would do such a thing?"

"You're upset. Maybe I should drive."

She glared at him, then shrugged.

"Maybe I'll have that drink *before* we *bench licht*."

***

"*Barukh ata Adonai Eloheinu Melekh ha-olam, asher kid'shanu b'mitzvotav v'tzivanu l'hadlik ner shel Shabbat.* Blessed are Thou O Lord, our God, King of the universe, Who has sanctified us with His commandments and commanded us to light the Shabbat candles."

"Amen," Ben said, admiring the flickering candles no less than the antique silver candlesticks on Susan's table. He felt profoundly grateful to be alive, to be a Jew, to be celebrating the arrival of Shabbat, to be in this lovely home with a warm, beautiful woman like Susan.

Susan handed Ben a small crystal goblet with a shot of an expensive single malt Scotch. She lifted her own glass.

Ben said, "Mazel Tov!"

"Mazel Tov!"

Susan downed her whisky in a gulp, made a face and poured another. Then she joined Ben on the couch, where he sipped and savored his drink. They sat in silence for several minutes, admiring the candles, munching on a tray of delicate sesame-seed cakes, Susan's special recipe.

Then Susan sighed and looked pointedly at Ben.

"Okay. But first I need a hug. Just a good hug."

Laughing, Susan embraced Ben, who sighed contentedly.

"Okay," he said, gently separating from her. "It was a hand grenade in a tennis ball tube with both ends removed. They painted it white and used white duct tape to hold it against the white wall.

"Then they pulled out the pin"—he mimed the action, using the whisky glass to represent the grenade—"and put the grenade in the tube. They tied fishing line to the top of the grenade and attached it to the door knob."

Susan looked solemn.

"Are you following this?"

"I think so. When you open the door, it pulls the grenade out of the tube. But why didn't it explode?"

"I came in through the window."

Susan threw back her head and roared. "That's the punch line to an old joke!"

"Tell me."

"I can't remember it!"

Susan grew sober. "You came through the window. Why?"

"It looked like someone had tampered with my door."

Susan poured more Scotch and offered Ben the bottle.

"Half. Then I really must eat—I'm starving."

"One more thing: How did you know what to do? Do they teach such things in Yeshiva?"

"In a way. My third year was in Israel. The IDF offers all sorts of self-defense classes. So do many *kibbutzim.* I took a seminar in counter-terrorism tactics."

"Booby Traps 101?"

"Close enough."

"And you've done this sort of thing before?"

Ben shook his head. "First time."

Susan stared at Ben, disbelief in her eyes.

Then she got to her feet, a little unsteadily.

"That's true? You just defused your first bomb?"

"As HaShem is my witness."

"And this sort of thing happens all the time?"

"Of course not. But really, there's no point in over-reacting. I saw a problem, I fixed it."

Susan sighed. "Everything's ready. Shall we go eat?"

***

They dined on a patio watching the dying sunset's magnificent purples and reds behind the entire San Fernando Valley, stretching dozens of miles toward the horizon, an endless myriad of twinkling lights framed by red and white ribbons of headlamp-and-taillight strewn freeways.

Ben had never tasted better food. The chicken was moist yet firm, marvelously seasoned. Each item in the salad was deliciously distinct in texture and flavor. The cornbread stuffing topped all—the best food he'd ever had. He took seconds, then thirds, meanwhile sipping on a robust, superbly fruity Baron Hertzog Zinfandel.

Relaxing into drowsiness, Ben marveled at how he felt—never more alive, more in control, more cogent, yet, somehow, he also felt himself drifting away, saw himself reclining on a patio chair with Susan nestled in his arms. It was as though he was in two places at once, viewing himself from high above and simultaneously feeling her soft lips on his own, the delicious weight of her breasts pressing against his chest...

Ben opened his eyes. Susan lay atop him, smiling.

Ben said, "What was in that stuffing?"

"Same as the sesame cakes—a little herb seasoning."

"What sort of herb?"

"Gary used to get it from that Mexican guy. The one in Pacoima, with the garage."

"Enrique?"

"No, silly. His name's Henry. Loco Henry."

"Gary buys marijuana from him?"

"I call it Mary Jane's Home Relaxer. He likes to smoke it. I *hate* smoking. It's so much better in food, don't you think?"

Ben sighed. Gary was out to get him, he was sure. He'd set him up to stay with Susan so she could drug him. Any minute he'd come to kill him. That was it. He couldn't say anything—Susan would tell Gary and he'd be finished.

Ben was fearful, but he didn't want to get up. It was too hard and he was too comfortable.

And something else was getting hard. Susan was gently stroking him through his trousers. Deep in his loins desire built, a buried tingling that grew more urgent by the second. It was wonderful. And dangerous. He knew that he should stop, but he was powerless to resist.

"I know what you're trying to do, Mrs. Robinson! You're trying to seduce me."

Susan laughed. He had never heard a sexier laugh.

"Damn right I am."

No, he thought. No, no, no. I'm high as a kite, but this is no excuse. Gently, he pushed her away and sat up.

"I shouldn't have let things go so far. Please forgive me."

"What?"

"You're a beautiful woman. I'd like nothing better than to make love with you. Gary was crazy to let you go."

"I let *him* go. He wanted his cake—me, and his little cupcake too. She's twenty-five, big fake boobs, legs up to *here* and she wants to open a chain of boutiques with his money. *Our* money! Well, screw him. Forget Gary. You're gorgeous! You defuse bombs, break bully's arms and give Torah lessons. And you're stoned. I'm stoned. Let's do it."

"Please, Susan, don't make it any harder."

Ben staggered to his feet.

"Tova was right! You're gay!"

"No. No. Please, don't do this."

Hating himself, Ben staggered inside and found his room. He kicked his shoes off and fell forward on the bed.

The room spun. A little sleep, he thought, and then I'll be able   to   think   straight.

CHAPTER 48

The screaming was too much. It came from everywhere. Louder and louder. So loud he couldn't stand it. Then he realized that <u>he</u> was the screamer. But why? The floor was covered with writhing black women. Blood and gore bubbled and oozed from where their faces should have been.

Ben sat up. He was clad only in a T-shirt and undershorts, both soaked with sweat. Indistinct in the pre-dawn light bathing the curtains, Susan sat at the foot of his bed wrapped in an oversized bathrobe.

"You were screaming," she said. "Off and on for hours."

"Sorry. Bad dream."

"I've never heard such pain! What happened to you?"

Ben took a deep breath. He still felt a little high. His mouth and throat felt dry and sore.

Ben put his feet on the floor and stood, swaying.

"I need some water."

"Stay on the bed."

Susan went into the bathroom and came back moments later with a glass. Ben drained it in a single gulp.

Then, in a few sentences, omitting all but necessary details, he described the bombing and the death of Rachel.

Susan wiped tears with her bathrobe sleeve.

"How awful. I had no idea."

"It's not something to advertise."

"It's not quite five. Can you sleep a little now?"

"I think I'll take a shower. Coffee would be nice."

***

Clad in bathrobes, Ben and Susan watched in silence as dawn slowly revealed the Valley's streets and structures.

Susan said, "Do you want breakfast?"

Ben shook his head. "Maybe just some bread?"

"Split a bagel?"

Ben nodded.

"Are you mad at me?"

Ben turned his head to look at Susan.

"Of course not. You were dealing with your own stress and you supposed that I'd also enjoy a little herbal medication. Then I ate too much of it."

"That was part of it. But actually, I'm lonely. And horny. You're a real hero. I did my best to seduce you."

Ben laughed softly. "Well, thanks. I don't think I'm any kind of hero, though. Sorry if I disappointed you."

"I was disappointed, yes. But now I understand. And Ben, now you're even *more* of a hero to me."

"What am I missing?"

"I undressed you and started to put your things away. I saw what was in the small suitcase. All those drugs. Antiretrovirals."

"So."

"So don't worry. I learned my lesson. It goes no further. Your secret is safe. Even from Tova."

"Especially from Tova."

"Yes. How did it happen? You have so many scars—from the bombing?"

Ben nodded. "I think so."

"But you seem so strong and healthy."

"I am healthy. I just need regular drug therapy to stay that way. And good nutrition."

Susan sighed. "What are you going to do today?"

"It's Shabbat. I'm going to Beit Joseph. I think they've got something special planned after services."

"They're dedicating the chapel in memory of Chang Rosenfeld's grandfather. He built a new ark and stuff."

"Yes, the *klei kodesh*—holy vessels."

"We'll drive down. Leave about nine?"

"I'm going to walk."

"But it's miles and miles!"

"Less than three. And all downhill."

The route to Beit Joseph was indeed all downhill, but by eight the pavement was warm and the air warmer. Clad in slacks, short-sleeve shirt and walking shoes, Ben's objective was to get to services without raising a sweat.

He abandoned that goal before reaching level ground near the Golden State Freeway.

Ben knew that on Shabbat he should concentrate on holy thoughts, but they were not yet in him. Instead he pondered what he'd learned the night before, that Gary Burkin had not only hired Loco Henry to restore his classic car, but regularly bought marijuana from him. Henry was the father of LaShonda's only child and she worked for Gary.

So how did a respectable lawyer, the president of a synagogue, meet a thug like Loco Henry? Did he represent him in a criminal case? Unlikely, Ben concluded. His fees were steep and his clientele affluent. So was it more likely that LaShonda connected them? Perhaps Gary asked her to find someone to restore his Mustang. Weed came later.

But that didn't make sense either. According to Ricardo, LaShonda wanted no contact with Henry. So who put the two of them together? That remained an open question.

Worldly and well-informed, Ben knew that using marijuana, though illegal, was not a criminal act in California. Many affluent professionals used it occasionally and preferred it to alcohol. Buying marijuana didn't make Gary a hardened criminal.

But if Gary wanted to stop LaShonda from learning that he'd laundered money through the cheder scholarship account, he might have paid Loco Henry to kill her.

Except for their son, Ricardo. Would any father, even a hardened criminal, accept a contract to kill his son's mother? Not impossible, but unlikely, he thought.

But if Loco Henry *did* kill LaShonda, did Gary then kill *him* to ensure his silence? Then Ricardo to get into her home?

Ben couldn't picture Gary going into Loco Henry's shop carrying a gun. Or cold-bloodedly stalking Ricardo. With his daughter as an accomplice. It just didn't fit with the man he knew.

On the other hand, most people have secrets. Gary was a successful attorney—but who knew what kind of beast lurked behind his façade of cultivated professionalism?

Gary knew where Ben lived. Was he driving the truck that tried to run him down? Did he booby-trap Ben's door?

Ben had only questions. Gary might be innocent.

He was no closer to finding LaShonda's killer than the day she died. Fighting despair, Ben forced himself to think about the joys of Shabbat. He would put aside worldly thoughts, he would consider God's great gifts of time for rest and reflection.

He walked on, perspiring, until the Fifties Suburban-Chic outline of Beit Joseph appeared ahead in the hot, shimmering, smog-thickened Valley air.

***

At most synagogues, Shabbat services begin with *Shacharit*, "morning light" at nine or so, but relatively few members arrive that early. Most trickle in an hour or so later, in time for the Torah service.

But when Ben stepped into the coolness of Beit Joseph's sanctuary at half past nine, most of the seats were filled. He took a *tallit*, a prayer shawl, from the communal rack, reciting the blessing for observing this mitzvah, and took a seat in a back row.

Noting the prayer being chanted, he found his place in the prayer book, and in a barely audible voice joined the chant. A flash of movement caught his eye—Aaron Ferguson, trailed by a woman, probably his wife, moving down the aisle toward his accustomed seat. He nodded and smiled at Ben.

Ben turned his head and looked around. There was Manny Seddaca with his wife and a younger man that must be his son, and there was Tova, and here and there some of the other members whose faces he knew.

Someone sat down next to him, but Ben was focused on the service. In a moment it would be time to rise for the Amidah, a prayer of praise recited mostly in silence.

The person next to him tapped his shoulder. Ben turned his head to find Detective Mendoza. A *kippah,* or skullcap, perched awkwardly on his head.

"What are you doing here?"

"We traced your grenade. You're going to be surprised."

Ben stood up. So did everyone else in the sanctuary.

Ben said, "Surprise me after this prayer."

CHAPTER 50

Mendoza followed Ben from his seat and into a dim corridor.

"What's so urgent it couldn't wait for tomorrow?"

"Captain Henderson left for Sacramento this morning for a seminar on law-enforcement and immigration reform. He's back Tuesday. Harris has choir practice today and teaches Sunday school tomorrow. I'm pitching in the Police League softball playoffs. First game starts in two hours. Unless we lose twice today, I'm busy until dark Sunday."

"And today is the Jewish Sabbath, a day of rest and retreat from worldly matters."

"Don't get your back up, Rabbi. This will only take a minute."

"Please, before people start asking questions."

"Which reminds me, why ain't you up there leading the services? You're the rabbi, right?"

"I'm *a* rabbi. The senior rabbi is Rabbi Kimmelman. And just so you know, rabbi means 'teacher.' A rabbi doesn't perform the service—he's not a priest. Jewish worship is participatory. And any adult Jew can lead the service."

"I get it now."

"Now, please tell me whatever you came to tell me."

"Okay. Short and sweet. About thirty years ago the Mafia tried to blow up another one of your fellow Jews, Frank "Lefty" Rosenthal, a guy who ran a Las Vegas casino, by putting a dynamite bomb in his Cadillac."

"I saw the movie. 'Casino.'"

"Yeah—Scorsese. Not one of his best. Anyway, about six years later, the LAPD, working a double murder—the Woodman case—gets a tip about one of the alleged killers.

"You know the twin towers in downtown L.A.? Used to be called Arco Plaza? Two black high-rise buildings between Fifth and Sixth on Flower?"

Ben shook his head.

"Anyway, LAPD is tipped by an informant that there's a hidden storage compartment in a basement barbershop in one of those towers. One of the guys they think was a triggerman in those murders supposedly keeps stuff there. LAPD is looking for something to tie this guy to the crime scene, so they get a warrant and go look for this compartment.

"Turns out it's about as big as a clothes closet and full of stolen crap—dozens of towels from a men's club gym around the corner, law books from the County Law Library—and several sticks of dynamite."

"Okay. So?"

"So dynamite needs to be stored a certain way. Has to be turned upside down every so often. This had just been sitting there for probably years and it was unstable. They evacuate the buildings, four thousand people out on the sidewalks and the bomb squad goes in. And underneath the dynamite they find a box of hand grenades."

"And the one in my apartment was one of those?"

"Uh-uh. LAPD brings in the Feds, the Bureau of Alcohol, Tobacco, Firearms and Explosives, and they take all that stuff someplace and blow it up. But first they photograph it. And pretty soon they track the dynamite to the same lot used in Lefty Rosenthal's car bomb, and the grenades to a theft from an Army base in upstate New York.

"Your grenade came from the same lot as the ones found in that barbershop."

"And that means…?"

"I forgot to mention. The guy who filled that locker with goodies and explosives had a brother, a stone killer who did contract hits for the Vegas Mob."

Ben considered this information for a long moment.

"The grenades came from a New York armory and passed through the hands of a goon working for the Mob. So, I am to suppose that other grenades from this theft remained with the Mob, or someone with ties to the Mob, and whoever tried to kill me is either one of those mobsters or he is somehow connected to them?"

"Something like that."

"Meaning, you have no idea who did this or why, but you thought by sharing the Mob connection with me you might find out where it leads?"

"You got me. What are *you* into, Rabbi, that would bring big heat from somebody with Mob connections?"

It was Shabbat. Ben tried to avoid lies on any day and Shabbat even more so. He thought for a long moment.

Even on reflection, he found it hard to believe that anything he'd been looking at—either the cemetery or the bank account—would be of much interest to a national crime syndicate. Or to Las Vegas mobsters, if there were still any around. One or two of his previous cases, however, might be a different story. He'd have to give it some thought. After Shabbat.

Ben looked at Mendoza, shook his head, shrugged.

"Go pitch your ballgame. If I think of anything that might be helpful, I'll call you. Either way, I'll come to your office Monday morning."

"Deal. And by the way, we've got about three hundred head shots for you to look at."

CHAPTER 51

Ben returned to his seat as the Torah service began. The ark was opened and from it Chang Rosenfeld took a Torah scroll dressed in a rich blue fabric with brocade embroidered with traditional Jewish symbols. Clutching it to his right shoulder, he went to the center of the raised area called the *bimah*.

Holding the Torah, he closed his eyes and chanted in a loud but melodious voice the six Hebrew words that together summarize all Jewish belief:

"Sh'ma Yis'ra'eil Adonai Eloheinu Adonai echad. Hear, Israel, the Lord is our God, the Lord is One."

The congregation responded with the same words. After another line of prayer and response, Chang descended the two steps from the *bimah*, and, followed by Rabbi Kimmelman, slowly made his way up and down the aisles, pausing to allow members to touch the Torah cover with fingers, prayer books or tallit fringes, each then kissing whichever had come into contact with the holy scroll.

Ben moved to the aisle and as the procession passed reached out to touch the Torah and saw Susan, smiling, across the aisle. He smiled back.

An hour later the congregation trooped the length of the synagogue and assembled in the smaller chapel near Rabbi Kimmelman's office.

People filtered in, arranging themselves in a semicircle around the new ark. Susan came to Ben's side to squeeze his hand. Tova came to his other side and smiled. They exchanged pleasantries as Kimmelman entered the crowded room. Ben looked for Gary Burkin, but the congregation's president was not around.

Kimmelman led Chang, carrying his enormous ibex-horn shofar, and three men and a woman, each with a much smaller shofar, to stand before the new ark, which was draped with a painter's tarpaulin. A table on high legs in front of the ark was similarly covered.

Kimmelman held up his hand for silence, but few members seemed to notice. The hubbub of conversation continued until Chang, sensing the rabbi's annoyance, put his long, curved shofar to his lips, puffed out his cheeks and blew the long, continuous blast called *Tekiah-Gedolah*, traditionally the last note blown on ritual occasions.

Ben was puzzled—to his ears, the tone issuing from Chang's instrument, while pleasing, seemed somehow different, less pure, than he recalled from the previous time he'd heard Chang blow. But that, Ben recalled, had *not* been *Tekiah Gedolah*, a long, uninterrupted blast.

The room quieted.

"Shabbat Shalom!" Kimmelman said, his voice hoarse.

"Shabbat Shalom!" returned the congregation.

"I've got a touch of laryngitis, so I'll be brief.

"We join together to dedicate this chapel to the memory of our late member, Chang Rosenfeld, *olav hashalom*. We also honor his grandson, who with his own hands has created a new ark to house our sefer Torahs, and a new table for reading them. In so doing, he elevates our chapel, which frankly has been a little shabby, to a proper worship space for smaller groups or for alternative services."

As Chang moved to the table, his students put shofars to their lips and together blew the single blast called Tekiah. With a flourish, Chang whipped off the tarpaulin, revealing a beautiful creation of fine wood. To shouts of "*yasher koach*," he removed the tarp from the ark, revealing a quilt of brightly-colored figures representing events in ancient Jewish history.

Kimmelman said, "And a big koach to the Sisterhood, who sewed the individual squares and then assembled them."

Several older women in the forefront of the crowd beamed with joy.

Chang said, "Now, the ark!" and drew back the cover to reveal a graceful, closet-like structure with Moroccan-style filigreed doors, through which came beams of light that bathed the Torah scrolls within with a soft glow.

The congregation applauded enthusiastically.

Kimmelman exchanged glances with Chang, who held up one thick, beefy hand for quiet.

"Join me, please, in saying Kaddish for my grandfather, in whose memory we dedicate this chapel and these sacred vessels, the *klei kodesh*."

After a sober, earnest recitation of Mourner's Kaddish, Kimmelman looked around the room until he found Ben, and beckoned him forward.

"In conclusion, Rabbi Ben Maimon, our visiting scholar, will share his wisdom on this solemn occasion."

Although they hadn't discussed this, Ben was not surprised—such ad hoc invitations, he had come to realize, reflected Kimmelman's sense of spontaneity and his confidence in others' abilities.

Ben moved to the front of the room and shook Chang's hand. "Yasher koach, and thank you," he said, quietly.

Chang smiled. "Thank you for coming. I thought you'd be gone by now."

"Soon, I think."

He turned to face the congregation. "Shabbat Shalom!"

In unison, the assembly replied, "Shabbat Shalom!"

"The first '*klei kodesh*,'" Ben continued, "were the sacred vessels used in the portable *Mishkan*, or Tabernacle, of the Exodus, and later those in Solomon's Temple and finally the objects used in the Second Temple. Today *klei kodesh* are the sacred objects we use in prayer services. Although we still recall the sacrificial nature of Temple worship, prayer now substitutes for ritual slaughter.

"Our great scholar Rabbi Abraham Joshua Heschel, of blessed memory, suggested that as Judaism has evolved from a male-dominated, Temple-centered religion led by *Kohanim*, priests, to a more inclusive and participatory religion dispersed among a multitude of congregations and led by ordinary Jews, instead of sacrificing livestock, oil or grain on a physical altar, the sacrifices God desires are the prayers of our hearts and souls. *This* is our way of crying out, of coming closer to the Holy One.

"As we honor our ancestors by using the terminology of Temple times, each of us should strive to fill our heart and mind with holy thoughts and to fill our lives with holy deeds. To put it another way, we should strive to *become* a sacred vessel—we ourselves, serve God as *klei kodesh*. It has been a great privilege to be a part of this wonderful community, and I thank you for welcoming me."

Trailed by their wives, Aaron Ferguson and Manny Seddaca pushed through the crowd to shake Ben's hand.

Ferguson said, "I heard you had to leave your apartment and you're staying with Susan Burkin."

Ben smiled. "She's a wonderful hostess."

Seddaca said, "I never thought it could happen here! People trying to kill rabbis—it's terrible."

Ferguson said, "Come stay with us—we have plenty of room and we keep a glatt kosher home."

Out of Ferguson's view, his wife frowned.

Ben clapped Ferguson on the shoulder. "I'll remember that when I get tired of Susan's cooking."

Seddaca looked like he'd just stepped in a dog's mess. "Rabbi! You're not..."

Ben laughed. "No, no. Nothing like that. She's still a married woman, after all."

Then food and was served and Ben, sampling delicacies from a long table filled with dishes, mingled with members, enjoying the moment, trying to forget the terrors he had felt, alone in a dim apartment, with a live bomb in his hand, and the horrific images of the mangled, lifeless bodies of a ruined Jerusalem café that writhed behind his eyes as he slept.

CHAPTER 52

As people drifted out and the chapel emptied, a handsome older man with a deep tan and a mane of silver hair approached Ben.

"I'm Sandy Feingelt," he said, extending his hand.

"I've heard so much about you," Ben replied, as they shook hands.

"And I, you. Your *drash*, Torah lesson, was inspiring."

"Thank you, Mr. Feingelt."

"Please, call me Sandy."

"Sandy."

"Listen, it's short notice, but my wife and I are hosting a little Havura this week—four couples. I'd be glad if you could find a couple of hours after Shabbat to drop by. I'm sure everyone would like to meet you."

"I'll try to find the time. Shall I call?"

"Not necessary. Just come by. I'm in the hills, a few streets over and a bit further up from the Burkins. Susan can show you where we live. In fact, she's welcome to join us as well. Any time before Wednesday afternoon."

"I look forward to it."

As Feingelt left, Ben felt exhaustion creeping into him. He wasn't looking forward to the long, hot hike back to Susan's home. Nor would he violate Shabbat by riding.

He caught Kimmelman's eye, and the two met near the chapel's back door.

Kimmelman said, "You look terrible. Do you need to lie down?"

"I was thinking...a nap would be perfect."

"Use the couch in my office. It's open. You know how to set the alarm when you leave the building?"

"The code is still Y-H-W-H?

Kimmelman nodded. "There's a little fridge behind the desk. Help yourself to anything."

"Thanks, Hank. *Shabbat Shalom.*"

"Go lie down."

***

Ben closed the office door behind him and locked it. The room was small and cluttered, and the couch littered with an assortment of items—a child's lost rain poncho, several books in a canvas bag adorned with *The New Yorker* logo, manila file folders holding synagogue papers, some music CDs, a man's rumpled necktie, a clean dress shirt in a dry cleaner's plastic bag, and under everything else, a brown accordion file.

A brown accordion file!

Excitement fighting fatigue, Ben carefully stacked everything from the couch on the floor, leaving the accordion file for last. Then he checked to see that the door was locked and sat on the couch.

He opened the file and peeked inside. It held fifteen years of bank statements from the Bank of B. Cohen, and Ben's note to Kimmelman, indicating that he might want to look through the statements again.

Ben had put the file on Kimmelman's desk, and Kimmelman had returned the checks to the file cabinet and kept the statements that, Ben thought, probably cost LaShonda and her son their lives.

He closed the file, put it under the sofa and pushed it back against the wall, out of sight.

These statements, he felt sure, would tell him why LaShonda was killed and perhaps by whom. He wanted to look at them, wanted to end this mystery and find justice as he had never before desired anything—but it was still Shabbat. He was exhausted, not thinking clearly. He felt sure that whatever secret lay hidden in the bank records would require a clear head and his best analytical skills.

Surely a few more hours would make no difference, he told himself.

Ben kicked off his shows, loosened his belt, and curled up on the couch. He closed his eyes and as his mind dimmed he felt a falling sensation, as though he was descending through an ever-darkening space into a bottomless pit. He forced himself to relax against the terror rising from the darkness as he fell into deep sleep.

CHAPTER 53

Ben opened his eyes.

Kimmelman's office was dark, its only illumination the creepy yellow-orange light of a sodium vapor street lamp filtering through Kimmelman's thin cotton curtains.

Shabbat was over.

Ben sat up, put his feet on the carpeted floor, gathered his wits.

The missing accordion file!

It all came flooding back. He tried, but failed, not to think of LaShonda's mutilated face, the horrific crime that took place just across the corridor from where he sat.

He tied his shoe laces, buckled his belt, stretched, and then dropped to hands and knees to feel for the cardboard file folder. He found nothing but floor and wall. Suppressing the urge to panic, he moved leftward, reaching deep under the sofa, probing, until his fingers felt cardboard. He grasped the file and pulled it out.

Ben squatted on the floor for a long moment, thinking.

What if someone had seen him enter Kimmelman's office?

What if the killer had been that person?

Ben told himself that he was paranoid. Doubtless last night's THC compounds lingered in his body. They might also explain his hunger pangs.

But even paranoids have enemies. And there was nothing imaginary about the bomb or the hit-and-run attempt.

Better to minimize risk, he thought. Leaving the lights off, he moved to the phone on Kimmelman's desk.

Susan answered on the first ring.

"Rabbi Kimmelman! Have you found Ben?"

Ben spoke in a low voice, almost a whisper. "Susan, this is Ben."

"Are you okay? Where are you? I was so worried!"

"I'm fine, Susan. I got tired and Rabbi Kimmelman offered me his office couch for a nap. I just woke up."

"Ben, hold on, I've got to take another call."

Several seconds passed in silence before Susan came back on the line.

"Sorry—my daughter calling from France. I better call Rabbi Kimmelman back. When it got dark and I didn't know where you were, I left a message at his home."

"Susan, do you remember where we stopped yesterday? On the way back to your home?"

"The supermarket?"

Ben thought he heard a click on the line. Was somebody listening on an extension? Or was it just his paranoia, the effect of cannabis lingering in his bloodstream?"

"Yes. There's something I have to do right now, but could you meet me there in half an hour?"

"It's a big store. Where will you be?"

"I'll find you."

"You're almost whispering. You're sure you're okay?"

"I'm fine. See you soon."

As soon as Susan hung up, Ben dumped the books from *The New Yorker* bag on the couch. He put the statements in the book bag. He shoved the empty accordion file back under the couch. Then he grabbed the bag and tiptoed to the door.

He listened for a long moment before cautiously opening it and stepping into the corridor.

It was empty. The front entrance was much closer than the back, but the alarm box was behind him.

Suddenly he had an idea. He'd switch on the office lights, and then leave by the back door.

He slipped back into Kimmelman's office, locking the door behind him.

The streetlight flared, and then went out. The room plunged into blackness.

Time for a change of plans, he thought.

Ben felt for and found the phone but couldn't make out numbers on the keypad. It took three tries to dial 911.

An operator said, "What is your emergency?"

Before he could answer, the line went dead.

Ben hung up, and then lifted the receiver. Still dead.

He thought furiously. If the 911 operator followed protocol, she would immediately call back. If there was no answer, the call would go to the synagogue's external voicemail. Hearing that, the operator should immediately dispatch a patrol car.

It was Saturday night—a period, in most cities, of high demand for police services. Burbank police had a relatively small patrol area, and much of it, the movie studio area, was all but deserted on weekends. There were probably only a few cars on the streets now. Ben realized that it might take several minutes for police to arrive—or much longer if all available units were on other calls.

He was on his own.

Quietly, Ben stepped back into the corridor and listened for a long moment. Gripping the book bag in his left hand, he crept to the alarm box to punch 9-9-4-9, the digital equivalent of Y-H-W-H. He walked quietly to the front door, opened it, closed it, then ran the length of the building and pushed the back door open.

He pulled it closed, heard the lock snap into place.

On the far side of the building an engine roared to life.

At full speed, Ben dashed toward the corner, into the empty parking lot and came out near the front door. Down the block he saw the back of a pickup truck, lights out, creeping toward brightly-lit Victory Boulevard. Ben went the other way, taking an alley that paralleled Victory until he emerged on the cross street. As he walked toward the supermarket, a police car sped by. Ben pivoted in time to see it turn into the street in front of Beit Joseph.

Ben wore no watch, but he was fairly sure that only about ten minutes had passed since he'd spoken to Susan.

He passed the first entrance to the half-empty supermarket parking area and continued down Victory to the second. This was the one nearest Susan's home, presumably the one she'd use. Nearby was a bus stop with a bench.

Ben sat on the bench for twenty minutes watching cars coming up Victory. When he saw Susan's Mercedes coupe he jumped up and flagged her down as she turned in. Ben opened the door, slid inside, and then buckled himself in.

"Where are we going?"

"I'll explain in a minute. Could you just sort of drive up and down the rows for a few minutes?"

"What are we looking for?"

"A car or truck that I might recognize."

They explored the lot for several minutes but saw no vehicle that looked familiar to either of them.

Susan said, "What's going on? Why didn't I just pick you up at Beit Joseph?"

Ben said, "Maybe I'm crazy, but I thought I heard a click on the line when we were talking. I called 911 and as soon as it answered the line went dead."

"My God. Ben, what's going on? Why would anyone want to hurt a rabbi?"

"I left my wallet and money at your house. Buy me dinner and I'll tell you all about it."

"Kosher Canyon? The better places are open late Saturday night."

"Sounds good. Could you swing by the shul first?"

"Are you crazy?"

"I'm just curious to see if the police ever came."

Minutes later, as Susan wheeled her car off Victory and toward the synagogue, they saw the flashing red-and-blue lights of a squad car stopped in front of Beit Joseph. Passing they saw Rabbi Kimmelman talking to a cop.

"Should I stop?"

"No, there's no reason. Did you call Rabbi Kimmelman?"

"I left another voicemail message."

"I'll call him tomorrow. Let's go eat."

***

Ten minutes later, speeding south on the freeway, Susan touched Ben's arm.

"Well? Why are people trying to kill you?"

"I'm trying to decide how much I can tell you."

"Gary told me that the shul hired you to fix a problem with some bank account—unauthorized deposits or withdrawals or something. I asked him why he didn't call the police and he gave me some double-talk about how it was too complicated to explain and the police would screw things up and anyway, they were launching a capital campaign and were worried about bad publicity."

"Gary wasn't supposed to tell you anything. Or tell anyone except the few people who already knew."

"But then I might not have let you stay with me."

Ben sighed. The cat was not merely out of the bag, it was playing marbles with the mice. "I guess since I already dragged you into this—what happened last night, the grenade booby trap, might be related. Probably is, though I'm still not sure who or how. So I might as well share what I know."

"Thank you."

"But you can't tell anyone."

"Not even Gary?"

"Especially not Gary."

"Oh—my God, is he involved? Did he try to kill you?"

"Let's not jump to conclusions. It's just that I can't rule him out yet. And believe me, I want to.

"But let me start at the beginning."

Feeling a sense of relief as he unburdened himself, Ben sketched out what he knew about the mysterious deposits and withdrawals, what he didn't know, and why he believed the odd activities of the now-closed bank account were related to at least two murders. He finished by describing the events at Beit Joseph that followed his entering Rabbi Kimmelman's office several hours earlier.

"And now you have the bank statements?"

Ben held up the bag.

"Can I help? I took an accounting course. For a while, until it got to be too much, I kept Gary's law office books."

"After dinner, we'll look at them. Together."

CHAPTER 54

Susan and Ben sat at opposite ends of her dining room table, each with a stack of bank statements before them, each peering in silence at a statement.

After a few minutes Susan took a new statement from her pile and began examining it. Minutes ticked by until Ben finished inspecting his statement and started the next.

An hour later Ben looked up from the last paper in his pile to see Susan watching him across the table.

Ben said, "Anything?"

Susan shook her head. "Same as last time."

Ben said, "It's almost two. Can you stand to do this one more time?"

Susan made a silly face. "We've already been through them twice. And the only thing we've found in looking at fifteen years of monthly statements is that almost every year there's one statement missing."

Ben nodded. "So there *could* have been an unauthorized deposit and withdrawal in each of those months."

"Sure. But Ben, the balances track from the statements before and after the missing statements. Isn't it more likely that the office simply lost or misplaced a piece of paper? Especially one that nobody paid much attention to?"

Ben nodded. Synagogue offices, he knew, were rarely centers of administrative excellence. He hated to admit it, but the statements had proven useless. He was no closer to finding LaShonda's killer than the day she was murdered.

Ben said, "Thank you for everything, Susan. I'm disappointed, but I feel like I've made a real friend."

"And I feel like I've finally met the kind of man that as a girl I imagined that I'd marry."

"I remind you of your father?"

Susan laughed. "In a way. He was tall and blonde and you're short and red-headed, but when he told you something it was true, and when he started something he kept at it no matter what got in his way. He was the one person that I knew I could always depend on."

"What was his name?"

"William Scott."

"Your maiden name was Scott?"

"Gary's blond trophy *shiksa*. I wasn't much of a Methodist anyway, so taking the *mikveh* didn't seem like such a big deal. But people change. Learning about Judaism made me change. My marriage didn't turn out the way I thought it would, but becoming a 'Jew by choice' is probably the best thing that could have happened to me."

"Better than having three children?"

"Better because it allowed me to raise those children in a wonderful, spiritual community."

"I don't see any pictures of your kids around."

"Two years ago we had a big family portrait done. Gary has it. My other family pictures are upstairs—in my bedroom. Come on, I'll show you."

Susan got up but Ben shook his head. "I'm still a little tired. Could I look at them tomorrow?"

"You're afraid to go into my bedroom!"

Ben laughed. "I guess I am. But tomorrow is soon enough. Sandy Feingelt invited me—us, if you want to come along—to his *havurah*, and I thought I'd go tomorrow morning. So I'd better get some sleep."

"Tomorrow, then."

Ben got to his feet and started to gather the statements into a single pile.

"Ben."

He looked up.

"You don't *have* to be celibate for the rest of your life. There are ways to express sexual feelings without actual intercourse. We could still get each other off."

Ben smiled. "I know. And I'm flattered. Truly. But I don't think it's a good idea right now."

"Right *now*, because I'm fabulous but fifty?

Ben chuckled. "You *are* fabulous. But right now you're still married to Gary."

"Legally separated! We have an interlocutory decree."

"Legal separation is not a category in *Halacha*, Jewish law; either one is married or one is not. In the absence of a *get*, a rabbinical divorce, you are still a married woman."

"Masturbation isn't sex. It can't actually be adultery."

"Technically correct. But even so, it's not conduct a rabbi should engage in with a married woman.

"I am tempted. You have no idea how much I miss sex."

"Then let's get naked, Rabbi."

Ben shook his head.

"Sow a thought and you reap an action;

Sow an act and you reap a habit;

Sow a habit and you reap a character;

Sow a character and you reap a destiny."

"Let me guess—Hillel."

Ben shook his head. "Ralph Waldo Emerson. Susan, please forgive me, but I just can't get sexually intimate with you now."

She sighed. "Okay. I get it. Still friends?"

"Of course. A hug?"

They met in the middle of the room for a long embrace.

Finally Ben said, "Tomorrow, will you show me where Sandy Feingelt lives? Come along with me?"

"I've got plans for tomorrow, but the house is easy to find. I'll draw you a map."

***

SUNDAY: JUNE 27

About six, just as the sun broke through the clouds to brighten his room, Ben sat up in bed and said his morning prayer, the *Modeh Ani,* with an addendum: "Master Of The Universe, thanks for opening my eyes and awaking my mind."

It was so obvious that he and Susan had missed it.

Ben had seen that all the missing statements were from February, May, August or November. And those months, he'd just realized, were each the second month of a quarter.

Interest on the cheder account was paid *quarterly* on the last business day of March, June, September and December. So a deposit in the second month of a quarter, followed within the same month by an equal withdrawal, would not affect the balance until the following month, when interest was computed. And that interest was computed on the *average* daily balance during the quarter.

So the presence, even for a few days, of two or three million extra in the account would inflate the average daily balance and increase the quarterly interest earned.

Ben got out the statements and compared interest rates. It varied somewhat from year to year but was the same from quarter to quarter within each year.

And the interest paid at the end of the quarter with a *missing* statement was *always* thousands of dollars *more* than the interest paid at the end of any other quarter.

Which meant that someone had been moving money in and out of that account for years.

He still didn't know who. But now he could find out.

Ben put the statements back in the book bag.

Then he changed into running clothes and laced on his Nikes. He strapped on his iPhone, put a credit card and his driver's license in his shirt pocket, took a sip of water and carrying the book bag, went outside to stretch before running. He was going to run five miles, get a good workout, and for the first time in days he felt good. Really good.

CHAPTER 55

After five miles, Ben finished his run with an uphill sprint to Wildwood Canyon Park, a leafy, green area offering spectacular views both of the Valley's urban vastness stretching westward and the deep canyon running east into the brown, brush-clad Verdugo Mountains.

He found the name puzzling—*el Verdugo* is Spanish for an executioner, specifically a hangman. A little iPhone Googling and he learned that in the lawless era before the U.S. occupation during the Mexican War, Californians resorted to vigilante justice. Those who disposed of suspected rustlers, horse thieves or other miscreants at the end of a rope were called "Los Verdugos,"—the Hangmen—a title of both fear and respect.

It was a sobering reminder to Ben. He must be absolutely certain of his facts before he brought in the police. Nothing could be worse than arresting the wrong person for the murders of LaShonda and Ricardo.

Or for washing money through the *cheder* account. To confirm what logic suggested, he decided to seek expert advice.

He craved coffee and food and wanted to make copies of the bank documents before sending them for safekeeping and confirmation of his suspicions—but on Sunday the Burbank FedEx Office didn't open until ten. Two hours to kill.

Ben found a shady bench and dialed Bert Epstein, his doctor. As he'd half-expected, the call went straight to voicemail.

"Bert, this is Ben. Hope you're enjoying the Commons or stuffing your face. Or whatever. Hey, I've been feeling a little run-down lately. Tiring easily. Couple of nights ago I didn't get much sleep and the next day, early afternoon, I got so tired that I almost passed out. So I'm wondering if I need to tweak my HAART. Maybe switch one of my NRTI's or ramp up my EVZ dose a little. Give me a call."

Suddenly Ben felt eyes on him.

He turned to see a tall, lean, good-looking young man a few feet away. He wore a helmed and straddled a mountain bike.

The man smiled. "I'm Link. Couldn't help overhearing. Hey, I'm HIV-positive, too."

"I'm sorry to hear that. But it's not something I'm comfortable discussing with strangers."

An impish grin creased Link's features. "Well, if we hooked up for a couple of hours we'd get to know each other and then we wouldn't be strangers, right?"

"Thanks, but I'm straight. Sorry."

"You're straight—or just not ready to come out?"

"I wasn't infected through sexual contact."

"Another self-hating closet queen! How do you live with yourself? Piss off, faggot!"

Ben watched, speechless, as Link rode away. What's with this place? Ben wondered. Is everyone obsessed with sex? Why are they so angry when they don't get what they want?

Ben decided that he'd enough of California to last him a long time.

***

An hour later, after jogging downhill to Burbank's business district, Ben nibbled on a bagel and sipped coffee in a neighborhood café down the block from a FedEx store.

He looked up to see Gary Burkin and a pretty, busty, blonde woman half his age standing in line. Both wore tennis togs. Ben waited until they had ordered, then waved.

"Gary!"

"Rabbi Ben!"

Arms linked, the couple approached as Ben stood up.

"Rabbi, this is my fiancée Cheryl... Cheryl, Rabbi Ben."

They shook hands perfunctorily and Ben gestured to the empty chairs at his table.

"Join me?"

"For a minute—we ordered lattes to go."

"Please."

"I guess I missed the announcement. Have you been engaged for a while now?"

Cheryl and Gary looked at each other, and then laughed.

Cheryl held up a hand to display a huge diamond ring. "He surprised me this morning. On the tennis court!"

Ben said, "My mother told me, 'Never give your heart to a tennis player."

Cheryl looked stricken.

"Because," Ben continued, "she said, 'love' means nothing to a tennis player."

Gary and Cheryl burst into laughter.

Cheryl said, "I never heard that before!"

The counter clerk called Gary's name and all three at the table got up.

Ben said, "Gary, a moment?"

Cheryl said, "I'll get the coffee."

When she was out of earshot, Ben said, "I missed you at the chapel dedication yesterday. Anything wrong?"

Gary scowled. "I heard Chang turned it into a shofar-blowing contest."

"I was a little surprised that Rabbi Kimmelman allowed the blowing, but it wasn't a breach of Halacha."

"Chang just rubs me the wrong way—leave it at that."

"Good enough. By the way, thanks for finding me a place to stay with Susan. She's been very supportive. I'm sure that asking her must have been a little awkward."

"Susan is... well, She often has an agenda. I'm sorry to say this, but I don't completely trust her any more. But I'm glad you've found a temporary home."

Cheryl returned carrying two lidded paper cups.

Gary said, "Good seeing you, Rabbi."

Cheryl said, "Nice meeting you."

Ben smiled and waved goodbye. What was *that* about? he wondered. Divorce often does strange things to people. But what had Chang done to earn Gary's enmity?

Ben finished his coffee, grabbed the book bag and went down the block to Kinko's. He made two sets of photocopies, wrote a note to Mitch Katz, whose wife was a CPA, and sent the originals to his medical practice office for safekeeping. He wrote a second note to David Siegel and sent it with a set of duplicates care of the warden's office at The Farm, the Joliet minimum security facility where, when not swapping kosher vittles for personal protection, Siegel the swindler was paying his debt to society. Or so he said.

Then Ben slowly jogged back to Susan's, wondering if there was anything on her agenda past jumping his bones.

CHAPTER 56

Ben let himself into Susan's home with the key she'd lent him. In his room he found her note: She was driving up the coast to Santa Barbara and would return Monday morning. The note included her cell number and directions to Feingelt's house.

After a quick shower and shave, Ben donned his summer rabbi outfit, topped by the Fedora, and set out on what proved to be a five-minute drive to an unmarked gate where he spoke his name to a hidden intercom. The gate slid open. He drove ahead to a second gate, which opened only after the first had closed behind him. Finally he was allowed to enter the grounds.

If the Burkin home was a provincial palace, the Feingelt estate was a petite Versailles: An enormous, three-story faux Georgian mansion, with separate guest bungalows, tennis courts, elaborate landscaping where delicate statuary peeked from niches in topiary hedges, gushing fountains, an outdoor spa and a huge swimming pool.

An olive-skinned young man wearing khaki slacks and a white polo shirt beckoned to Ben. He stopped.

"Good afternoon Rabbi, and welcome to Fine Gold. I'm happy to park your car."

Ben left the keys in the ignition and climbed out.

"Do you have luggage, Rabbi?"

Ben shook his head. "I'm not staying that long."

The valet pointed to the great house. "That way, please. Mr. Feingelt is expecting you in the chapel."

The *chapel*, thought Ben. He has his own prayer space.

Following a pathway paved with something that seemed to add spring to his step, Ben moved rapidly to the enormous house, climbing three steps next to a gentle ramp wide enough for a wheelchair. The door opened at his approach. Another man, older than the valet but clad in identical slacks and polo shirt, greeted him respectfully.

"Straight back, then left, Rabbi."

Inside the house Ben found himself in an atrium, lit by a multi-pane skylight that was itself a work of art. Dominating the far wall was an enormous tapestry, which on close inspection so much resembled the Chagalls hanging in Israel's *Knesset* that Ben concluded it was either a heroic copy or an original from the same hand. His head spun thinking about what it must have cost.

The chapel was at the rear of the house and traditional except for a high, curving stained glass ceiling. An ark rested on a small *bimah*. Three rows of seven seats provided comfort with generous leg space.

The room was empty, but a door to one side of the *bimah* was open. Ben went through it to find himself in a sculpture garden surrounding a reflecting pool.

At the near end, in a loose circle of chairs, was Sandy Feingelt with four men and five women. Feingelt rose to his feet, smiling.

"Wonderful, wonderful! So glad you could come, Rabbi."

As if summoned by mind waves, yet another servant, dressed like the valet and the butler, appeared.

"Can I get you something, Rabbi?"

"Just some water, please. Tap water."

The servant looked inquiringly at the others, who shook their heads.

Feingelt guided Ben to the center of the circle.

"May I introduce our visiting scholar, the grandson of the great Rabbi Salomen Maimon, *olav hashalom*, Rabbi Moshe Benyamin Maimon."

"Please, just call me Ben, or Rabbi Ben."

Feingelt went around the circle, introducing each couple in turn, and ending with his wife, Malka. She seemed to be Ben's age, slim, dark, and pretty, dressed modestly and wearing no makeup except a trace of pale lipstick.

The others appeared to be in their sixties and seventies, as fit and healthy-looking a group of seniors as Ben could ever recall meeting.

A man whom Feingelt had introduced as Mordechai said, "How well did you get to know your grandfather, Rabbi?"

"I pretty much grew up in his home. My father died when I was an infant and my mother, *olav hashalom*, about ten years later. So *Bubbe* and *Zaideh* were my family. But I knew them as a child knows parents—we had a close, loving relationship, but I had no sense of what their problems were, what they aspired to, their fears, their limitations.

"In a way—and I've never really thought about this until just now, so thank you, Mordechai—my relationship with my grandfather was akin to our relationship with God."

Feingelt smiled.

"Sit down and tell us more about that, Rabbi."

Perched on the lip of the reflecting pool, Ben faced the circle.

"It seems to me that parents must seem godlike to young children. They provide everything the child needs, but most children are shielded from knowing what that entails. We know that our parents go and come, that food appears in kitchens and on tables. Clothes and toys arrive and we are bathed and groomed. We have no sense of the toil required to buy that food, that clothing, or even to prepare it for the table. We don't know what worries our parents, what makes them afraid.

"We may be scolded for bad behavior, perhaps punished, but rewarded for good behavior, for carrying out our parent's commandments: brush your teeth after eating. Don't hit your brother. Put your toys in a box when you're finished—all the little stuff we learn in our family society.

"Yet as children, we don't know how such a code of behavior comes about. We are told only to accept and obey the rules.

"If we have good parents, we think of them as all powerful, all-wise, almost godlike in their powers.

"Grandparents, because they are still older than our parents, wiser, more experienced, more patient, more filled with loving kindness—grandparents are even more godlike.

"But as we grow from children to adolescents and into adulthood, our perceptions change. Parents or grandparents are no longer gods. They are ogres who stop us from doing whatever we please. Who limit us. Who don't understand us or our needs.

"We ask for money for some trifle we're desperate to have, must have at any cost, and they won't give it to us!

"They demand to know who we spend time with, where we go and when we will return. And we hate them for this. We feel misunderstood, controlled, punished for no reason.

"Later, much later, as adults, we realize that our parents' resources had limits. Their abilities and powers had limits. To put food in our bellies they often had to do work that they disliked for people who exploited them.

"And we learn that there were times when they had money to give us but wanted us to earn our own, to learn the value of work and sacrifice. As then, in our maturity, we come to appreciate the deep and abiding love our parents bestowed on us. Our relationship becomes deeper, more loving, and more thoughtful.

"I think our personal relationships with God are like that. We think of God as all powerful, as possessing limitless resources, but ultimately we learn that this is not so.

"And we think of God as imposing limits on our behavior for arbitrary reasons that are no longer relevant in our changed world. Eventually we learn that God's laws are rooted in *chesed*, loving kindness, and intended to make us better people, better parents, better Jews. Only then we can begin to truly understand the nature of God."

"*Yasher koach!*" said Feingelt, and the others echoed him. "Thank you for sharing your wisdom, Rabbi."

Ben shrugged. He didn't feel wise at all. He had merely shared an insight that appeared spontaneously.

"Mordechai, you asked how well I knew my grandfather, and I gave you, perhaps, not the sort of answer you expected.

"When I was in my teens—when *Zaideh* was approaching the end of his life—and I could read Hebrew and knew some Yiddish, I had a better sense of what he did with his days. And I noticed things that still bother me."

Mordechai said, "And will you share that with us?"

Ben nodded. "For most of the years that I remember him, my grandfather was the most cheerful of men. He laughed often; he encouraged me to find joy and happiness in everything. When I was sad or discouraged about something, he quoted Rabbi Nachman of Breslov to me."

"'A great *mitzvah* is to always be happy,'" said Feingelt.

"Exactly. Or he'd tell me to get my bank, a jar where I put my nickels and dimes and quarters, and when I brought it he'd tell me to take some coins and put them in the tzedakah box on the mantle. And then he'd tell me, again, where that money would go and who it would help."

Mordechai said, "'Essential joy comes from *mitzvot.*'"

Ben said, "Yes, Nachman again. For most of his life that I remember, Zaideh read the Gemara, the commentaries, every day. I know as fact that he could recite pages and pages from memory. And from the Mishnah as well. He knew the entire Talmud as well as any man who lived, I think. Certainly anyone in the last five hundred years.

"But in the last months of his life he put his beloved Talmud aside and read mostly from *She'elot u-Teshuvot–*"

Feingelt interrupted. "That is, *The Responsa.*"

Ben said, "Yes. The written decisions and rulings provided by the rabbinical sages on practical matters of law in the many centuries following the Talmudic era.

"I asked him about this once, and he told me, in a sort of roundabout way, that he was less interested in the rulings than in what the questions and the circumstances of each case revealed about the evolution of Jewish customs and practices, about joys and sorrows and the changing social mores over the millennia.

"But I noticed that the more he read, the more the joy seemed to fade from him. He didn't laugh as much. He didn't tease me and *Bubbe,* and he no longer spoke about Nachman."

Feingelt said. "What did you make of that, Rabbi?"

Ben shook his head. "I have an idea, a glimmering, but I'm not sure what made Zaideh change, what he found, what he was looking for in the Responsa."

He made a sweeping gesture, encompassing the group. "You are my elders. You're closer to the ends of your lives than to their beginning.

"What do *you* make of this? What insights do your years give you? I'd like to know."

The servant returned with a glass of icy water. As Ben sipped, the servant whispered to Feingelt.

Feingelt said, "Chef Alon has prepared a special lunch in your honor, Rabbi. I hope you'll join us?"

Ben smiled. "An offer I can't refuse!"

CHAPTER 57

It was indeed a wonderful lunch, Ben thought. A thin but surprisingly rich chicken broth, small mounds of finely-chopped chicken liver with slivers of almond served on tiny, perfect, red lettuce leaves, half a boneless Chinook salmon, poached and topped with a mustard sauce faintly suggesting garlic, a chicken salad with walnuts, bits of Portobello mushrooms and sliced Kalamata olives, followed, European style, by a salad of lettuce, spinach and the most flavorful tomatoes Ben had ever tasted.

As the last course was served, Feingelt left his seat at the head of the table and approached Ben.

"After lunch, some of us will take a walk around the grounds, and then enjoy a nap. I can have a bed brought to the library for you, if you wish."

"I won't be napping—I have other business to attend to. But a walk sounds great. Perhaps we might chat along the way—there are a couple of things I'd like to ask you."

***

Ben watched as Malka Feingelt led the four couples out of the dining room and toward the front of the property. Sandy clapped an avuncular hand on Ben's shoulder and pointed to the chapel.

"Let's go this way. We'll meet the others later."

Ben followed him through the chapel, into the sculpture garden, and then up a steep path fifty yards to a tall cyclone fence topped with electrified barbed wire. With Ben on his heels, Feingelt moved off the path to a wild thicket of oleander. Ben watched in amazement as Feingelt pulled a branch and the "thicket" swung back to reveal a gate with a heavy combination lock.

Ben felt the foliage—plastic. On close inspection it seemed almost identical to the real oleander growing nearby.

Feingelt unlocked the gate and followed Ben through it, pulling the faux thicket back against the gate and pushing a second, identical thicket away. From ten feet up the path it looked like a patch of shrubbery growing through both sides of the fence.

Feingelt paused a little way up, then pointed to a faint trail that traced the hillside's contour, rising and then disappearing into thick brush a hundred yards above.

Feingelt said, "My property ends at the crest of the ridge—where the path goes into the brush."

Ben said, "You've taken extraordinary measures to ensure your privacy."

"It's more about safety than privacy. I was kidnapped, many years ago."

Ben's surprise showed on his face.

"There was one other kidnap attempt, more than ten years ago. Or, one that I know of."

"I can see that you're wealthy—is that why you're worried about being kidnapped?"

"Partly. And partly because I support a number of particular causes in Israel and around the world. But mostly, I suspect, because I control a private bank."

"A great segue. That's what I wanted to chat about."

"I thought so. You're not *just* a visiting scholar, are you?"

"There was some hanky-panky with the cheder account. Money appearing in the account, then disappearing."

"So Burkin decided he couldn't trust members to investigate this, and brought in an outsider. Smart."

"Sandy, what exactly is a private bank, and why would someone want to put a synagogue account there?"

"Private banks are for those who have a lot of money and want to protect their privacy. And who, perhaps, would like to invest this money safely and intelligently. We have a small staff and we pay good salaries, not commissions, to advise our clients. There are no-pie-in-the-sky brokerage tips, no early insider IPO buy-ins. Just the best market and investment intelligence we can gather from public and private sources. We bundle external investment transactions and pay a fraction of the charges that an individual investor bears.

"And because we are *not* F.D.I.C. members, our accounts are not insured. They're also not subject to audit without a court order."

Ben nodded. "I'm supposing that your customers need to meet a certain financial threshold."

"When I bought the bank about twenty years ago, it was two hundred thousand. We grandfathered existing accounts but over several years incrementally raised the minimum for new money to half a million."

"But why does owning or controlling a bank put you, personally, at high risk?"

"Because terrorists and kidnappers imagine that abducting someone like me would give them the keys to unlock my customers' accounts and steal the contents. In fact, I know no such details. We have elaborate systems to keep account information secure and compartmented. I have no reason to be privy to anyone's account information."

"But thieves believe otherwise."

"As you and I believe in *Ribono Shel Olam*, the Master of the Universe. And there are parts of the world, unfortunately, when those in positions such as mine do, sometimes, out of greed or thirst for power, compromise internal controls to harvest information. But not me."

"Thanks, Sandy. Here's what I want to ask you. I can show you written proof, signed by Gary Burkin, that I'm authorized to look into the cheder account. Unfortunately, he closed it and moved the proceeds to another bank."

"I don't need to see paperwork. And that is one account that I am personally familiar with. Several years ago there were a couple of times when all the authorized signatories were either out of town or otherwise unavailable. I added myself as a signatory, with the president's blessing, to sign a couple of checks."

"Do you keep records of closed accounts?"

"For a time. Come by next week—just call me a day before—and I'll show you what we have."

"I've stopped by the bank a few times, but it's always closed. Even during business hours."

Feingelt chuckled. "Yes, that's a problem. You should have called me. Basically, we never close. A bank officer and a guard is always on duty and available by phone, email or Telex. If a customer needs to access, for instance, a safe deposit box, they go to a rear door and after properly identifying themselves, we let them in.

"But the last thing we want or need is the public coming in and out of our lobby. So that door is never opened to the public. At the same time, we don't want to call attention to ourselves by seeming *too* exclusive. We don't want the City coming around with lots of questions, and we don't want developers eying our property and looking for reasons to have it condemned. So we allow people to peek through the windows, but what they see could as well be a movie set. Everything goes on upstairs.

"Opening a new account requires a personal reference from a member or an employee. We do a background check on the individual and if they pass muster, credit wise, we invite them in for a chat.

"Would you like to open an account?"

Ben's mouth flew open. He laughed. "I'm not sure I'd qualify."

"*I'm* sure. Aaron Ferguson asked me to check you out before you ever came out to be interviewed. At the time I didn't quite understand why, but now I see it, of course.

"You went through M.I.T. and Yeshiva on scholarship, so you have no student debt. Your grandparents left you money—not a lot—and you received a life insurance settlement on your late wife, *olav hashalom.*"

Ben murmured, "*Olav hashalom.*"

"Over the last several years you've earned a series of fees-for-service that range from a few thousand to over a hundred thousand dollars.

"You own a car, you lease an apartment, you have good credit but no significant debt, you're not married, and you have no children. If memory serves, you're now worth about three-quarters of a million. Or a bit more. Most of that is in bonds, mutual funds and money market accounts."

"Why would I want to move my money to your bank?"

"I can't promise a better return on your funds, although I expect that you *would* see one. I *can* promise to save you the nickel-and-dime fees and commissions charged by brokerage houses—thousands of dollars annually. I can also promise total confidentiality: No one will ever learn about your assets what I learned in less than a day."

"I don't know what to say."

"Say you'll think about it. And say you'll call me next week and we'll make a time for you to look at the cheder account records."

Ben smiled. "I say, skip the phone call. Tuesday morning at ten?"

CHAPTER 58

MONDAY: JUNE 28

Harris said, "Donuts? Last time you brought bagels."

Ben said, "And you kvetched because they weren't donuts and I didn't understand cop cuisine."

Mendoza said, "That's because in that distant, long-ago, best-forgotten era, Detective Harris thought a bagel was something frozen from Ralph's or Von's that you put in your moldy kitchen toaster. He'd never tasted a *real* bagel."

Harris said, "Like *you* had."

Mendoza looked hurt. "I spent my formative years grazing *bodegas* and delis. Certainly I know that a *real* bagel is what you get at—"

"H&H," Ben finished. "Broadway and 80th."

Mendoza said, "Exactly. The last honest bagel."

Ben shook his head. "Not so *honest*—couple years ago, one of the owners couldn't keep his hands off the employees dough—embezzled their withholding taxes."

Mendoza said, "The Hectors ripped off their people?"

Ben looked blank.

"Hector and Hector. H&H. Puerto Rican brothers-in-law."

Harris said, "I thought you were Mexican?"

"I grew up in the Bronx. I'm a genuine *Nuyorican*."

Ben handed the donuts to Harris, "Next time, bagels."

Harris looked carefully at the donuts, selected an Original Glazed, and bit in.

"Not bad," he said, mouth full. "Randy's are better."

Mendoza shook his head. "But not worth the drive to LAX. C'mon, Rabbi, let's go look at some pictures."

***

Ben looked up from a stack of glossy head shots on Mendoza's desk and shook his head.

Mendoza said, "Will you look through the email again?"

"A few of them. I starred the messages so I could find them quickly."

Ben turned in Mendoza's chair and with several key strokes brought up a photo embedded in an email.

"She's a brunette here, but at first I really thought this was her. But now I see her eyes and mouth are different—a little bigger, I think."

Mendoza frowned. "I'm pretty sure that's a porn actress named Joy Owed. Been making blue movies for eight, ten years now, so she's gotta be breathing on thirty."

Ben closed the file and pulled up another, revealing a beautiful, green-eyed blond girl. He stared at it for a long moment, and then closed the file.

"Nope. And one more."

Ben clicked open a third file and the screen filled with a pair of pouting lips and wavy blond tresses.

"This looks a *lot* like her, but her stats say she's five feet, eleven. The girl I saw was about five-four. I guess you could cheat a few inches, but not that much."

He clicked the email closed and turned to see Harris leaving Henderson's office and unhurriedly approaching.

"Got something for you, Rabbi. You, too Mendoza."

Mendoza said. "Don't make a production out of it."

Harris looked annoyed. "LAPD just called the captain. Looks like the Glock we found with the kid—Ricardo—was *not* the gun that killed Loco Henry."

Ben said, "Same model, but different guns?"

Harris said, "Yeah. So now we got nothing to tie the kid to shooting his old man."

Mendoza said, "Which is cool. Not our case, anyway."

Ben said, "What did the coroner say about Ricardo?"

Mendoza said, "Sorry. Should have called you about that. Homicide—death at the hands of another."

"That's all?"

"Well, no. His front teeth were broken, like someone forced the gun barrel into his mouth. And time of death, probably—the body was badly decomposed from heat—was within a few hours of when he was supposed to fly out. That fits with somebody following him to the roof and killing him then and there."

"What about the airport security tapes—did anything turn up on the other cameras before and after the time the paint ball took out the roof camera?

Harris said, "Nothing that helps. The stolen Avis car doesn't show in the parking structure."

"What about when it was stolen?"

"That was a cagey boost. Whoever grabbed that car waited until a group of people came by on the terminal sidewalk, and, I think, slipped behind them and got into the car when they were masking him—or her—from sight.

"The camera can't see inside the car, so when it drove off there was no clue. Could have been anyone."

Ben said, "So, we've got nothing but the girl."

Mendoza said, "I thought sure that fake casting notice would pay off."

Ben said, "Maybe she's not an actress at all."

Harris said, "Or maybe she's got an agent who won't send her on cattle calls."

Ben said, "And what about LaShonda? Anything new?"

Mendoza chewed his lip. "You're our only suspect."

Harris said, "Unless you start bringing bagels, we're gonna have to slap the cuffs back on."

Ben said. "Funny. And what about the bomb in my apartment? The hit-and-run? Henry's murder?"

Mendoza said, "I probably shouldn't say anything, but we do appreciate your help. And the bagels. LAPD has a description for a guy who might have popped Loco Henry."

"And what is it?"

Mendoza shook his head. "You got to get that from the OC—organized crime—squad at their Foothill Station."

Harris said, "Things were peaceful in Burbank until you showed up. Now we're getting wild stuff like gals taking FedEx trucks down in broad daylight."

Ben said, "What? When?"

Mendoza said, "Sunday, about one. A white woman drove off with a truck after it picked up from the FedEx store."

Harris said, "About three hours later the fire department found it burning, up in Brace Canyon."

Ben said, "What about the packages?"

Mendoza said, "Mostly ashes and cinders."

Harris said, "Good thing you're leaving soon."

CHAPTER 59

Processing what he'd just learned about the stolen FedEx truck, Ben drove toward Beit Joseph.

If Burbank police were investigating the stolen truck, then it had been stolen in their jurisdiction, Burbank. If it had been stolen after picking up at the Burbank FedEx, then both the envelopes he'd sent among its cargo.

If that was so, it was either coincidental or because someone knew he sent something from that particular FedEx store a little earlier that day.

If not a coincidence, then either someone had staked out the store, or someone had followed him.

The latter was more likely than the former.

Only Susan knew that he had the cheder documents. But Gary, Rabbi Kimmelman, Sandy Feingelt, Ferguson, Seddaca, their wives and perhaps others knew that he was staying at Susan's home.

Ben parked at Beit Joseph and found Rabbi Kimmelman in his office. After exchanging greetings, Ben asked about the previous Saturday night.

"On Shabbat my wife and I usually have a quiet lunch at home, just us, and then take a nap."

This was, Ben knew, a well-worn euphemism for the ancient Jewish custom of husbands and wives enjoying each other's bodies on Shabbat.

"So we unplug the phones and take our nap. When we wake up, after dark, we decide to go out for dinner.

"We're getting ready to leave the house and my wife plugs the phones back in. We've got two voicemails from Susan Burkin, where are you, she can't find you, and then she found you. And then two messages from the police, there's been a break-in here or something."

Ben said, "Somebody shot out the street light?"

"Police said it was a pellet gun. And they cut our phone lines. Sawed the lock off the box and then sliced right through the cable."

"Did they take anything?"

"Not as far as I can tell. My office looked neater than I left it—I guess that was your doing?"

"I cleaned up your couch before I took my nap."

"So aside from that, everything seems fine."

"Do the police have any idea who cut the lines?"

"They think it was kids. There's been a few incidents like this in the last few months—churches and synagogues. All over the Valley."

"Thanks, Hank. Now I need to ask you something. I'll understand if you don't want to answer. But it's important to clearing up some details on the cheder account mystery."

"You're still on that? I thought we agreed that the matter had resolved itself."

"Yes, but lately I've been learning things that suggest there was more to it. Just between us, my poking around about that account might be the reason behind the hit-and-run, and then the bomb."

"Bomb? You didn't tell me about that!"

With a few sentences Ben described the booby trap left in his apartment, explaining that he'd gone back to get his things when he found it.

Kimmelman said, "My God! A bomb—here in America!"

"I'd appreciate it if you didn't mention it to anyone."

"The police know about this?"

Ben nodded. "The bomb squad is investigating."

"What was it that you wanted to ask me?"

"Is there bad blood between Gary and Chang?"

Kimmelman looked thoughtful. "I'm not sure. They used to be very close, but for the last year or two, not so much. Nothing overt, mind you, but I think they had some kind of falling out."

"But you don't know details?"

"Honestly, I try *not* to concern myself with such things. You can't take sides, even if one party is clearly right and the other wrong, unless both people ask you to resolve their dispute. And then you must try hard to find a middle road. But nowadays, it's very rare that people turn to a rabbi to settle such issues. They'd rather go to court. If you're ever fortunate enough to get your own pulpit, you'll see why it's vital to appear completely even-handed."

"I understand. Thanks Hank."

"You're going back home soon?"

"I hope so. Maybe another week or so."

"Please, come by and see me before you go. You've performed a great service to our community."

"Not so great, but thanks. I'll see you before I go."

***

Ben drove into Susan's garage and parked next to her Mercedes. He touched the hood as he walked by: It was warm.

Barefoot and wearing a stunning yet conservatively styled suit, Susan greeted Ben with a wave of the hand.

"How was Santa Barbara?"

"Fabulous! I drove up with Rifka and we spent the whole day at Sea View Spa!"

Ben tried not to look interested.

"We had mud packs, a deep massage, a facial, colonic cleansing—I feel ten years younger!"

The kitchen phone rang and Susan answered it, and then chatted happily for a few minutes before hanging up.

Susan said, "That was Rifka. Congratulations!"

Ben said, "Excuse me?"

"You're going to open an account with Sandy's bank. Does that mean you might be staying in California?"

Ben held up a hand, palm outward. "Back up, please. You just spoke to Rifka—Sandy's ex-wife—and she told you what?"

Susan laughed. "Rifka and Sandy get along much better as ex-spouses than they ever did as a couple. She still works at the bank—VP customer service, or something. She said that you and Sandy talked about opening an account, and that you're coming in tomorrow. I think it's wonderful!"

Ben stifled a sigh. Clearly there were few secrets in this community.

"Yes, I'm going in to see Sandy in the morning. And I don't think I'll be staying in California—but who knows?"

"You're right—who knows? Anyway, I'm working today so I need to leave soon. Can I make you a sandwich?"

Suddenly ravenous, Ben sat at the kitchen table while Susan spread Whole Foods tuna salad on toasted Tuscan pane.

Piled in the center of the table were framed pictures.

Susan put the sandwich in front of Ben and sat down.

"You won't come to my bedroom, so I brought the pictures down to show you."

She held up a framed photo of a handsome, fair-haired young man in tennis togs. "Nathan is a junior at Yale. He just landed a summer internship in Senator Sanders's office."

Susan put the photo down and picked up another. "This is our son Noah—he'll be starting his third year at Stanford Law, and this summer he's clerking for Alioto & Alioto in San Francisco."

Ben said, "How are your kids handling the divorce?"

"The boys are a little confused, but they understand that I couldn't be their father's wife and ignore his girlfriend. They don't like it, but they get it. Our daughter is another story.

"Naomi was daddy's girl. Worked in his office all through high school. For her, Daddy can do no wrong."

Susan laid the photo back on the table and held up a much larger picture that showed the whole family—Susan, Gary, Nathan, Noah, and a petite, blond beauty in her late teens. Everyone wore paint ball gear.

Ben said, "Paint ball?"

"This was about five years ago, when she was a high school senior. She graduated from USC film school last month. She's the one who called me from France the other night while I was on the phone with you."

Ben took a bite of his sandwich and chewed, slowly, trying to mask his excitement, to show no emotion.

"Naomi was such a tomboy. Nothing scared her. When she started talking about film school, we worried that she would become a stunt woman."

Naomi Burkin was older, more poised and her body had filled out since the family picture was made, but Ben didn't think she was in France.

The girl in the picture, the recent film school grad, was almost certainly the one who'd called herself Roberta Towne when they met outside LaShonda's apartment.

CHAPTER 60

Ben ate slowly, watching Susan finish her pre-departure ritual, retouching her makeup, putting on shoes, then rinsing Ben's dish before putting it in the "dairy" sink—the other was for meat dishes, pots and utensils—then gathering her purse, briefcase and keys.

They hugged at the door and Ben watched through the living room window until Susan's Mercedes emerged from the garage, the door swung down and locked, and she drove out through the security gate.

Meanwhile his mind was churning furiously. He had telephoned from Kimmelman's office about nine on Saturday night. Seconds into that call, he remembered, Susan had taken another call that she said was from her daughter in France.

Shortly after that, he recalled, he'd heard a click on the line in Kimmelman's office.

Had Susan told Naomi she was talking to him and that he was in the rabbi's office at Beit Joseph?

And had Naomi then called someone else? Someone waiting outside who could tap into the synagogue's phone lines from the external terminal box?

If someone was still after him, Ben wondered, why hadn't they simply attacked him when he left the building?

The street light went out, Ben recalled, after he returned to Kimmelman's office from the hallway. The phones went dead a minute or two later—as long as it had taken him to find Kimmelman's phone and clumsily dial 911 in the dark. Was that time enough for one person to shoot out the light and then cut the phone cable?

It was, he thought, if they had earlier cut the lock off, and opened the box. Which they would have done if they wanted to listen to his call. A pellet gun used compressed air or CO_2 and was almost silent. The phone box was on the side of the building and only about thirty yards from the street lamp. It was possible to have done both while he was fumbling in the dark.

But why?

Ben decided that its purpose had been to panic him into running, so he could be attacked as he left by the front door. So that whatever happened to him wasn't *inside* the synagogue and wouldn't automatically be linked to LaShonda's murder.

But instead of going through the front door, Ben had paused to set the alarm, opened and closed that door, then left by the rear entrance. Instead of dashing for brightly-lit Victory Boulevard, he had stayed in alleys and run parallel to Victory. The driver of the lights-out truck creeping down the street expected to catch him before he got to Victory.

But then what?

Run him down, Ben supposed. Or take him prisoner and kill him elsewhere.

Five minutes had passed since Susan left. He examined the kitchen phone but it had no Caller ID. Nor did the one in the living room.

Ben went upstairs and found a small office. The multiline phone on the desk included a Caller ID display.

Ben scrolled backward through Monday, then Sunday until he found his own incoming call at eight before nine Saturday evening. One minute later there was a call—but the caller had blocked name and number.

Would a caller in France be able to block outgoing caller ID? Or could Naomi have used a satellite phone?

The former was possible, Ben thought. Except that it was likely she had called either from a public phone or a phone in a hotel or *pensione*, a sort of rooming house, in which case it was virtually certain that caller ID would *not* be blocked. Ben had never used a satellite phone, but he suspected that, given the cost of airtime, caller ID for incoming calls would be a valuable feature. But would a daughter block her number when calling her own mother?

A caller from any U.S. or Canadian number, Ben knew, could block outgoing caller ID by dialing 67 before the number to be called. He concluded that it was more likely that the call that Susan took from Naomi had originated locally.

But he couldn't be certain.

He was sure, however, that he had to leave Susan's home, where his comings and goings were somehow being tracked.

Ben went to his room, packed everything in his two bags, and then put them in his rented Toyota.

The last thing he put in the car was the New Yorker book bag he'd taken from Kimmelman's couch. He pulled the photocopied pages out and glanced at them.

He saw off-center copies of somebody's term paper. Too-faint copies of pages from a lawsuit. Wrinkled copies of news clippings.

But no cheder bank statements.

Either Susan was part of this ugly scheme, or—would Naomi have a key to her parents' house?

Of course she would. And she knew he had made copies of the statements—that's probably why the FedEx truck was hijacked. If so, then she would have suspected that he'd keep a copy.

Naomi, Ben concluded, had slipped in to her mother's home and stolen the documents while both he and Susan were gone.

CHAPTER 61

Ben went back into the house. In the upstairs office he booted up the desktop PC. After logging on to Facebook he found Naomi Burkin's page: A private profile, no friends, no Causes, no Likes.

The page had been scrubbed.

Ben made a note of the page location, its URL, then logged onto the "Wayback Machine," an archive that provides access to deleted web pages. He searched through some ten *billion* web pages for Naomi's Facebook URL; in seconds he was looking at what the page had been less than two weeks earlier. Dozens of photos. Hundreds of Facebook friends. A link to her page on the Alpha Epsilon Phi Sorority Website. Links to her student films. A link to her Twitter page.

Ben now had no doubt that Naomi was the young woman who had coolly called herself Roberta Towne and who had, perhaps, participated in Ricardo's murder.

He copied the Wayback Machine link to his iPhone and emailed it to Mendoza with a short note:

The girl I met outside LaShonda's apartment is Nomi Burkin, age 22. Nomi is short for Naomi. Daughter of Gary Burkin. Her home address is 3225 Rimcreste Lane, Burbank. Parents believe she is traveling in France. I think she is here in the Valley, or in L.A. somewhere.

This is a link to her erased Facebook Page. I'll explain more when I see you.

Ben erased his Internet browsing history from the Burkin computer, deleted everything from the web page cache, and turned off the machine.

Then he went back downstairs and into the garage. He found a flashlight and with the garage doors shut carefully searched the rented Camry. Under the dash, secured by a ribbon of masking tape, he found a battery-powered silver box the size of a business-card and less than half an inch thick: A real-time GPS tracker that broadcast a signal that could be followed by anyone with a Web connection.

Ben had seen such devices in so-called "spy shops." They cost, he recalled, only about a hundred dollars.

He carried the tracker inside, laid it on the window sill and used his iPhone to take a close-up picture. Then he looked the device over carefully until he saw how to disassemble it. Inside he found the serial number, which he also photographed. Then he put it back together.

He got into his Toyota and drove to a gas station near the freeway, where he called Aram Takarian, the man from whom he had rented the car, and arranged for him to pick up the rental from the station. Then he called a cab and with the GPS tracker in his pocket, put his bags in the trunk. He slipped the tracker into the cab's taillight panel and snapped a shot of the cab's license plate.

Ben left the taxi a block from his former sublet and walked to the curb in front of the building where police had left his Honda, still missing its driver-side door.

He put his suitcases in the trunk and drove to Glendale, where he sold the Honda to a used car dealership for five hundred dollars. The dealer took him to the Burbank Airport. He hid in a restroom for half an hour, then went to the Hertz counter and rented a red Ford Focus.

Then he drove east through Pasadena and deep into the San Gabriel Valley, where he checked into a small motel across the street from a three-story mini-mall with a vegetarian Chinese restaurant.

Ben spent a sleepless night, eventually deciding that he should let the police find Naomi, deal with her disbelieving parents, and ascertain the extent of her involvement with whoever had killed LaShonda and Ricardo.

He dozed off just before dawn, only to be awakened by his cell phone: Bert Epstein returning his call from two days earlier.

Bert said, "Are you still in California?"

Ben said, "Yeah. Another few days, I think."

"How are you feeling now?"

"Crappy. I haven't been getting much sleep."

"Even a completely healthy man who doesn't get enough rest or eat the right food is going to feel tired."

"I guess."

"Well, I went through your last blood work and didn't find anything worrisome. Get more sleep, make sure you eat enough meat, and when you get home I'll run a few tests."

"Thanks for calling me back, Bert."

"Ben, wait, don't hang up."

"I'm still here."

"Listen, this may seem like a strange time to ask this question, but do you know how to blow the shofar?"

"Well enough not to make a fool out of myself on Yom Kippur."

"Well, the High Holidays are coming and my son wants to learn. Do you know a teacher? I'll pay, of course."

"I know the perfect guy—but he's out here. Anyway, I'd be happy to show him the basics. And I'll start taking your money when you start taking mine."

"Thanks Ben. I really appreciate it. See you when you get back."

Bert hung up and Ben got out of bed and into the shower. Standing under the hot water, he realized that he knew who killed LaShonda, had known it for several days. And even if he no longer had the statements, the documents that were proof of guilt were in Sandy Feingelt's bank.

A great burden lifted from Ben's soul. He left the shower, toweled off, and dressed for his five mile run.

***

TUESDAY: JUNE 29

At nine Ben checked out of his room and took the Foothill Freeway west through Pasadena into Glendale and then dropped down into Burbank.

Taking no chances, he parked on a residential street two blocks away and used an alley to enter the small, nearly empty parking lot behind Bank of B. Cohen. Following Sandy Feingelt's instructions, he found the door marked "Employees" and rang the buzzer.

A metallic voice asked for his name.

"Rabbi Ben Maimon."

A buzzing noise issued from the door.

As Ben reached for the handle someone very strong pinned his arms to his sides. A rag was thrust over his mouth and nose. Sickening-sweet gas flooded his lungs.

Ben felt his *ruach*, his life force, draining away, and tried to recite the Sh'ma. He got as far as "Adonai" before the world went black.

CHAPTER 62

Ben fell into agonizing consciousness, a bottomless pit of pain. Every muscle, joint and bone in his body shrieked. He tried to open his mouth to groan but it was taped shut. He opened his eyes. The world was a dark blur. His glasses were gone.

Ben willed himself to stretch, slowly relaxing his muscles. Over interminably excruciating minutes the pain eased, became almost tolerable.

When he was able to focus on things external to his body, he learned that his arms were taped to his sides and his ankles similarly joined. He realized that he lay on a textured surface and pushed his face into it until he recognized the tight weave of industrial carpet.

Ben rolled to his left but after two revolutions bumped a wall. Rolling and squirming, after much painful effort he pressed his shoulders to the wall, agonizing work that soaked his clothes with sweat. His mouth and throat silently shrieked for water.

He rested for several minutes, catching his breath, and then steeled himself. Arching his back he pulled his legs under him and stood. Now he saw, across darkened space, an array of tiny colored lights. Squinting to help sharpen his focus, he decided they were diodes, the type found on electronic devices.

Maybe a computer. A way to call for help.

He considered the wisdom of hopping toward the lights. They seemed very distant, though he had no way to tell. If he lost his balance, he had no hands to break his fall.

But it would take a long time to inch around the wall.

He hopped toward the lights, one hop, two hops, three—and tripped, trying to twist as he fell. Something smacked his face before he landed on the carpet.

Tsunamis of pain gushed from his nose. Warm fluid blocked his nostrils until he rolled sideways, raised his head and blew as forcefully as he could muster. Surely his nose was broken, he thought.

The faintly metallic taste of blood triggered a wave of nausea. He forced himself to choke back the burning bile rising into his throat, suppressing the urge to vomit, knowing that his tightly-sealed mouth ensured that he would choke to death.

The nausea passed.

The inchworm routine is better, he thought, angry that he had overruled his cautionary instincts.

Ben rolled back to the wall, stifling a scream each time his nose hit the carpet.

Six revolutions and he returned to the spot he had left. But something was different. He tasted blood on his lips. Had the tape across his mouth loosened?

Trying to ignore the throbbing agony that was his nose, he pursed his lips, then raised his head to drag his mouth across the rug, long strokes in one direction—pain.

Again—pain. Again—pain. Again—pain.

Dizzy with hurt, he tried to push his tongue through his lips. He tasted the thin edge of the tape.

Ignoring the pain, he again dragged his face across the carpet, again and again and again until the tape had partly peeled away.

He coughed blood and saliva through his lips, rejoicing in the simple act of being able to open his mouth. But now his thirst was overwhelming.

He considered yelling. He didn't know where he was. If his captors heard him then his ordeal would be wasted.

He would remain silent, for now.

Again he wriggled and endured the agony and effort required to get his shoulders against the wall. Again he rested and again he slowly mustered the strength to pull his legs under him and push upward until he stood more or less erect, shoulders and back pressing the wall.

He slid his torso leftward a few inches, and then brought his legs back under him. He repeated the action, inch-worming sideways until, after a few minutes, he encountered a vertical crack in the wall. Then a round objects. A doorknob. A door! He slid sideways until he was near the center of the door. He grasped the knob in his right hand.

And twisted. The knob turned freely, but the door opened inward, or toward him. Teetering, he forced his back against the wall, regained his balance.

Ben inched back the way he had come and moved his left shoulder away from the wall until he could hold the knob with two fingers of his left hand. He pulled the door toward him, twisting away as he did so.

He started to fall and slammed his back against the door until he could regain his balance.

The door shut.

He tried again, more cautiously, letting the door open just a bit, less than an inch, and then pivoting on his heels until his right shoulder rested against the wall.

He leaned back, fumbling for the door's edge with his right hand, and finally touched it with an index finger.

He pushed the door as hard as he could and it opened.

Now he had to turn around.

Inch by agonizing inch Ben turned until he was almost facing the partly-opened door. The faintest of light came from the room behind the partly-open door, just enough to make out the door itself.

Moving shoulders and then feet an inch at a time, he transferred his shoulders to the door jamb. Slowly he turned the corner and edged away from the door until he felt something hard against his upper arm.

He stood on his toes, raising his body slightly, moving the hard object upward.

Light flooded the room.

Blinking as his eyes adjusted, Ben peered left and right. To his right a heavy shade was drawn over a window. Before him was something white and boxy.

He closed one eye and squinted with the other, resolving, if he survived this ordeal, to get the eye surgery he had put off since his teen years.

The object in front of him was a flush toilet.

To the left of the toilet was a mirror above a sink and commode.

He was in a bathroom.

Ben took a deep breath. Quietly he chanted in Hebrew,

"Adonai ro-i, lo ehsar.

Bin'ot deshe yarbitseini,

Al mei m'nuhot y'nahaleini,

Naf'shi y'shovev..."

"The Lord is my shepherd, I shall not want.

He maketh me to lie down in green pastures..."

Finishing the psalm, Ben carefully hopped to the sink. His momentum almost carried him into the mirror fronting the medicine cabinet, but by shifting his upper body backward at the last moment he remained erect.

The face staring at him from the mirror was a stranger, a wild man with a nose oozing black, dried blood, puffy eyes shrouded in purpling bruises, a bloody chin rubbed raw with abrasions, tape hanging from his lower lip and caught in his unruly hair.

With his chin Ben opened the medicine cabinet. Moving in until his eyes were inches from the shelves, he scanned the contents: Toothpaste, a toothbrush in a case, dental floss, tweezers, aspirin bottle, Tylenol bottle, tube of Preparation H, tube of antifungal cream, Gillette Mach Three razor blades, and finally, a large nail clipper.

Bumping his aching nose on the shelf above, he gripped the clipper between bloody teeth, then bent and deposited it on the edge of the sink. He turned around. Standing on tiptoes, teetering at the very edge of his balance, he grasped the device in his right hand.

He turned, slowly, got his balance, then one dizzying hop at a time, moved to the toilet commode. He sat as far back as he could, back braced against the tank, willing his muscles to relax until slowly, very slowly, he could again painfully pull both legs under him.

Now he shifted his weight forward until his body rested on his folded knees, hands above his ankles.

With thumb and forefinger he cautiously unfolded the nail file, rotating it until it was at right ankles to the cutting edges. Bending backward as far as he could, he probed with the file until he found the edge of the tape binding his ankles, then worked the flat edge of the file under the tape. To his surprise and relief, it lifted easily from his trousers. After regrasping the clippers and using his numbed fingers to rotate the clippers, he cut into the tape.

Hoping he'd guessed right, he palmed the clippers with three fingers and used his thumb and forefinger to tear the tape across its width.

It took more strength than he'd imagined he still had, but instead of stretching, the tape *tore.*

He had guessed right: It was gaffer's tape, a cloth backed tape used by movie lighting technicians. It tore instead of stretched, making it easier to apply and remove quickly from coils of cord or lighting setups.

In a few minutes of tearing Ben freed his ankles.

He stood, and then froze.

Somewhere beyond the bathroom window a diesel engine coughed to life. After a moment he heard the distinctive beep-beep-beep emitted by heavy equipment on the move. The roar grew louder as the machine approached, then faded as it passed and moved away.

Where on earth could he be?

He wondered if the light could be seen through the window, then decided that anyone watching that window would *know* someone was in the room if he turned the light *off.*

He pushed the door open and cautiously returned to the other room. The bathroom light revealed a desk with a few manila folders, a computer, and a phone. It was a windowless office that seemed somehow familiar. Had he been here before? He couldn't place it.

Between him and the desk a chair lay on its side. That was how he'd tripped. He'd hit his nose on that chair.

To his right was a door. He moved quietly to it. The knob turned but the door wouldn't budge. He explored the door frame with his shoulder and found three nail heads protruding inside. The door was nailed shut.

He took that as a good sign. His captors did not intend to return soon. But then he thought a little more. He had no idea how long he'd been in the room. Hours? Days? He couldn't be sure. They could come for him at any time.

He moved to the desk and using his chin, knocked the phone off its cradle. He bent to put an ear next to the receiver. No dial tone. The phone was disconnected.

In search of a scissors or something that he could use to free his arms, he tugged on a drawer knob. Locked.

He tried another drawer. Also locked. All locked.

He turned and looked at the desk again, recognizing its type. When the top drawer, in the center of the desk, was closed, all the other drawers were locked.

All he had to do was open the center drawer.

He turned his back to the desk, sat on the top and squirmed until one hand encountered a file folder. Inside he found a sheaf of paper held together with a metal clip.

He pulled the clip off and patiently, using the fingers of his right hand to press it against the desk top, straightened it. He left it on the desktop, wriggled to his feet, turned around and after bumping his sore nose several times, gripped the wire between his teeth.

Then he moved around the desk, knelt, and pushed one end of the wire into the desk drawer lock.

After several tries and much pain the lock turned a little. A second attempt moved it all the way to the right.

Ben turned until his bound hands faced the desk drawer, found the center knob and pulled. The drawer slid open. He pulled it out as far as it would go without falling, then searched through it, finding little except pens, pencils, a tiny stapler, rubber bands and paper clips.

He pushed the drawer part way in. Bending his knees he pulled out another, deeper drawer, pulled it all the way out until it fell to the carpet. With a foot he turned it over, and squatted, his thighs complaining as he felt through the drawer's contents.

He stood up, a scissors in his left hand. It was about eight inches long, with plastic-coated finger rings and sharp blades. Backing up to the top drawer, he put the top finger ring and blade inside and pushed the drawer in with one hand until it stopped, leaving the lower blade, sharp side up, sticking out of the drawer and pointed upward.

Carefully he stood, and then slid down until he could get the blade under the tape.

Straining, he pulled the tape binding his arms taut and sawed against the blade until his arms were free.

He stretched until his numbed hands began to tingle. When he was able to use them as nature had intended, he found the power switch for the computer and turned it on.

He ran to the bathroom and urgently relieved himself.

Moving to the sink, he opened the cold water tap. It was vibrating and as he washed his face and rinsed his mouth, Ben realized that the pipe feeding this room was connected to another pipe moving a lot of water. A *lot* of water.

Under the sink he found a stack of paper cups. He drank three cups of water before his thirst abated.

He put his nose to the window shade and saw the outlines of a heavy metal mesh. He wasn't going through that window any time soon.

Returning to the office, he righted the chair and switched on the room lights. He sat in the chair and looked around. He *had* been here before. He had sat in this very chair. And behind the desk, he recalled, had been Lawrence Mint, executive funeral director of Shabbat Tamid.

He was in a cemetery.

And if that was so, he reasoned, then the diesel vehicle that had gone by earlier was probably a backhoe.

A machine used to dig holes in the ground.

But why would a backhoe dig a hole in a cemetery closed to burials? At night?

The answer chilled his blood.

It was digging *his* grave.

Chapter 63

Ben hurried to the computer. It was, as he now recalled, far from new. He found and clicked open its Internet browsing program. Endless seconds ticked by before the program loaded and was ready to use.

An error message appeared: The browser couldn't find an Internet connection. Ben examined the back of the computer and found an ordinary modular phone line terminating in the computer's built-in, dial-up modem. He tugged on the line until the plug on its far end appeared. He knelt to find a single-line receptacle on the baseboard behind the desk.

He shoved the connector in, then removed the near end from the computer modem and plugged it into the telephone.

No dial tone.

No telephone service in this room.

No dialup Internet access.

No way to call for help.

He was on his own.

He took a deep breath and thought. There was something about this room, he recalled. Something he'd noticed once before. It had to do with the bathroom.

Yes.

He ran to the bathroom, returning to pluck the scissors and the nail clipper from atop the desk.

In the bathroom he stood on the toilet seat, then, bracing himself against the wall, stepped atop the tank. Affixed to the wall just below the ceiling, between toilet and sink, was a square of white wallboard held in place with strips of baseboard secured by screws in each corner—the entrance to a crawl space, he hoped. Unfurling the nail clipper and squinting, he used the edge of the nail file to turn the first screw. He let it drop to the floor.

Suddenly faint with hunger, Ben's head swam.

A murmur of voices through the office door sent frigid waves of fear racing up Ben's spine.

As he jumped down he heard the loud crack of splintering wood—a hammer or crowbar prying loose the first of the nails holding the door shut.

In the office Ben snatched up the chair he had earlier stumbled over, turned out the room lights and returned to the bathroom, locked the door, then laid the chair flat in front of it, hoping that if someone entered the room it would buy him a little time. A second or two.

Again the ripping sound came from the office. Ben returned to his perch atop the toilet tank and removed the second and then the third screws before he heard the office door crash open behind him. A man's voice, at once familiar and strange, yelled his name.

Before taking the last screw out, Ben grabbed the scissors from his back pocket and snapped it apart. He put one half between his teeth like a pirate's cutlass and the other into his back pocket.

Something big crashed against the bathroom door. As the last screw came loose he heard the wood door splinter behind him. Ben pulled the wallboard away, revealing a hole about thirty inches square.

He crouched, then jumped as high as he could, seizing the bottom lip of the crawl space with first one hand, then another. He pulled himself up.

An explosion blew a hole in the door. An even bigger hole appeared above the toilet tank where Ben had stood seconds earlier.

The shotgun fired a second time and the door flew from its hinges.

By then Ben was on his stomach, legs in the hole, head and arms out. Cone—the thuggish assistant funeral director whom Ben met on his first visit to Shabbat Tamid—kicked the chair aside. Ben hurled his makeshift cutlass at Cone's chest, and then scuttled backward into the crawl space.

Cursing, Cone pulled the half scissor out of his left shoulder and leaped up on the sink, lost his balance and grabbed the bottom edge of the crawl hole.

Ben slammed the second half of the scissors through Cone's right hand, impaling him.

Cone screamed. Ben scuttled backward until his feet encountered the far wall. Twisting himself supine, he pulled his legs up and kicked. Again. A third time and the thin wallboard broke from its screws and fell into the public bathroom on the other side.

Legs dangling, Ben sat in the hole, and then dropped, bouncing off the sink ton land on outstretched hands and arms. The shotgun fired through the crawl space but by then Ben was at the door, twisting the simple deadbolt open.

He dashed into the darkened cemetery, trying to get his bearings. Up the path to his left, he recalled, was a pedestrian gate. The gate whose lock he had picked on his earlier visit.

Could he get it open?

Wrong question. A dark shape appeared ahead of him. A flash and a bang and something hot whizzed by his head, very close but not close enough.

Ben turned and ran deeper into the cemetery, the gunman on his heels.

Ahead, moving back and forth between headstones, Ben saw a light. As his pursuer fell behind, Ben ran toward the light, weaving around graves and finally turning into a lane between rows of headstones. To his left, a dark shape against the faintly glowing sky, was a wall. He guessed that it was at least twelve feet high. He hesitated. Could he get over that?

Another shot and another bullet buzzed by his ear. He'd never make it over the wall without getting shot.

Ben ran toward the back hoe, approaching the old-style machine with its massive shovels fore and aft from its flank. As it passed, moving backward, a load of dirt in its raised front bucket, he seized the startled driver's arm and pulled him from the rolling vehicle.

Ben leaped into the seat, grabbed the wheel and turned it to his left. He'd never driven a backhoe, but he was going to learn. Still backing, the vehicle angled to the right, narrowly missing the fallen operator. Squinting through the darkness and the fog of his vision and touching each object before him with foot or hand, Ben explored the levers, then stepped on what he hoped was the brake. The backhoe slowed but swerved, rolling on, riding over a headstone. Ben realized there were *two* brake pedals and applied feet to both, bringing the machine to a halt.

Another shot rang out, and sparks flew as the bullet ricocheted from the machine's steel frame. Ben found the gear lever and shoved it forward, lifted both feet from the brakes, turning the wheel and stepping on the accelerator.

The backhoe lurched forward, its raised shovel framing the top of Ben's vision as he wove between rows of graves. The gunman was almost upon him when Ben saw a wider path ahead and swerved right, picking up speed as he headed toward the bright lights near the mortuary and the main gate.

As the mortuary came into view Ben saw it was far larger than only a few weeks earlier—construction had finished and the building had quadrupled in length and doubled in height.

Another shot clanged off the shovel at the backhoe's rear end. Ben fed more fuel to the diesel, mindful of the load of dirt bouncing before him. He felt with his left hand, located a lever, and pushed forward. The bucket rose.

He pulled the lever back a bit and the bucket fell.

Ahead a big brown step van blocked the way to the gate.

Ben knew that van. It belonged to Chang Rosenfeld.

A shotgun fired and the backhoe's right front tire blew. The machine swerved right and Ben, out of habit honed on icy Massachusetts roads, steered right, into the skid.

The machine pivoted sharply. Cone dropped the shotgun and scrambled sideways to evade the bucket swinging toward his head.

Ben hit the right brake and the right turn tightened, the vehicle describing a big circle through the all-but-empty parking area until Chang's van re-appeared to his left.

Removing his foot from the right brake pedal and placing it on the left as he whipped the wheel back, Ben headed straight for the gate.

The van backed into his path. Ben lowered the shovel and as the ungainly machine lurched forward, leaped leftward from the driver's seat just before the shovel struck the van.

Ben landed on his feet, turning in time to see the van roll on its side, the backhoe glancing off its rear and crashing into the corner of the new mortuary structure, punching through its thin stucco.

A fountain of water erupted from the hole, a geyser rising eighty feet into the sky and soaking the bundles of paper money that had tumbled out of the van.

Ben turned to see Chang pointing a Glock at him. At his side, in a dark jumpsuit and clutching a Canon HD video camera, was Naomi Burkin, her pretty face a mask of rage.

Nomi and Chang. Just as Ben had suspected: A forty-something like Chang dating his college-age daughter was enough to piss off most fathers—and especially Gary, who was hypocritically living with a girl not much older than Naomi.

Chang said, "Sorry I gotta do this, Rabbi—you're pretty much the coolest—"

The cemetery's massive, wrought-iron gate flew from its hinges and sailed inward, followed by a huge black armored car sporting a long, thick battering ram.

A dozen helmeted men in black body armor and carrying assault rifles followed the armored car into the cemetery.

A man's amplified voice yelled, "D.E.A.! Federal agents! You're all under arrest! Hands in the air!"

Ben froze, hands skyward. From the corner of his eye he saw a rotund jump-suited figure that he decided was Lawrence Mint depositing an AK-47 on the pavement.

Someone said, "You can put your hands down, Rabbi."

Ben turned to see Mendoza, wearing an armored vest, stepping through a phalanx of D.E.A. officers.

Ben said, "I sure hope you didn't forget to bring the bagels."

CHAPTER 64

Ben said, "Where are you taking me?"

Mendoza said, "Saint Joseph."

"You mean, *Beit* Joseph. It's closed now."

"I mean, *Saint* Joseph, the hospital. You're a mess."

"Can we stop somewhere? I'm really starving."

"Hungry enough to eat *cochina criolla*?"

"Come on—you can't get *real* Puerto Rican food out here."

"Hell you can't—Mofongos in North Hollywood."

"Do they have *bacalaitos*? *Surullitos*?"

Mendoza laughed. "Hell yes. Even *caldo gallego*!"

Ben shook his head. "Fish, I'll eat. And vegetables. But I only eat meat when I know it's kosher."

"You don't know what you're missing, Rabbi."

"But, I know *why* I'm missing it."

Mendoza turned onto Lankershim Boulevard and stopped at the light. "Someday you're going to have to explain the whole kosher deal to me."

"First tell me how you came riding in with the cavalry just as I was about to join my ancestors."

Mendoza snorted. "Good, old-fashioned police work."

"Explain."

"You sent soil samples up to a lab in Bakersfield?"

"Couple of weeks ago."

"And they told you what was in them?"

"Methamphetamine precursors, cocaine, opiates, THC..."

"Well, they also told the DEA. You gave a Burbank address, so the Feds contacted us."

"When?"

"This morning. Then about ten minutes later some bank calls and says you've been abducted by two guys in ski masks.

"Harris and I go to the scene, find your glasses—which reminds me."

Mendoza fished in a jacket pocket and handed Ben an unsealed envelope containing his spectacles.

Carefully, Ben put them on. The world swam into focus. "Thanks."

"Ever think about getting that LASIK surgery?"

"As soon as I can get an appointment."

"Anyway, the bank has video—big guy grabs you from behind, small guy with blond hair sticking out around the bottom of the ski mask—so maybe a girl—shoves a rag in your face. You go down. They drag you away. End of video.

"But we've got your email from the day before, ID-ing the blond as Naomi Burkin."

"So maybe that takes you to noon."

"Yeah, then we get a call from Burbank Taxi, our one local cab outfit. They found a GPS device rattling around in a tail light. And you hired that cab yesterday."

"So you cracked it open and ran the serial number."

"Manufacturer keeps a database. We call the dealer, he says he sold it to a Chang Rosenfeld.

"Meanwhile, Harris is talking to your lawyer buddy, Gary Burkin, who says his daughter Naomi is making a film in France. Harris says no, she's running around the Valley stealing cars, shooting sailors and kidnapping rabbis.

"Burkin starts screaming that it's this guy Chang, that he seduced his innocent baby girl with drugs and money.

"So we sit on Chang's place, and then he and the girl come out of the building next to the office and load some bags in the van and drive to the cemetery. We call DEA and follow them. DEA takes a while to get ready. The Feds have a lot of fancy hardware and they like to go in with all their toys.

"So here we are. Now I gotta ask: Why did they kidnap *you*?"

Mendoza slowed his car, than parked at the curb. Down the block the restaurant's multi-hued neon beckoned.

Ben said, "I should start at the beginning. But first I really must eat something."

Twenty minutes later, after wolfing down *pastelillos de Queso*—cheese dumplings, *tostones*—crunchy plantains, and *yuca frita*—fried Yucca, Ben drained his water glass and sat back in his chair.

Mendoza chewed a chunk of his *Pollo Empanizado*, chicken strips. "You know your Puerto Rican food."

"I grew up in Williamsburg and spent four years at JTS—ten minutes from Spanish Harlem. A New York Jew does not live by bagels alone."

"So tell me your story, Rabbi. Who did what to who, and why they did it."

"Okay. Maybe fifteen years ago, there was this pious old Korean Jew—"

"You're kidding, right?"

Ben shook his head. "*Not* kidding. Korean orphan, adopted in the Fifties by a Jewish couple. Grows up, goes to college, does well in business, and leaves Beit Joseph two hundred grand in the Bank of B. Cohen. A private bank, mind you. The interest goes for scholarships to the synagogue cheder—the Hebrew school. His name was Chang Rosenfeld."

"So *our* guy Chang is—"

"His grandson, Chad. Changed his name to Chang after the old man died. He did so because—I'm guessing here—he's making dirty money and thought of a way to wash it."

"What kind of dirty money?"

"I'm pretty sure he runs a gambling operation in an outbuilding next to his shop. And gambling means—"

"Loan sharking. And maybe drugs. And he can't do that without giving a cut to one local gang or another. Did Chang know Loco Henry?"

Ben's head bobbed up and down. "Enrique—Loco Henry—restored Gary's Mustang. I think Chang must have put them together."

"I just had a thought, but I'll tell you later," Mendoza said. "Chang washed money through the synagogue—how?"

"The old man's will specified how the bequest was to be invested and that the interest would go to the cheder. Chang must have personally opened the account and made himself a signatory. But nobody at Beit Joseph knew *that*. Over the years they added or removed signatories, but they had no reason to suspect that Chang himself had access to the account.

"He makes one or two big deposits a year, cash, then has the money, which is now clean because it comes from a synagogue, wired to another bank. Maybe to an offshore bank."

"How could he get away with that?"

"He served on the board and knew that neither the office staff nor the treasurer pay much attention to that account. It paid interest quarterly, but they withdrew it only once a year, when they gave out scholarships. If he made deposits and withdrawals in the same month, a month chosen because no interest was paid in that month, and picked up that statement at the bank before it was mailed, odds were no one would notice.

"Plus, Beit Joseph has accounts in several banks. One missing statement from one bank a year—hardly missed.

"But a couple of months ago the synagogue decides they're using too many different banks. They want to look at maybe moving that account, but they can't find the most recent statement. They call the bank and get a duplicate, and there's this huge deposit. And then a second deposit. About three million, all told. And then that mystery money is withdrawn."

"That's why the synagogue brought you in?"

"They needed an outsider. But then the funny money disappeared and they moved their account to another bank.

"But Chang was worried. He'd guessed that I might be looking into this so he found reasons to be around the synagogue a lot. He starts refurbishing the chapel, an hour or two every day. And he creates a shofar-blowing class—"

"That's that little cow horn you blow on New Years?"

"Sheep or goat horn. And not all of them are so little. Chang has a four-footer made from the ridged horn of a Nubian ibex. That's what he used to kill LaShonda—I'm certain of that, and I think I can prove it."

"Back up. Why did he want to kill her?"

"I don't think he planned it. I'd called her just before closing—I was stuck in traffic—and asked her to leave the cheder account file out for me. She couldn't find anything but the cancelled checks and the most recent statement. I think Chang panicked when he saw them on LaShonda's desk. He didn't know that the statements, which showed that his deposits and withdrawals went back many years, were misplaced under a pile of stuff on Rabbi Kimmelman's office couch."

"So after his shofar class, Chang comes into the office, probably carrying his great big shofar, sees LaShonda with the checks and thinks she's reading the file. He knows that we're good friends and jumps to the conclusion that she's helping me investigate. She wasn't! He grabs his shofar and clubs her to death."

"And you can prove that?"

"Each shofar's sound is unique. I heard Chang blow his before the murder and again after it. A different sound. Probably cracked it when he beat LaShonda. You can repair horn with Super Glue, but the tone will never be the same."

Mendoza said, "So if I send that big shofar to the lab, they might find traces of LaShonda's blood?"

"I believe so. And, horn is made from keratin. Like fingernails. Same stuff. You'll probably find that the keratin traces that the autopsy turned up in her wounds were from that kind of horn. I'm not current on the technology, but I suspect they can match the keratin to a particular horn."

"Okay, so Chang kills LaShonda. Why kill the kid?"

"Chang takes the file from LaShonda's desk but can't find the statements. They're not in the filing cabinet either. He thinks LaShonda hid them and wants to search her apartment, but Ricardo is there. When he leaves, Chang, maybe with Naomi, follows him to the airport and kills him for the keys."

Mendoza interrupted. "By the way, we ran the keys through fingerprint—no prints. None at all."

Ben said, "Then Naomi wiped them after she put them back in the apartment. Chang had ransacked the place a couple of days earlier. Probably she went back there to straighten it up so it wouldn't look like it was connected to Ricardo's murder."

"But then you show up."

"She has to get out before I come to the door."

"Here's another thing we didn't tell you. Didn't know until today. Ricardo was shot with his father's gun."

"The gun you found with his body?"

"Yeah. Loco Henry's prints were on the cartridges and the magazine."

"Then maybe the Glock that Chang pointed at me was the one he shot Henry with."

Mendoza smiled, a coyote about to dine on rabbit. "Here's what came to me a minute ago: Remember I told you that the LAPD had a description on a guy who might have killed Loco Henry?"

"Yeah, but you wouldn't share that with me."

"Sorry. I couldn't. Anyway, it was from a little kid who saw a guy go into Loco Henry's shop a little before he was shot. Kid said he was big man and that he had 'Chinese eyes.'"

"That could very well be Chang."

"Okay. But why does Chang kill Henry?"

"At one time, Loco Henry was Gary Burkin's weed connection. Gary is mad at Chang because forty-something

Chang is dating his innocent little girl, Naomi. But he can't make a fuss about it because *he's* dating someone almost the same age.

"After Chang kills LaShonda, he worries that Gary will figure out the money laundering scheme, then tell Loco Henry that Chang killed LaShonda—she was his son's mother, and he cared about them. But Chang doesn't want Loco Henry or his Pacoima Cholos coming after him."

Mendoza said, "So kill him before *he* kills you?"

"Right. Preemptive strike. Then Chang used Loco Henry's gun on Ricardo so it would look like the gang's revenge for Loco Henry."

Mendoza scratched his head. "How do you remember all this?"

"If you think this is convoluted, spend an hour or two with *Baba Metzia*—Talmudic discussions of tort damages."

"I'll take your word on that. So now, how does Chang and his money-laundering tie in with your soil samples?"

"I didn't know that until just before the DEA arrived. By the way, where's your partner?"

"Harris is playing nice with the *Federales* and looking out for the City of Burbank's interests in this case. There could be a reward for recovering the Mob's dirty money.

"So, what did you learn just before we busted in?"

"When I ran the backhoe into Chang's van, it rolled and bundles of money fell out. The backhoe crashed into the mortuary and cut a high-pressure water pipe."

Mendoza put a piece of chicken into his mouth. "So?"

"So let's back up again. A few weeks ago, before LaShonda was murdered, I went to a funeral at Shabbat Tamid.

Afterward I noticed some empty plots that looked like they'd recently been dug up. I've been doing research on Jewish cemeteries—"

"So you're a Kung Fu rabbi *and* a visiting scholar?"

"*Not* Kung—never mind. Yes, a visiting scholar. Anyway, I began to take an interest in this cemetery, because something wasn't quite right."

"Like what, exactly?"

"Well, it was almost full, there were almost no empty plots, but they were building a huge addition to the mortuary. Then they made it almost impossible for people to visit graves.

"I got Chang to make me a long, thin, wooden probe, and one night I snuck in there and stuck the probe into the plot I'd noticed. There was something buried there, three or four feet down, made of iron or steel. It couldn't be a Jewish casket—they *must* be made of wood. And something buried in the next two plots as well.

"I took soil samples from that plot because I suspected the box held something *other* than human remains.

"A friend analyzed the samples and came back with pretty much what the Bakersfield lab reported.

"But then I needed samples from other parts of the grounds to compare with that one. If all were similar, then I'd suspect the box held a body that was not supposed to be buried in a Jewish cemetery. But if the samples were different, that might point to drugs in that steel box."

Mendoza swallowed. "Hold on. *Chang* made you that probe?"

"Before LaShonda died, I had no reason to suspect him."

"Go on."

"Chang had washed his money through the synagogue for years. But three million seems like a lot for a small gaming room. Maybe he also washed other people's money—like the Cholo gang that was taking a cut of his action. Their drug money.

"Then his scheme is revealed. He has to find a new way to clean his money.

"Chang has gang connections. The gang sells drugs, so they're connected to suppliers and the suppliers are connected to bigger criminal enterprises. I'm guessing again, but I think Chang reached out to the Mob for help in laundering his money.

"Now, hold that thought, because I have to come at this story from a still different angle."

"Go for it."

"Not long ago, the cemetery was purchased by a privately-owned East Coast company headquartered in the Bahamas. Now, why would they want to buy an old cemetery?"

"Maybe they thought it would be nice to have a place where burying bodies wouldn't seem suspicious?"

Ben grimaced. "Maybe. I can tell you that the company they bought the cemetery *from* had already looted its 'perpetual care' endowment, which after fifty-odd years of burials must have been worth a lot."

"That's a bust-out. Kind of thing the New York Mob used to pull: Buy a hurting company with a small down payment, agree to pay the rest over a few years, and then loot the company's assets, the employee pension fund, walk away and stiff the seller."

"Not only mobsters. There are supposedly legitimate operators who look for companies they can buy cheap and break up—sell off the pieces. So what happens to Shabbat

Tamid after the bust-out is interesting: Another company buys it. A cemetery with no expansion capability and no endowment. Why?"

Mendoza smiled. "I give up. Why?"

"Probably the owners used a shell company to insulate themselves from the looting, held a sham sale to transfer the cemetery from one dummy corporation to another, to make it *seem* like new ownership, and then put their asset to another use."

"If they were making meth or crack that could explain the contaminated soil."

"It might. The cemetery is isolated behind high walls and lots of shrubbery. It buys all sorts of chemicals for embalming. And they're a well-established business with, probably, multiple banking connections."

Mendoza chewed his lips. "Not so fast. You start depositing lots of cash, sooner or later most banks will call the Feds and the DEA will come in and test the currency for residue, which is a tipoff to dealing activity."

"Do you read the Bible, Detective?"

Mendoza puffed out his cheeks. "That's Harris. I belong to the church of four bases. We pray softball."

"I went out for baseball at M.I.T. My eyes are so bad I couldn't make the bench at Egghead-Geek U."

Mendoza laughed.

"Anyway, in *b'midbar*, the Book of Numbers, is Parshat Parah, the story of the so-called Red Heifer."

"Never heard of it."

"A cow that meets certain very strict standards of purity is slaughtered in a ritual manner. The entire animal—hide, meat, horns, bones, even the dung—is burned. A sweet-smelling herb called hyssop, some cedar and the extract of a red worm are added to the fire. This produces a mound of ash, which is then, in very small amounts, added to water."

"Why?"

"It becomes 'Water of Lustration.' The Torah says that anything or anyone 'impure' becomes pure by washing them in the Water of Lustration. But here's the kicker: The Torah also says that anyone involved in the preparation of this water becomes impure in the process."

"Say what? I don't understand any of this."

"Neither does anyone else. It has bedeviled rabbis for thousands of years. Even King Solomon was stumped."

"What does it have to with dirty money?"

"The soils lab found chemicals from different drugs: Meth, pot, heroin and cocaine. A meth lab in a cemetery I might believe. Or a heroin factory. But not multiple labs making different drugs."

"So then..."

"They built out the mortuary to make *impure* money, tainted with drug residue, clean—*pure*. When the DEA looks inside that building they'll find industrial-sized washing machines and some kind of great big air dryers."

Mendoza's mouth flew open. "They were *washing* money! Literally washing it in water!"

"Then they could deposit it in banks through front companies without arousing suspicion. Like through a casino, for example. Or a grocery market. But the process of purifying that unclean money breaks many laws. The purifiers became impure."

"And then you come poking around. Did they know?"

"They had suspicions. I'd been to the cemetery a few times before, but the night I snuck in and took soil samples they almost caught me. Chased me, but I got away."

"Say they wanted to know what you were up to. If they thought you might be a rabbi—"

"I'm sure they did."

"Then they find someone who has your 4-1-1—"

"Chang, their laundry customer."

"Chang tells them you're more than a rabbi, that he made a probe for you, that you're interested in their cemetery. He tells them where you live."

"Thus the hit-and-run, followed by the grenade booby trap."

"I see all that. But, why was there drug residue in the soil? Why not dump the dirty water down the sewer?"

Ben shut his eyes for a long moment. He was far beyond exhaustion and his whole body ached. "They were using a lot of water. This is the fourth year of a statewide drought. There's mandatory water rationing. Burbank Water & Power would notice a spike in usage and offer to look for leaky pipes and show them ways to conserve—whatever."

"They didn't want that kind of attention, so they recycled dirty water through the landscape sprinklers?"

"Exactly. One thing more. Naomi had a video camera."

"They let her in to film?"

"Maybe she was making a commercial. Maybe they wanted to expand their business. Instead of bringing prospective clients to visit their laundry, show them a movie."

Mendoza shook his head. "I'll be damned."

Ben stood up. "I'm really tired."

Patting his pockets, he frowned. "They took my wallet—I don't have any money."

"No problem. They never let me pay here."

"But that's corruption!"

Mendoza shook his head. "It's only corrupt if someone gives me something of value and I'm in a position to do something illegal or unethical for them."

"And you are!"

"No way. This is North Hollywood, part of Los Angeles. I'm Burbank PD. I've got no jurisdiction here, no authority, no influence. I couldn't beat a parking ticket."

"Do they know that?"

"I sure hope not."

Harris said, "So you actually live in Boston?"

Ben said, "Near there. Cambridge."

Mendoza said, "You checking bags, Rabbi, or going with all carry-ons?

Ben said, "It's worth a few bucks to check them."

Mendoza nodded and pulled up to the curb in front of the skycap stand at Bob Hope Airport's main terminal.

Ben leaned in from the backseat. "People see me get out of this, they'll think I'm being run out of town."

Harris said, "Sorry, but all the unmarked units were recalled for some fool problem with their gas pedals."

Mendoza said, "Rabbi, it's been a pleasure working with you. Even if you have funny ideas about food."

Ben said, "Thanks. Buy you guys a cup of bad coffee?"

Harris said, "Can't be worse than the squad-room swill."

Mendoza said. "Sorry—we're meeting the DEA guys at two."

Ben said, "That reminds me. Were they able to identify those bodies? The ones buried in the plots that Beit Joseph had sold back to the cemetery?"

Mendoza said. "A guy named Lawrence Mint, a guy named Michael Cone, and a guy named Arturo Jung. The executive funeral director, the head mortician, and the accountant."

Harris said, "Pretty slick. They needed state-licensed people to operate a cemetery, so they killed the management team and took over their identities."

Ben said, "What about their families? Why didn't someone report those people missing?"

"Jung was single, here on a green card from Argentina. Mint and Cone were a gay couple—the gang recruited them from Sebastopol, way up north, near Santa Rosa. No family or friends in this area."

Ben said, "I'm lucky to be alive."

"Damn straight! They were gonna plant you right next to Jung. Had the hole almost dug," Harris said.

Ben said, "There's one other thing I wanted to ask you. Remember the night you had me in the interview room?"

Harris groaned. "You're not still holding that against us?"

Ben shook his head. "No, no. It's just that you threw out some very specific crimes. Chapter and verse, it sounded like the record of a professional con man."

Mendoza said, "Gotta be honest, I thought that was one of our best performances. We just had the wrong audience."

Ben's own moment of truth had arrived. Cohorts of centipedes crawled up his spine. "Where did you get all that? Those crimes? Was it real, or were you guys making it up as you went along," he asked, dreading the answer.

Harris said, "That? A for-real rap sheet. But it went *way* back. To when you were in diapers. Maybe before, even."

Ben said, "So you knew it wasn't me?"

Mendoza said, "Of course. But the reason we used it—the way we got it from the FBI—was that you and that guy had the same name. Legal name, I mean."

"Mark Thompson Glass?"

Harris said, "Yeah, that was it."

Ben's mind was a planet knocked off its axis, spinning out of orbit into uncharted darkness. His mysterious father had been despicable predator! His mother, his grandparents— they must have suffered endless anguish. How many lives had his father ruined?

No wonder his family had kept Ben in the dark. Why they shielded him from the awful truth of his patrimony. Why he had never even seen a picture of his father. Why his family had never called him anything but Ben, never used his legal name.

Ben took a deep breath. This was now ancient history. He would have to find a way to move on.

Mendoza said, "I remember wishing how sweet it would be if you were actually *that* Mark Thompson Glass."

Ben said, "Why is that?"

Mendoza said, "Because we only just skimmed that file. It was maybe two or three times as long. The guy is only sixty-something now. There are open cases and rewards still posted for his arrest and conviction."

Ben said, "Nobody's ever going to collect those rewards. But I know where you can find him."

Later, waiting to go through pre-boarding security, Ben recalled the pebbles he'd noticed on his father's tombstone. Who could have left them? A wife? Children? Since the death of his grandparents and then Rachel, Ben had believed he was alone in the world. But now—was it possible that he had siblings? A half-brother or a sister?

Might they not live somewhere near where they chose to bury their father?

Somewhere in this area?

He cocked his head, considering the wisdom of stepping out of line.

CONGREGATION BEIT JOSEPH of BURBANK

Member of the United Synagogue of Conservative Judaism

325 East Chandler Boulevard, Burbank, CA 91509

FOR IMMEDIATE RELEASE:

MEDIA CONTACT: Dr. Tova Levine, (818) 311-9499

Congregation Beit Joseph proudly announces acceptance of an $8.75 million reward from the Department of Justice for its employees' role in recovering over $30 million in funds derived from racketeering, and for the arrest and convictions of seven individuals from a criminal organization operating across five western states and in Mexico.

The reward is one of the largest ever paid under a federal program designed to reward citizens who cooperate with authorities in identifying criminal activities that result in the seizure of unlawful assets.

Half the reward will be used to re-develop the synagogue's campus. New or refurbished facilities will include the Valley's largest Jewish Day School, a modernized sanctuary, a playground and underground parking. Additional redevelopment funds were donated by the Bank of B. Cohen.

CONGREGATION BEIT JOSEPH of BURBANK

Member of the United Synagogue of Conservative Judaism

325 East Chandler Boulevard, Burbank, CA 91509

FOR IMMEDIATE RELEASE:

MEDIA CONTACT: Dr. Tova Levine, (818) 311-9499

Congregation Beit Joseph proudly announces the establishment of the LaShonda Harris Memorial Restitution Fund. Ms. Harris, 35, Beit Joseph's Synagogue Administrator, was murdered last year.

Led by Executive Director Susan Scott, the Fund will seek out victims and the heirs of victims of certain classes of crimes and confidence schemes nationwide and compensate them for losses. The Foundation's initial funding is over $4 million. Administrative support and additional funding will be provided by the Bank of B. Cohen.

— The End —

ABOUT THE AUTHOR

Before his 21st birthday, Marvin J. Wolf had served as a U.S. Army drill instructor, taught hand-to-hand combat to Army officers, ran a weapons squad in cold-war South Korea, sold encyclopedias door-to-door, worked in a junk yard, walked three miles through a blizzard to pay a family debt, and served with distinction as a delicatessen pearl diver. While serving as a combat photographer in Vietnam, Wolf was awarded a battlefield commission, one of only 62 such awards during the decade of that war. Back in civilian clothes, he became a globe-trotting photojournalist; when he regained custody of his adolescent daughter and was forced to choose between frequent travel and single parenthood, he turned to writing. He is the author of more than a dozen nonfiction works and a series of mystery novels. Two of his teleplays, written with Larry Mintz and based on stories from his nonfiction books, were produced as made-for-television movies. Wolf lives in Los Angeles with his adult daughter and her ferocious Chihuahua/terrier mix, Samson.

Made in United States
North Haven, CT
16 July 2023

39103110R00196